MW00897901

RED SKY IN THE MORNING

J. Walter Ring

Red Sky in the Morning

Copyright 2015 by J. Walter Ring
All rights Reserved

ISBN-10: 1514241056
ISBN-13: 978-1514241059

No Part of this book may be reproduced in any form or by any electronic or mechanical means, including information storage and retrieval systems, without permission in writing by the author

This is a work of fiction. Names, characters, places, locations, and incidents are purely fictional and bear no relationship to any real life individuals, living or dead, or to any actual places, business establishments, locations, events, or incidents. Any resemblance is entirely coincidental.

AUTHOR'S NOTE

This book is dedicated to my wife, Erina Bridget Ring, and our children, Jennifer, Joseph, and Julie.

Thank you to Ken McNany and to Helen and Thom McDermott, and a special thanks to my friend and editor Carolyn Woolston for her help and support.

J. Walter Ring
Napa, California 2015

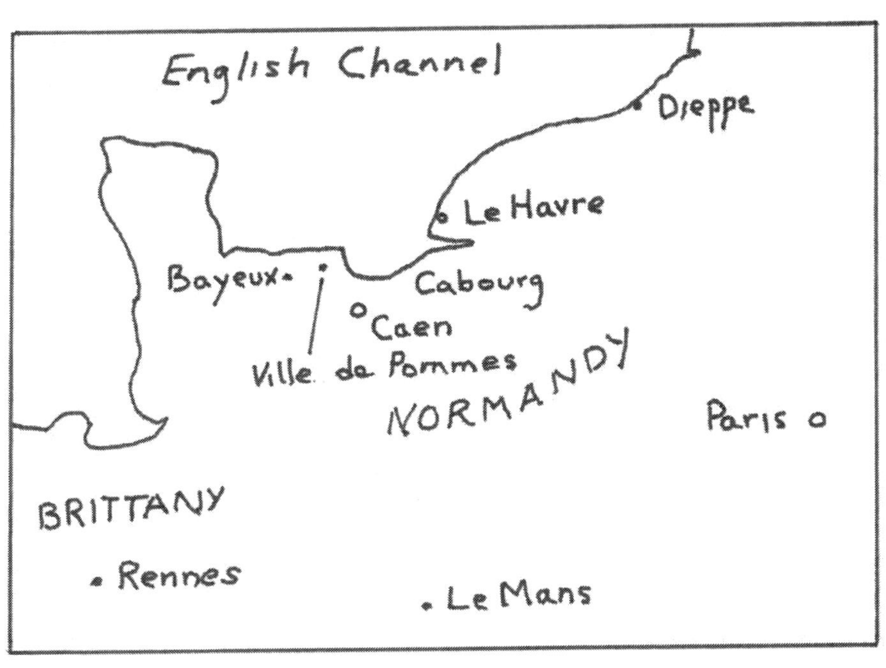

Map of Northern France

"May you live in interesting times."

-Chinese curse

CHAPTER ONE
RED SKIES

June 1940

A siren wailed. A second siren joined the first, then silence. Marguerite heard a faint boom, followed a few seconds later by another, and her mother froze. "*Mon Dieu,* what was that?"

Aunt Germaine led them out onto her tiny apartment balcony and pointed to the eastern sky. "Look above the smoke, see those black dots? Those are German bombers. The Nazis are bombing the airport!"

"*Madame* LaFluer, we need to get you out of Paris," Richard said, his voice tight. "We came to take you to the country, where you will be safe. I hope it's not too late. We have to get to the train station."

Marguerite scarcely knew Richard. He had come from Spain just weeks ago with Uncle Pierre and her cousin Bérénice, supposedly to work on Pierre's farm, though she suspected other things were going on there. Richard was Irish, tall, in his mid-forties, with bold blue eyes and ginger hair that peeked from under his beret. She liked him but she was unsettled about him. And, she wasn't sure she could trust him. There was something hidden about him and the rest of the people at Perdu farm.

Germaine and *Maman* hurriedly filled two suitcases and a duffel bag with her aunt's clothes, and all four of them clattered down the stairway onto the street to join a crowd of silent people hurrying toward the train depot. It looked as if everyone was leaving Paris—bent old men, young women tugging children along by the hand, mothers pushing infants in baby carriages. Marguerite hadn't been scared up until now, but the sight frightened her.

The train station doors were locked and police guarded the entrances. Richard stopped and asked one of the gendarmes, "Why is the depot closed? Where are the trains?"

"The army has commandeered them. Move along."

Maman touched Richard's arm. "We need to find a telephone, call the farm, and ask Antoine to pick us up."

Tall, elegant Germaine dropped her suitcase and approached the gendarme. "Excuse me, where could we find a telephone?"

"There are none, *Madame*. The bombs have knocked out the electric power and the telephones."

She caught Richard's gaze. "We have to find a working telephone." She pointed down the crowded street. "That way."

Aunt Germaine always knew what to do. She was the only woman Marguerite knew who was divorced; she lived alone and supported herself working as a nurse at a hospital in Paris.

Marguerite picked up the duffel bag. "How far is Ville de Pommes?"

"Too far to walk," Richard said. "But we have no choice. Let's get started."

They joined the throng of pedestrians surging down the main thoroughfare out of Paris. The sidewalks were so crowded they had to walk in the street, and at one point had to step aside as a column of French army transports loaded with soldiers overtook them. A few seconds later, another packed convoy sped by with uniformed soldiers hanging off the trucks or riding on the guns and caissons.

Richard picked up the pace. "Those trucks are running *away* from the front. We have to hurry."

More overloaded military transports passed them, but now they were no longer organized in convoys. Military vehicles of all sorts roared by, fleeing the battle outside Paris. Then came French soldiers quick-stepping, almost running, their uniforms filthy, their faces pale and dirty, their eyes vacant.

Streams of people and vehicles converged from the side streets, swelling the throng on the main artery out of the city. Ahead of them a sea of shoulders swayed as refugees clogged the sidewalks. Cars and trucks jammed the streets.

On the main boulevard, honking vehicles filled all four lanes while people slogged forward on foot. Farther on, buildings gave way to meadows and plowed fields, and the highway became a crowded two-lane road so thick with people Marguerite couldn't help bumping into them. *This is madness.* She felt claustrophobic. Where were they all going?

Late in the afternoon they stepped out of the shuffling crowd and sprawled on the edge of a grassy pasture. Cattle grazed nearby and Marguerite sucked in fresh air. Richard sat down at her elbow, and when his coat fell open, she glimpsed a shoulder holster and the butt of a revolver.

Her heart stopped. There was something dangerous about the group Uncle Pierre had brought back from Spain, and now here was this gun. She drew closer to Richard. "Where did you meet my Uncle Pierre?" She kept her voice low.

"In Pamplona," he whispered.

"What did you do for him in Pamplona?"

He shifted away from her. "That's not the kind of question you ask a man in my line of work."

She edged closer. "What line is that?"

He looked away.

"What did you do in Spain?" she pressed. "What were Uncle Pierre and my cousin doing in Spain?"

Richard hesitated. "It's not important that you know, Marguerite."

"Tell me anyway."

He hesitated, then expelled a long breath. "I was a member of the Irish Free Army. The IRA assassinated my brother, mistaking him for me, so I had to escape. I got involved smuggling guns to Ethiopia, then I joined the Loyalists against Franco. That's where I met your uncle."

She thought for a moment. "It seems to me you're always on the losing side."

"I will forget you said that." He sent her a wry smile.

She let out a resigned breath and watched the cows in the pasture, but curiosity gnawed at her. She leaned toward him again. "Bérénice said she was knifed in Pamplona."

His ginger eyebrows shot up. "She told you about that, did she?"

"*Oui.* She said her friends hid her."

"I was the one who found her. The Loyalist with her was dead. She was bleeding and unconscious, so I took her to safety." He glanced at her mother and Aunt Germaine, talking quietly a few feet away. "Your cousin told me you have medical training. Maybe you can help us."

She shook her head. "*Non.* I don't want to be involved. Besides, I cannot treat people. I am training with a veterinarian, learning to treat animals. I could hurt someone and I don't want to risk it."

"We would use you only in an emergency."

We? Who is 'we'? She clenched her jaw. "Richard, I am not qualified to work on people, and that's all there is to it."

He nodded and leaned back and closed his eyes. "I understand."

Marguerite studied him. She had a feeling this discussion wasn't over. It wasn't easy saying no to this man.

Suddenly he stood up. "Let's go."

They picked up their bags and fell back into line. Farther into the countryside they passed four men pushing an automobile onto the side of the road; steam gushed out of the radiator. The farther they walked the more abandoned vehicles she saw; she assumed they had run out of petrol. Discarded clothes, packages, and boxes of dishes, sheets, even lamps were scattered along the road edge.

All at once an explosion erupted behind them, and cries rose from the crowd. People bolted forward, but Richard stepped into their midst and raised his arms. "Don't run!" he shouted in a commanding voice. "Don't panic."

The jittery mob quieted down.

Marguerite gazed up at the huge ball of grey smoke in the sky behind her. "What was that?"

"Artillery burst," he said. "Maybe two kilometers behind us. We need to keep going."

Mon Dieu, this is a nightmare. A buzzing noise overhead made her look up where a single-engine airplane flew low above them, following the road. Black German crosses were painted on its silver wings. She instinctively ducked as it passed directly over her head and began to climb.

"Richard, what is that plane doing?"

He watched it climb, bank, and circle back around. "I don't know. It's a German fighter, a Messerschmitt, I think. Odd that he's out here by himself."

The plane flattened out and dove even lower, its machine guns exploding. Screaming people scrambled off the road into ditches, and Marguerite dropped her duffel and dove for the roadside, protecting her head with her arms. Bullets tore up the center of the pavement.

The plane roared past, and when it circled for another attack she tried to make herself as small as possible. *God, oh God, help us.* The guns exploded again.

Richard jumped to his feet, ripped out his revolver, and fired until the weapon was empty. The plane's engine sputtered, then it banked and disappeared toward Paris. Marguerite leaped to her feet. "You hit it!"

"Maybe. I had to do something." He holstered his revolver and reached down to help her mother and Aunt Germaine to their feet.

"Doctor!" a woman a few feet away from them shouted. "Is there a doctor?"

Aunt Germaine pushed through the crowd. "I'm a nurse, what can I do?"

"Over there, in that car." The woman pointed to a black Citroen with a pattern of bullet holes from back to front. Germaine crawled into the back seat where a young boy was clutching his thigh and screaming. An old man slumped in the front, covered in chunks of glass from the windshield. Marguerite wriggled into the front seat, carefully brushed the glass off the man, and immediately saw that his arm had been severed below the elbow.

Germaine leaned over the front seat, saw what confronted Marguerite, and then backed out of the car. "I need something to tie off this man's arm," she yelled. A woman threw a long-sleeved white blouse to her, and together she and Marguerite wrapped one sleeve around the mangled arm and tied it tight. The bleeding stopped, and Germaine returned to the back seat to work on the boy.

Marguerite remained with the old man. All at once he shuddered and lay still, and she stared down at his open eyes, then checked his neck for a pulse. Nothing. *God in heaven, he was dead.* Gently she placed her hand over his heart, closed her eyes, and offered a short prayer. Then she wiped her bloody hands on her dress and wept.

"Marguerite?" Germaine didn't look up. "How's he doing?"

"He's gone," she sobbed.

Her aunt straightened and leaned forward to study her face. "Are you all right?"

Marguerite wiped her hand across her eyes and shook her head. "*Non*. I feel faint."

Richard poked his head in and helped her out of the car. "Let's go over here and sit down." He walked her to the shoulder, where she sat down and dropped her head onto her knees.

Maman knelt next to her. "Lie down, *chou-chou*. If your head is level with your heart, you cannot faint." Marguerite stretched out on her back and covered her eyes with her arm. *How could Maman know such a thing?* Then she remembered that her mother had been 17 during the Great War, the same age as herself. She would know a great many things.

"Marguerite," *Maman* said quietly. "How did you know what to do?"

"From Doctor Morel," she said in a monotone. "I learned it from him." Every summer and on weekends Marguerite worked with the veterinarian as an apprentice, setting bones and suturing wounds. Someday she hoped to be a nurse, like Aunt Germaine.

"I am proud of you, *cherie!* You saw what had to be done, and you did it."

Marguerite rolled over onto her stomach and rested her head on her folded arms. "But I couldn't save him," she wept.

Maman rubbed her back as Aunt Germaine emerged from the Citroen. "Who was driving this car?" she shouted to the crowd.

"I was," a middle-aged man answered. His trouser was torn, his bare leg bloody.

"Find a doctor for the boy as soon as you can." She tipped her head toward the front seat. "I'm sorry about him. Can you take care of his body?"

The man nodded and took a deep breath. "*Oui*."

Germaine knelt on the ground beside Marguerite and stroked her hair. "You couldn't have saved him, Marguerite. We were too late. He had lost too much blood before we got here."

Someone offered water and clean rags, and they washed their faces and hands and dried them on their blood-stained dresses. Marguerite glanced back at the bullet-riddled car. "Richard, why would that plane fire into a crowd of unarmed civilians?"

He shrugged. "Maybe he was blood-thirsty or insane. Or maybe he was bored."

That made her smile, and the helpless feeling began to lift. She got to her feet and moved on, but she felt sick at what she had seen. *This isn't war, it's butchery.* She tried to distract herself by concentrating on the pastures around her, cows and horses lazing in the late afternoon sun, shoots of young corn poking up in the nearby fields. The vineyards were green with fresh leaves shading clusters of tiny green grapes.

"It will be dark soon," her mother called. "We must find a telephone."

Richard scanned the horizon, then pointed to a knot of buildings some distance off the road. "Do you think you can walk a little farther? See that telephone line going into the farmhouse? Maybe they'll let us use their phone."

Marguerite released a sigh of relief. She was so tired she felt dead inside, and her steps were unsteady. To her surprise, neither her diminutive mother nor Aunt Germaine showed any signs of the exhaustion she felt. She walked on.

The farmhouse was flanked by a milking shed, a weathered grey barn, and an open-sided structure to protect farm vehicles. Cars and trucks jammed the driveway leading up to the house.

"Looks like we're not the only ones to spot the telephone line," Richard said. "I'll go in and call Antoine and see if I can buy us something to eat."

Marguerite sat down beside the dusty driveway and watched the farmer's dairy herd amble toward the milking shed. The normality of cows walking in to be milked restored her sense of reality, but everything seemed like a terrible dream. She wished she would wake up and find that none of it was happening.

Slowly the sky turned to shades of orange and red. When Richard returned it was dark, and his arms were laden with bread and cheese. "I called your husband, *Madame* Auriol. I told him we had Germaine with us and that we were all right. He agreed to meet us at the intersection with Rue de Verdun, about two kilometers farther on."

Maman tore the bread into chunks and passed it out with pieces of cheese. Richard chewed thoughtfully. "While I was in line for the phone, I listened to the farmer's wireless. The British Army has retreated to England from Dunkirk. That leaves us all alone to fight the Germans. The French Army is backed up to the outskirts of Paris, but supposedly they are holding firm."

He took another hunk of cheese from *Maman.* "What we saw this morning was a routed army fleeing the front lines. I saw the same look in the defeated Spanish Republican Army outside Madrid." He shook his head. "My guess is the Germans will be in Paris in a matter of days."

Marguerite flinched. "How could this happen? France was supposed to be the most powerful country in the world, with the most powerful military." A sense of dread swept over her and tears stung behind her eyelids. "What will happen to us?"

Richard looked at her for a long moment. "I don't know. Unless a miracle happens, within a few weeks the Nazis will be in Ville de Pommes."

CHAPTER TWO
WHAT NEXT?

June 16, 1940

After their harrowing trek out of Paris, feelings of despair and helplessness nagged at Marguerite. The German army was in Paris. Soon they would occupy the whole of Normandy, and the townspeople of Ville de Pommes braced themselves. Food markets sold out, businesses shuttered their windows, and Jean LaVaque locked the doors of the bank and disappeared. Rumors circulated that he took the bank's money with him.

Richard and the other workers Uncle Pierre had imported from Spain stashed food and weapons in a secret cave they had hastily constructed beneath the storage building on Perdu farm. When all the supplies were secured, hundreds of casks of calvados were rolled in to camouflage the secret space.

The radio announced that President Lebrun had appointed Marshal Henri Philippe Pétain, the Lion of Verdun, as premier, and that evening Marguerite listened to his first national address on the radio in their parlor.

"I offer to France the gift of my person that I may ease her sorrow. It is with a heavy heart that I tell you that we must halt the combat. Last night I asked the adversary whether he is ready to seek with us, in honor, some way to put an end to the hostilities."

Was the war really over? Marshal Pétain claimed he had saved the country, but now they lived in Occupied France. Every day she heard rumors about atrocities the Nazis committed in northern France and now they were coming to Ville de Pommes. She clenched her hands in her lap. What would the Nazis do to them?

* * *

Marguerite stood at the edge of town with her cousin, Bérénice, and her *lycée* classmates Simone LaVaque and Yvonne Callion, along with the rest of the townspeople of Ville de Pommes. The Germans were due to arrive that morning. It seemed unreal, as if she were watching the cinema.

A military convoy rumbled into view, eight motorcycles side by side, followed by four troop carriers. Then two more motorcycles appeared, escorting an open staff car. The soldiers looked clean and disciplined but, Marguerite thought with disgust, they were Germans. Nazis.

The lead motorcycles throbbed past her, and she studied the men. They looked confident, even arrogant. One of them stared boldly at Simone, who was tall and pretty with long blonde hair. Her father, Jean LaVaque, was the wealthiest man in town and Simone always wore stylish clothes.

The soldier smiled at Simone as he passed the Hotel Eau-de-Vie. He had blond eyebrows, Marguerite noted. Simone smiled back, and when the soldier touched the brim of his helmet with two fingers, she waved.

"*Mon Dieu*, they're handsome! Did you see that one? He saluted me!"

"You idiot," Bérénice hissed. "They're here to occupy our town!"

"But Simone is right," Yvonne whispered. She wore a forest green frock that set off her dark hair. "They are good-looking, and they look so self-assured. Do you think we'll get to meet any of them?"

Marguerite was ashamed. "Do neither of you have any pride?"

"We have to get along with them," Yvonne retorted. "They're our government, now."

Bérénice shook her head. "*Non*, we don't, you fools. They are the enemy. Stop panting after them."

Marguerite stared at her cousin. She knew Bérénice would not passively accept Nazi occupation, not after fighting in Spain. She worried that being so outspoken would put her cousin in danger.

Yvonne pointed at the open staff car bringing up the rear. "That must be their commander."

The two accompanying cyclists thundered down the main street; the commander sat erect in the back of the car until they reached the hotel. His left arm was missing; the sleeve of his uniform was folded up and pinned to his tunic. His face was unsmiling. *Callous,* Marguerite thought. She shivered.

An aide snapped a salute and opened the car door, and without looking down the officer stepped out and marched to the police station next to the hotel. He stopped directly in front of Lieutenant Lastrange, standing at attention in front of his men. Snapping a riding crop under his injured arm, the commander leaned into Lastrange's face and looked him in the eye. "*Heil* Hitler," he shouted. Then he gave the straight-armed Roman salute.

Lastrange awkwardly touched the brim of his kepi. "*Bonjour*, Colonel."

The colonel brushed past him and strode to the main entrance of the hotel. "This will be my headquarters," he shouted. Two soldiers took up stations at the front of the building; the rest followed him into the hotel. To Marguerite's horror, a moment later a huge blood-red Nazi flag was unfurled from a third-floor window.

Mon Dieu, France is no more.

Bérénice and Marguerite stared at each other and began moving away from their simpering friends. "Will you join us?" her cousin murmured.

"*Non.*" Bérénice was different since she had returned from Spain. More self-assured. Harder. She didn't know her cousin anymore. Sometimes she wasn't even sure she liked her. She swallowed hard. "*Non*, I cannot join you. But . . . let me know if you need any help."

She had to do *something*. Volunteering to help her cousin gave her a small sense of control.

* * *

September 1940

For the rest of the summer Marguerite stayed away from her cousin's farm. In September she began her final year at the *lycée*, in *Mademoiselle* Huet's classroom, to prepare for her baccalaureate exam. The first morning, she surveyed the schoolroom, the chalkboard, the bookcases, the oak cabinets that lined the walls and breathed a cautious sigh of relief. How normal everything looked!

"*Bonjour*," *Mademoiselle* Huet said. "Welcome back to school. This year we have some new responsibilities. We will all learn to speak German, and our curriculum will include . . ." She hesitated ". . . racial studies. We are also required to take daily attendance." She glanced down at her class list. "Is everyone here?"

The students looked at each other and then at the teacher. *Mademoiselle* Huet was young and pretty, with deeply waved short brown hair. Today she wore a dark blue high-necked dress trimmed with white lace. "Is everyone present?" she repeated without looking up. *Mademoiselle* was strict but fair, and she was a stickler for details. She always reported absences, even late arrivals, to the administrative office.

"*Oui*," a single voice called out from the back of the room.

Marguerite counted at least ten empty desks.

"*Bon,* perfect attendance." With a flourish, *Mlle*. Huet ran her pencil down the list and checked off all the names.

Perfect attendance? But it was nothing of the kind! Marguerite then understood her teacher's passive resistance, and she felt a rush of pride.

"Today we will start our classes in German. We will speak German as often as possible, and we will converse with each other only in German. That goes for your parents, as well. We have been asked to report anyone not speaking German, either in public or in private. Is that clear?"

Silence.

Mlle. Huet's voice rose. "Is that clear?"

"*Oui*," came a chorus of voices.

"The word for '*oui*' is '*ja'*." She lifted her arms. "Now, all together."

"*Ja*," everyone repeated.

"*Gut.*"

Yvonne raised her hand. "*Mademoiselle* Huet, how long before we are required to speak only German?"

"That is not known at this time, probably a year."

"To whom do we report people speaking French?" someone on the other side of the room asked.

Mlle. Huet ignored the question. "Now, the words for '*bonjour'* are '*guten Tag*'."

After class, Marguerite walked into town with Simone and Yvonne. "We're supposed to learn an entire language in one year?" Yvonne complained. "Are they serious? Learning German isn't how I want to spend my free time."

Simone twisted a long strand of her blonde hair. "It'll be easier if we practice together." She glanced up. "Well, look who's here."

"*Bonjour*," Bérénice said as she joined them. Her cousin had decided not to attend the lycée this term, so why was she here?

"What's going on?" Bérénice inquired.

Simone frowned. "We're going to learn German in school. And we're supposed to report anyone speaking French."

Bérénice stared at her, then at Marguerite. Then she pointed to the sky. "Look up there. See those long white clouds? Those are bomber contrails."

"What are you talking about?" Simone shaded her eyes and looked up.

"Look! Look at them! Don't you listen to the radio? The Nazis are bombing England from airfields here in Normandy. Those airplanes are killing people like us, destroying towns like ours."

Simone wagged a finger at Bérénice. "You're not supposed to be listening to the BBC."

"You get that finger out of my face," Bérénice snapped. "Are you going to report me? Maybe you can turn me in for speaking French, along with your parents. That way you can be the perfect little French Nazi."

"Stop it!" Marguerite hissed. "No one is going to turn in their parents for speaking French. And we're not going to turn in our friends, either, are we?"

Simone glared at Bérénice, then shrugged her shoulders. "I guess not. Why don't you give the Germans a chance?" she said defensively. "France is Germany's natural partner. We're all Aryans. Look what Hitler did in Germany during the Depression. The man is a genius. We could use his help here. Life would be better for everyone."

"*Seig heil!*" Bérénice clicked her heels together and snapped a straight-armed salute.

Simone shot her a look. "Don't do that! If anyone sees you, we'll all be in trouble. The Nazis only want us all to speak the same language. They're trying to be efficient."

"Simone, they're trying to stamp out French language and culture." Bérénice shook her finger in Simone's face. "You watch yourself and keep those opinions to yourself. Others are watching."

Simone flushed. "Who do you think you're talking to, Bérénice?"

They stared at each other, and then Bérénice stalked away, her hands clenched.

"This isn't a game, Simone," Marguerite whispered angrily. "Don't get in too deep."

"You need to be careful, too," Simone said, her voice tight.

Marguerite's chest tightened. Was Simone threatening her? She edged away and caught up with her cousin. "Bérénice, what does she mean, *I* need to be careful?"

"Stay out of it, Marguerite. I can handle Simone."

Marguerite dropped her chin to her chest. "I think Simone has no pride in being French." She met her cousin's eyes. "She is self-centered, and Yvonne is even worse. All they think about is how to advance themselves and get along with the Nazis."

Bérénice pressed her lips together. "At some point we're going to have to choose sides. They've chosen theirs."

"I'm going to have to give up my friendship with them, aren't I?"

"*Non*, Marguerite, just the opposite. You need to get closer to them, become like them, at least on the outside. Then you can help us. We could also use someone with medical skills."

"We? Who is 'we'?" She studied her cousin's face. "What are you doing in town, anyway?"

"Don't ask questions."

Marguerite rolled her eyes. "Don't ask-- ? Bérénice, for pity's sake, I am your *cousin!*"

"All right, then. Tell me what happened in school?"

"*Mademoiselle* Huet said we have to learn German and we will speak only German."

"Really? How long do you have to learn German?"

"She said probably a year. We started today."

"Could you steal a German textbook for me? You can help me with pronunciation. What else happened?"

"She took attendance, but even though there were about ten missing, she didn't mark anyone absent."

"*Bon!*" Her cousin grinned. "She's resisting. We need people like *Mademoiselle* Huet to do more."

Marguerite puzzled over her cousin's words. What was 'more'? What was Bérénice involved in? Something inside her felt sick. She knew in her bones that people she cared about were going to get hurt.

She pedaled her bicycle home, and just as she wheeled it into the driveway, a black police Citroën drove out of the farmyard. She dropped her bike and raced inside. "*Maman!* What were the police doing here?"

Her mother smoothed back her dark hair and grabbed Marguerite's arm. "They were looking for your Uncle Pierre. Quick, run over to Perdu farm and warn them. I telephoned, but no one answered."

An icy hand gripped her insides. Marguerite slipped out the back door and ran the shortcut all the way to Perdu. At the back door and she shouted for her cousin. "Bérénice? Bérénice, where are you?"

"Right here." Bérénice took her hands out of the washtub on the porch and dried them on her apron. She looked pale and her hands shook.

"Are you all right?"

"*Oui*, I'm fine," she snapped. "What are you doing here?"

"The police came to our house looking for your father."

Bérénice leaned her lanky frame against the washtub. "We know. They've already been here."

"Did they arrest him?"

"*Non.* We have lookouts watching the roads around Perdu. They saw the police coming and signaled the house. Papa hid while they were here, and after they left, he went to Creully to go underground. As far as anyone around here is concerned, he went back to Pamplona."

"But— "

"*Réfugié* will live on. It has to."

"*Réfugié*?"

"Oh!" Bérénice clapped one hand over her mouth.

"What is *Réfugié*? Tell me."

"That was a mistake. Really, Marguerite, it's best if you stay out of this. You know too much already. And stay away from Perdu. If you want to talk, telephone me and I'll come over."

Marguerite changed the subject. "I haven't seen the new tunnel your workers are constructing under the storage building. Is it finished?"

"How do you know about that?"

"Papa told me."

"Well, don't ask about it. As far as you're concerned, it doesn't exist."

Marguerite studied her cousin's pale face. "It doesn't exist? Of course it exists. That's all Uncle Pierre and Papa have talked about for weeks."

Bérénice turned away without answering.

Exactly what was going on under her uncle's storage building?

CHAPTER THREE
THE CAVE

After school the next afternoon Marguerite was sitting in the kitchen sipping a cup of tea when she heard a vehicle enter the farmyard. Through the front window she watched the orange Perdu pickup truck rattle to a stop. It was only seven years old, but the rigors of farm life showed in its dents and loose fenders.

She walked out to the porch, and Bérénice slid out of the passenger seat. One of her uncle's workers, slim, dark-haired José Castello, waited behind the wheel.

Her cousin grabbed her arm. "Marguerite, you have to come with us."

She wrenched her arm away. "Why? What's going on?"

"There's been an accident. There's a man hurt at Perdu. He's bleeding and we need you to get it stopped."

"Did you call the doctor?"

Bérénice yanked her arm. "We can't let anyone know about—." She broke off. "There's no time. It has to be you."

"Stop pulling on me! I need to get my emergency kit. Wait here."

She raced upstairs, snatched her veterinary medical kit from under the bed, and returned to the yard.

"Hurry," Bérénice yelled.

She jumped in the truck next to her cousin, and José sped out of the farmyard. "Where is this man?" Marguerite panted.

Bérénice braced herself as José barreled around another curve. "In the Cave."

"What?"

"He's in the Cave, under the storage building."

Marguerite hung on as José took another fast turn. "How did he get hurt?"

"We're almost there," her cousin barked. Marguerite noticed she didn't answer the question.

The truck turned down a lane hidden between two dense green hedgerows and parked near a leafy thicket at the base of the hill. Bérénice jumped out and waved for Marguerite to follow. José scrambled ahead, reached into the thicket, and tugged on something mechanical. The greenery swung away.

Bérénice touched her arm and guided her into a dim passageway. José pulled the outer gate closed and darkness engulfed them; then he slipped past them and opened an interior door. Light poured in and cold, damp air washed over her. She rubbed warmth into her upper arms and gazed around the chamber.

The enclosure was about 10 by 20 meters with cots, tables, and chairs scattered in the open area and calvados casks stacked three high against the walls. A threadbare brown carpet covered the floor and worn tapestries decorated the walls. A large French tri-color hung over one of the tapestries. Marguerite hadn't seen a French flag in months.

Wooden stairs led upward into darkness, and the only light came from bare electric bulbs hanging from the ceiling. The room smelled of oak and fermenting fruit turning into the apple brandy known as calvados. In the center, Uncle Pierre stood over a man lying face down on one of the cots. His shirt had been ripped open, and Richard bent over him, a bloody rag in his hands. Both their shirts were blood-stained.

"Marguerite, quick!" Richard called over his shoulder. "See if you can stop this bleeding."

She froze. "I… I am not sure I can."

Richard snorted. "I've seen what you can do. Now get over here."

"Richard, please. Remember, that man outside Paris died when I tried to help."

"Marguerite, just try!"

She took his place and pressed the cloth hard onto the man's bleeding wound, slowly released pressure, and peeked underneath. Blood oozed from a neat, round hole. Quickly, she reapplied pressure. "Is this a gunshot wound?"

"*Oui,* it is."

"What is he doing here?"

"I brought him," her uncle declared.

"I thought you went to Creully?"

Uncle Pierre stared at her.

She closed her eyes as understanding dawned. "Oh!" She looked down at the injured man. "Get me some clean cloths, hot water, and some alcohol."

"I'll get them," said Bérénice. She raced out the tunnel entrance.

"Is a doctor coming?"

"*Non.* We can't bring anyone here," Richard said tersely. "We have a doctor in Creully."

"You'll never get him there. He'll bleed to death."

"Then you're going to have to patch him up here."

Marguerite took a deep breath. She decided she needed to cauterize the wound. "Richard, get me a sharp knife, narrow enough to fit in this bullet hole. And I need heat. I need to get the blade red hot."

"I'll do it." Her uncle disappeared up the dark stairs and returned with a penknife and a candle. Marguerite shook her head. "The knife is good, but the candle will take too long."

"Wait here." Richard pounded up the stairs two at a time and returned with an electric hotplate. He plugged it in and held the penknife against the coil.

Marguerite's confidence grew. "I'm going to push that knife into his wound. When I do, he's going to jump, so you'll need to hold him down."

"I'll do it," her uncle offered.

"You won't be enough. Richard, straddle his legs, then hand me the knife. Uncle Pierre, put your arms around his head and shoulders. He'll jerk hard, so hold on tight."

"What about the bullet?" Richard asked. "Aren't you going to take it out?"

"*Non*. I don't know enough. I'll leave it until you can get him to a real doctor."

Richard heated the blade until it glowed cherry red. Marguerite took a deep breath. "All right, hold him."

Richard climbed over the man's thighs and deftly handed her the penknife. Her uncle hugged the man's shoulders and waited. She grasped the knife, lifted the rag, and plunged the red hot blade into the open wound. He screamed and jerked, but Richard and her uncle held him still. Quickly, she pressed a clean cloth onto the bullet hole and he groaned and went limp. She smelled burnt flesh.

After a moment, she peeked under the compress, watched the bullet hole for a moment, and reapplied pressure. "The bleeding has stopped," she murmured. "Now, I need to clean the wound."

All at once she felt light headed. She stepped away from the cot and sank onto a chair, then had the odd sensation that she was watching herself work on the man's back. She shook the image out of her mind and sucked in a lungful of air.

The tunnel door opened and Bérénice returned with clean cloths, hot water, and a brown bottle of alcohol. Marguerite forced herself onto her feet and sponged the man's back with warm water. "Who is he?" she asked. "Why was he shot?"

"He's someone important to our movement."

She paused, an alcohol-soaked cloth in her hand. "*Réfugié*?"

Richard shot her a look. "*Oui*. How do you know that name?"

"It's not important. Is he Spanish?"

"*Non*, he's French."

"He's a Communist?"

Richard tilted his head and shrugged. "He is a good man who needs our help."

Marguerite's mind spun. She was involved with an illegal operation, in a secret hiding place, doctoring a fugitive. "Richard, what if the police catch us? We would all go to jail, including me."

"We do what we have to. You were our only choice, Marguerite. We're grateful you are here."

Richard's comment sent a wave of warmth into her chest. Whoever or whatever this man was, she knew she had saved his life. But she had to think. If the police had shot him or, worse, the Nazis, they could all be arrested.

"Do my parents know what you're doing down here?"

"We haven't told them," Richard said, his voice flat.

"Try to understand," Bérénice pleaded. "Without you, LeBel would have bled to death. A doctor or a nurse would have to report a gunshot wound to the police, and then the Nazis would get involved. LeBel hasn't hurt anyone or stolen anything. He's done nothing wrong."

Marguerite's stomach churned. She had saved a life, but deep inside she knew it would mean trouble. "I don't want to be involved."

"You won't be," Richard promised. "Just keep this to yourself."

She finished cleaning LeBel's wound. "I need to put in a couple of temporary stitches. Hand me my medical kit." She sterilized a curved needle and silk thread with alcohol and sutured the man's wound.

"You're going to have to keep him here for a while. If you move him too soon his wound could reopen."

"How long?" Richard asked.

"Two days at least, maybe three. But Richard, you need to get him to a doctor, understand?"

Richard nodded.

"*Bon*. He's lost a lot of blood, and when he wakes up, he'll be thirsty. Give him some water, and when he's stronger, some chicken broth. I've done all I can."

Her uncle smiled and laid a gentle hand on her shoulder. "*Merci*, Marguerite."

Richard stepped in close and hugged her shoulders. "*Merci,*" he said quietly. When he released her, she looked down at her blood-stained dress.

"Bérénice, I need to change."

Her cousin nodded. "You could be valuable to us, Marguerite."

"I can't get involved with this. I'm glad I was able to help this man, but I can do no more."

Bérénice glanced at her father, then at Richard. "France is your country, Marguerite. Sooner or later you will have to choose sides."

Marguerite clenched her jaw. She wasn't going to make a choice. She didn't want to get involved in something that could threaten Papa and *Maman*, something that might interrupt her schooling or her work with Dr. Morel. She loved France, but she was only one person, and a frightened one at that. What possible difference could one person make?

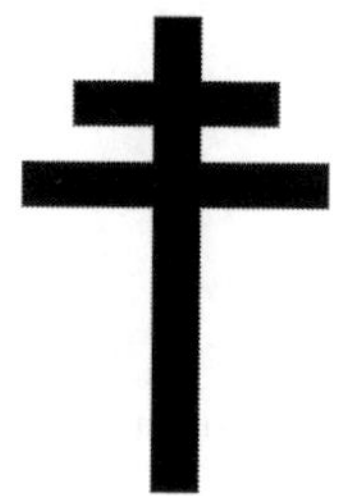

CHAPTER FOUR
CHOOSING SIDES

May 1941

Marguerite graduated from the *lycée* and passed her baccalaureate examination, but she agreed to stay on at Charentais, her family's farm, for a year to help her father. The Nazis had occupied Ville de Pommes; now, even the French police were required to speak German. Every Sunday evening when she walked to Perdu to hear de Gaulle's BBC broadcast from London, she felt more pulled toward working with Bérénice and Richard and getting involved with whatever they were doing.

She was restless and unsatisfied. Something was stirring inside her, a kind of reaching inward. She mourned what happened to Ville de Pommes, to all of France, and she hungered for significance in her life, for connection to what was real. It wasn't enough to bake bread with *Maman* every other day and help Papa on the farm. She wanted to be a patriot.

For the past week she had felt especially unsettled. On Sunday night after supper she was about to leave to visit Bérénice when her father stopped her at the kitchen door. "Where are you going?"

Marguerite froze at the accusation in his voice. "To Bérénice's."

He paced back and forth on the tile floor. "I told you to stay away from Perdu."

"I only visit on Sunday night, Papa. Bérénice is like a sister to me."

Her mother stacked the plate she had just dried. “You’re going to listen to the radio, aren’t you? To the BBC. You know that the Germans have banned Radio London.”

“We don’t listen to the radio,” Marguerite lied. “We just talk.”

Her father leaned against the kitchen counter and folded his arms across his chest. “Marguerite, *we* need to talk.”

“All right,” she retorted. “Let’s talk about my nursing internship. You agreed that if I worked on the farm for a year I could go to school. It’s been almost a year since graduation.”

“I said that after a year we would talk about it. I never said you could go.”

Anger flooded her. “We had an agreement, Papa! I promised to wait a year, and I did.”

“It’s that Dr. Morel and his animal clinic, isn’t it?” he grumbled. “There is no way a veterinary school will accept a woman. That is a man’s job.”

“No, Papa. I do not want to be a vet. I want to be a nurse.” Her parents didn’t understand about nursing. In a medical clinic or a hospital she would feel needed, and the work would be important. Exciting.

He gave her a long look. “Marguerite, you are my only child. What will happen to you if you leave Ville de Pommes? What will happen to our farm when your mother and I are too old to work it?”

“Sell it.” The words flew out of her mouth before she could stop them.

Her mother’s lips twisted. “We will not sell this farm. Never. This was all we had during the Depression, and you want us to sell it?”

Marguerite put her arms around her mother. “I am sorry, *Maman*, but nursing is what I want to do, not farming.” Farming was endless drudgery, and it required no special skill, like nursing.

She glanced at her father. “May I go now?” Papa angrily waved his hand and tramped out of the kitchen. Clamping her lips together, Marguerite closed the kitchen door behind her and started down the hill to the shortcut. She had to go to Perdu tonight, not only for the radio broadcast but to talk to Uncle Pierre about the Vidals.

* * *

“Bérénice,” she called at her cousin’s back door. “Are you there?”

“In here. You’re late.”

She joined her cousin, José, and Richard in the parlor, taking her usual place on the sofa. She looked up when the front door opened.

Bérénice bolted from her seat. "Papa! What are you doing here?"

Uncle Pierre stood in the doorway. "Richard said Marguerite wanted to talk to me."

Richard and José rose to shake hands with Pierre. Marguerite went to her uncle and kissed both his cheeks. "Uncle Pierre," she murmured.

"Please, sit down," her uncle said. "Has the broadcast started?" He slipped off his jacket and hung it in the closet.

Bérénice dialed the BBC frequency and tuned into Radio London's French language program, which aired every Sunday night. "It's starting now, Papa."

"And now, ladies and gentlemen, the leader of the Free French Government, General Charles de Gaulle."

Marguerite liked de Gaulle. He defied the Vichy government and presented himself as a legitimate alternative. The general represented the real France, the France that chose to fight and not capitulate. It was De Gaulle who had inspired her to help the Vidal family.

"Tonight I address the members of the Résistance. You are the heart of a great people, the heart of the struggle. Persevere! No matter how long it takes, France will be free again because of you. Vive la France!"

Marguerite leaned back and let the general's words wash over her. Her parents' don't-get-involved attitude irritated her. She wanted her country to be free.

After the broadcast, Uncle Pierre leaned toward her, his elbows on his knees. "You wanted to ask me something?"

"*Oui.* Do you remember Paul and Sarah Vidal, the old couple who own the bakery?"

He nodded.

"They've always been kind to me, especially Sarah. They are the only Jews in Ville de Pommes, and three weeks ago someone denounced them to the Germans."

"How do you know this?"

"Simone mentioned it at our auxiliary meeting last week."

"Auxiliary? What auxiliary? Who are the members?"

"There are only four of us because Simone wants to keep it small. You know her father, Jean; he owns the bank, and he got Simone a clerk's job at Nazi headquarters. Simone says it helps her do favors for Ville de Pommes citizens. There's also Yvonne Callion; she works for her father at Callion Construction, which just won a big contract from *Organisation Todt* to build beach defenses for the Germans. And there is also Yvette Rounet. Her father is the attorney who works with Papa and the Growers' Association. We meet once a month at Café Angéle."

Pierre's dark eyes bored into hers. "Why do you meet?"

"Because we want to help. Simone is friendly with the German soldiers, but she admits she loves France. We all do."

"They are all daughters of collaborators," Bérénice sniffed.

Marguerite glanced at her cousin but said nothing.

"What about the Vidals?" Pierre asked.

"Last week their bakery was vandalized. Someone broke the windows and painted swastikas on the walls and *Juden* on the front door. Then two days ago Simone overheard someone at Nazi headquarters say the Gestapo was finally going to do something about them."

"When?"

She bit her lip and shook her head. "Soon I would guess. Sarah told me they're afraid they'll be arrested and shipped to one of those work camps in Germany or Poland."

"What do you want me to do?"

Marguerite swallowed. "Could you get them out of Ville de Pommes before they're arrested?"

Pierre's eyebrows shot up. "That's a pretty big request."

"I know, Uncle. But remember, you owe me a favor for saving LeBel's life. That was a year ago, but you still owe me."

Pierre rubbed his chin and glanced at Richard.

"She's right," Richard said with a shrug. "We do owe her."

Her uncle gazed thoughtfully at her for a long minute, then slapped his thigh. "Done! I'll make the arrangements. Richard, send Miguel to talk to the Vidals."

Marguerite sat up and smiled. "*Merci*, Uncle Pierre."

Later, she hiked back home, feeling good that she could do something for her friends. And for France.

Three days later, the Vidals simply vanished. Marguerite heard a rumor that the Gestapo had arrested them, but Simone confided that the Gestapo knew nothing about it. Marguerite spread the Gestapo rumor anyway.

* * *

Marguerite knew her cousin avoided Charentais because her parents made her feel uncomfortable, so she was surprised on Monday afternoon when

Bérénice showed up at the house. "Bérénice! What are you doing here?"

"Happy birthday, Marguerite!" Her cousin threw her arms around her, then handed her a small box. "This is for you."

She opened it to find a chain with a medal attached. "What's this?"

"It's a *Jeanne d'Arc* medal. She's my patron saint, and I wanted to share her with you."

Marguerite held the medal up to the light. "But things didn't work out too well for poor Jeanne," she quipped. She glanced at Bérénice, expecting a smile, but instead her cousin's face looked somber.

"What's the matter?"

"I don't believe I will survive the Occupation. Each day I pray to Saint Jeanne that my death will be meaningful, that in some way it will help to restore France."

"Don't say that!" Her cousin's fatalism frightened her. "Bérénice, you will make it. You have to."

Her cousin smiled. "I'm sorry. I came here to give you a gift to cheer you up and instead, I've made you uncomfortable. By convincing myself that I will not survive, I am more effective. It is only once in a while that I feel sorry for myself."

Marguerite touched her cousin's shoulder. "It's a thoughtful gift, Bérénice. *Merci*. And we'll get through this together. Agreed?"

Bérénice gave her an unconvincing nod.

Her cousin fastened the chain around her neck and Marguerite dropped the medal inside her dress.

She gave her a hug and Bérénice's face brightened. "Do you really like it?"

"*Oui*, I do. *Merci*." She smoothed her hand over her chest.

Bérénice touched her arm. "Can we talk privately? I have something to ask you." She led Marguerite out the back door where they could sit and enjoy the cool evening air. "Have you heard about Guy Massu? He's escaped from a German prison camp, and we think he's somewhere near Ville de Pommes."

Marguerite folded her arms on her knees and tilted her head to study her cousin. "Why are you telling me this?"

"Didn't you like him when we were at the *lycée*?"

She hesitated. "That was a long time ago. I doubt he would remember me."

"We thought you might help us find him."

"Me!" Marguerite gaped at her. "How could I do that?"

"You could ask Doctor Morel. He visits all the farms, and he might hear something."

Marguerite hesitated. She was grateful that the Vidal family was safe, and she did want to help France. Asking questions was a small thing, and it wasn't risky. "Very well, I will ask him tomorrow."

The next morning, Marguerite bicycled into town and found Dr. Morel behind his clinic, cleaning out the back seat of his Citroën. "Marguerite! I didn't expect you today. Why are you here?"

"*Bonjour*, Doctor Morel. How are you?"

He narrowed his eyes. *Trés bien*, and you?"

She scanned the alley and the fenced yards surrounding the clinic backyard. "Do you know if Guy Massu is in the area?" she whispered.

The tall, slow-moving vet raised his head. "So that's what this is all about." He jerked his thumb over his shoulder. "Let's go inside." He led her into his office and carefully closed the door.

"Marguerite, you are asking dangerous questions."

"Perhaps. But I know some people who could help Guy."

His narrow face looked puzzled. "*Réfugié*?"

She gasped. "How do you know about that?"

"I hear things." He took a deep breath. "We've been trying to make contact with *Réfugié*. I didn't know you were with them."

"I'm not. But they asked me to talk to you, as a favor." She leaned back in the chair and folded her hands.

Morel looked at her steadily for a time. "Tomorrow is Saturday. Pick up Guy behind the building next door."

"Oh? All right. Very well."

"What's the matter?"

"I didn't think it would be that simple."

"What is your code name?" he asked suddenly.

"My code name?" She touched the medal under her blouse. "Uh, Patrice. Patrice Cerne."

"Why Patrice?"

She thought for a moment. "Saint Patrick drove the snakes out of Ireland. Maybe as Patrice I can help drive the snakes from France."

Dr. Morel chuckled. "After the clinic closes tomorrow, Guy will come from next door, looking for Patrice Cerne."

"Doctor Morel, I think he will recognize me. Why not tell him he's meeting Marguerite Auriol?"

"Because if he is arrested, he'll tell them he was meeting Patrice Cerne. He won't know it's you, Marguerite, until he sees you. That way, you and *Refugie* are protected."

Marguerite stuffed her hands in her pockets and dried her suddenly sweaty palms. "Can't one of the *Réfugié* people pose as Patrice?"

He shook his head. "*Non*, you don't understand. I must know the person who is meeting him, and I need to trust that person."

She slipped her hands out of her pockets. "I usually prefer not to get involved. Not directly, anyway."

He held her gaze. "If you are not here, Marguerite, Guy won't be, either. It has to be someone I trust, and I trust you. I am also risking *my* life."

"I understand," she said, her voice quiet.

"*Bon.* Now, come and help me clean out my car."

Later, she rode her bicycle back to Perdu and reported to Bérénice. "Guy will be behind the building next to the animal clinic after closing tomorrow. We need to meet him there."

"*We*? I thought you didn't want to get involved."

"I don't. But Doctor Morel says I have to be there. He trusts me. If I am not there, Guy will not come."

Her cousin nodded. "I will arrange it."

CHAPTER FIVE
THE FUGITIVE

Marguerite liked working on Saturdays because it was clinic day. This morning she parked her bicycle inside Dr. Morel's back door and put her lab coat on over her blue-flowered dress. All day long the villagers brought in a steady stream of ailing cats, dogs with thorns in their paws, even a pet monkey. Their last patient of the day was a Brittany spaniel with a skin disorder, brought in by a young woman in a calf-length burgundy dress and a floppy sun hat. Marguerite didn't recognize her. Perhaps she was the wife of a German officer?

Dr. Morel was ahead of schedule, so Marguerite gave the woman a tin of medicated cream and explained how to apply it. Before she was done, the vet came in and chatted with the woman. Impatient with the conversation and uneasy about Guy Massu, Marguerite left the examination room to dust the storage cabinets and settle her nerves. When she heard the woman leave, she found Dr. Morel in his office. "Is everything ready next door?" she whispered.

He didn't look up. "I don't know what you're talking about. Lock up when you're finished in the storeroom."

Marguerite busied herself restocking drawers and arranging shelves. *Madame* Benault, the receptionist, stuck her head in to say goodbye; Marguerite then heard the vet turn the key in the back door lock. She checked every room in the clinic to make certain she was alone. She had just finished when a knock startled her.

She looked out the back door window. "Bérénice! *You're* my contact?"

Her cousin wore a buttoned blue cardigan over her skirt and her kick-fighting shoes, the ugly black ones she got when she learned savate in Spain. "We thought it would look less suspicious if we knew each other."

"Isn't it a little warm for a sweater?"

Bérénice shouldered past Marguerite into the clinic and unbuttoned her sweater to reveal a revolver in a holster under her arm.

Marguerite blanched. "Wait! We don't need that."

Her cousin re-buttoned her sweater. "I got knifed during a rendezvous in Spain. I have been to my last rendezvous unarmed."

Suddenly a series of sharp pops broke the silence. "What was that?" Marguerite pushed past her cousin to look outside, but instantly Bérénice pulled her back and slammed the door.

"Gunfire!"

Marguerite caught her breath. "*Mon Dieu.* You don't think . . . ?"

"I don't know, but we have to be careful." Her cousin peeked out the window. "Someone's coming."

They ducked down and waited in silence. It went on so long Marguerite's heart began to pound. Finally a male voice outside murmured, "Is Patrice Cerne in there?"

Bérénice yanked open the door and Marguerite pulled the young man inside. "*Oui*, come in, quickly." He hobbled into the clinic dragging one leg and sagged against the wall. Oh, yes, she recognized Guy Massu. He wore torn, filthy trousers and a black cap; his narrow face looked white and he clutched his left thigh with both hands.

"Can you help me? I'm hurt."

"*Oui*," Marguerite whispered. "Bérénice, go outside and see if anyone's around."

Her cousin slipped out the back door and Marguerite turned her attention to Guy. "Can you stand?"

"Only on one leg."

She lifted his left arm around her shoulders, helped him into the middle treatment room, and eased him down onto the floor. Bérénice returned to report all was clear.

"Lock the back door and turn off the lights," Marguerite ordered. "We'll use this room because there are no windows." She knelt over Guy and moved her fingers along his thigh. Guy jerked and gritted his teeth. She could feel his thigh bone was broken, and blood welled from a bullet wound just below the break. *Mon Dieu, can I really do this?*

"Bérénice, bring me Doctor Morel's medical bag, it's by the back door. He— "

She heard pounding at the front door and broke off. Quickly she moved to the waiting room window and peered out the window.

Her insides went cold. "It's Lieutenant Lastrange! Quick," she whispered, "Bérénice, try to stall him." Frantically she searched for a place to hide Guy. When she heard her cousin unlock the front door, she fought panic.

"*Guten Tag*, Officer," Bérénice said. "May I help you?"

Hurriedly Marguerite emptied the large cabinet below the sink and made a space to hide Guy. "I need you to crawl in there," she whispered. She grabbed a sturdy splint and quickly wrapped it tight against his thigh to keep it straight, then helped him across the floor and into the empty space. When she bent his knees to fit, he sucked in his breath and clenched his jaw. She stacked cleaning supplies in front of him and closed the cabinet doors.

Then, as calmly as she could, she walked into the waiting room.

"*Guten Tag, Fraulein* Auriol." The tall, thin police lieutenant rose up on his toes to peer over her head. "Is everything all right back there?"

"*Ja*," she and Bérénice answered in unison.

He cleared his throat. "What are you two doing here?"

"I work here with Dr. Morel," Marguerite explained. "My cousin came to meet me so we could go into the village after work. I was just locking up."

Lastrange drew his revolver. "I'd better have a look around."

"*Ja*, of course," Marguerite said, working to keep her voice steady.

The officer's suspicious eyes searched the waiting room and the office areas; then he moved down the hallway toward the treatment rooms. Bérénice quietly pulled her revolver from inside her sweater and followed him.

Mon Dieu, she's going to shoot him.

She stepped in front of Bérénice to screen her from the lieutenant's view. Her cousin placed the flat side of the revolver against her back and nudged her forward. *What is she going to do?*

Lastrange searched the storeroom. Marguerite felt a sudden surge of terror and jammed her hands in her lab coat pockets to hide their trembling. The lieutenant then crossed the hall to the front treatment room and stepped inside.

Bérénice leaned in the doorway, watching him, but she kept her gun hidden. Marguerite shot her a glance and caught her breath; her cousin's eyes had the cold look of a predator, her entire focus on Lastrange.

The lieutenant grasped the door handle of the middle treatment room and opened it. Bérénice lunged toward him, but Marguerite blocked her. She watched the officer open the cabinet below the sink and her heart sank. She had to do something, but what?

She moved toward him. “Lieutenant, those are just supplies. What are you looking for?”

Frowning, he studied the cleaning supplies under the sink. “We shot a criminal earlier today, but he escaped. I believe he was meeting someone near here.”

“Meeting someone?” Marguerite echoed. “Who?”

“That we don’t know. Have you seen any strangers?” He closed the cabinet doors.

Marguerite shot a glance at her cousin and they both shook their heads. Lastrange proceeded to the last treatment room, and Marguerite stayed right behind him. Her legs felt rubbery, but she did her best to walk normally.

The lieutenant stroked his bony chin and peered into the room. After a long minute he shrugged and holstered his gun. “I see no one here.” He turned and marched toward the door, and Marguerite and Bérénice flattened themselves against the wall to let him pass. Before he had taken three steps he suddenly turned to confront them.

“Keep this door locked and report anything suspicious.”

Marguerite gave him her best wide-eyed look. “*Danke*, Lieutenant.”

“*Auf Wiedersehen*,” he replied. He touched his kepi visor and strode out.

With a sigh of relief, Marguerite locked the door behind him. Bérénice pulled her around to face her. “What did you do with Guy?” she hissed. “Where is he?”

Marguerite rushed to the middle treatment room, opened the cabinet doors, and pulled out the supplies to reveal Guy’s hiding place. “Quick! Help me get him out of there.” The two of them grasped his shoulders and carefully dragged him out of the cabinet. Bérénice accidentally bumped his leg, and he yelped.

They stretched him flat on the floor. “How are you doing?” Marguerite whispered.

His face was ashen and sweaty. “My leg really hurts.”

She looked at her cousin. “Go outside. Make sure Lastrange is really gone.”

“*Non!*” Bérénice snapped. “The police know Guy is near. They’ll be watching outside.”

Marguerite wrenched her attention back to Guy. “Bérénice, get Doctor Morel’s medical bag, by the back door.”

Bérénice darted out and returned with the bag, unbuckled it, and slid it close to her.

"You're Marguerite Auriol, aren't you?" Guy said suddenly.

Marguerite smiled. "*Oui.* I didn't think you'd remember."

"I wouldn't forget a face like yours."

Marguerite knew her cheeks were turning red. *Mon Dieu, I haven't blushed since I was ten years old.* She bent to untie the splint and slit his trouser leg above the knee. "Bérénice, there's a large cup in that bag with some long straps on it. Pull it out and set it over there. Now, find the brown bottle labeled chloroform."

"What's the cup for?"

"We use it to anesthetize horses."

"Horses! You're going to kill him."

Exasperated, Marguerite glared at her cousin. "We also use it on colts, calves, sheep, and dogs--whatever animal we need to anesthetize."

Guy rose up on one elbow. "Marguerite, do you know what you're doing?"

She gently pushed him back down. "*Oui*, I do. Bérénice, help me get his trouser leg off."

When the bullet wound was exposed, she checked the underside of his thigh. "Just my luck," she muttered. "No exit wound." She tried to lift his leg and he screamed. "Guy, you're in so much pain I'm going to put you to sleep. Bérénice, take the cup and fill it with cotton. Now, add about half a finger's width of chloroform. Don't breathe it in or you'll be on the floor next to him. Now, hold the cup over his nose for a few seconds."

She waited for Guy's body to relax into unconsciousness. "*Bon*. Now, let him breathe some air, and every time he stirs, put the cup back over his nose . . . and look away. Don't watch me cutting and probing his wound."

Perspiration rolled down her forehead and she blotted it with her sleeve. "I'm not sure about this, Bérénice."

"Why? You've taken out a bullet before."

"*Oui*, but I don't know whether his thigh bone is shattered, and that makes this complicated. Otherwise, I could just remove the bullet and set the bone."

The color drained from her cousin's face. "Don't tell me about it, just do it." She turned her head to one side.

Marguerite sterilized a scalpel and a pair of forceps with alcohol, then cleaned Guy's injury, spread the edges of the wound, and poked around with a probe looking for the bullet and debris. It looked clean, but the bleeding started again, so she applied pressure with a clean piece of linen.

"Let him breathe normally. Bérénice, are you still with me?"

Her cousin nodded, but her face was pasty.

"I have to cut open the wound a little more. If I hit an artery, I'll need you to hand me one of those clamps."

Bérénice did not reply. Using the scalpel Marguerite sliced the torn flesh down to the bone, inserted the forceps, and located the bullet. She extracted it and dropped into a metal bowl with a clink, then sucked air into her lungs. Next she stitched and bandaged the wound, placed sturdy wooden splints on each side of his thigh, and wrapped them tight.

"Now, put the chloroform away and let him wake up."

Bérénice removed the cup and sealed the chloroform bottle.

"You look pale, Bérénice."

"I feel faint."

"You're through with the tough part, now stay with me. How are we going to get him out of here?"

"Red, I mean Richard, planned to bring the pickup. I'll go out and look for him. I need the air anyway." She returned in a few minutes and Marguerite noticed some color had returned to her cousin's face.

"Feeling better?"

Bérénice nodded.

"Is Richard here yet?" Her cousin shook her head and Marguerite's blood turned cold. There was nothing to do but wait, so she steeled her nerves, methodically cleaned her instruments, and repacked them in Dr. Morel's medical bag. Then she bent over Guy, listening to his shallow breathing.

Suddenly a key scraped in the back door lock and she heard Lieutenant Lastrange's muffled voice. "Where are you going, Dr. Morel?"

Marguerite shot a terrified look at Bérénice, who signaled her to be quiet, then reached under her sweater and pulled out the revolver.

"Oh! Lieutenant," Dr. Morel said in a loud voice. "You startled me. What are you doing here at my clinic?"

Thank God it was the vet and not Richard. With a trembling hand she smoothed Guy's sticky forehead. *Please, please don't let Guy make any noise.*

"I'm searching for a wounded man, a criminal," the lieutenant replied. "I checked with Doctor Kunard in town. He said the man might come here."

"I treat only animals, Lieutenant. I do not treat people."

"Why are you here so late?"

"There is an emergency at the Baillard farm. I stopped to get my medical bag."

Marguerite froze. She looked across the room at Dr. Morel's bag just as

Guy moaned and moved his arm. Her heart somersaulted into her belly. She knelt beside Guy and laid her hand over his mouth. "Shhhh," she whispered.

"May I go with you on your call, Doctor?" Lastrange asked.

"Certainly, I'd appreciate the company. Let me get my bag."

With her foot Marguerite shoved the leather bag past Bérénice into the hallway, praying Dr. Morel would see it. She heard his measured footsteps and saw him pick up his bag without looking in the room. Then he retreated down the hall and out the back door. The key turned in the lock and she heard his voice. "Let's go, Lieutenant."

Bérénice holstered her revolver and Marguerite tried to stop shaking. She bowed her head over Guy's chest and listened to her pulse thunder in her ears.

Guy covered her hand with his and squeezed weakly. "Well done," he whispered. He reached up, curled one hand behind her neck, and pulled her head down. "You saved my life today, more than once today. How can I thank you?"

"There is no need to thank me."

Guy looked as if he wanted to say more, but out of the corner of her eye she caught Bérénice shaking her head with an unmistakable look that said *not now.*

Someone tapped at the door. "That has to be Red," Bérénice said. She darted out and returned with the tall Irishman. He studied the figure on the floor.

"Can we move him?" he asked.

"*Oui*," Marguerite answered.

Guy tried to sit up, but he was too weak, so Richard and Bérénice ducked under his arms and helped him hobble outside. She saw the pain in Guy's eyes when they loaded him in the bed of the truck, but he made no sound. Brave man.

Marguerite picked up her bicycle and waited while Richard rearranged sacks of potatoes to clear a space and settled Guy into it. "I'm piling these sacks over you, Guy. Any questions?"

"The police ambushed me but I got away with a bullet in my thigh. How did they know I was coming here?"

Richard shrugged and arranged potato sacks up to Guy's head.

"Where are you taking me?"

"Out of town. The police will be scouring Ville de Pommes for you. Any more questions?"

"How long will it take?"

"Not long. Less than an hour."

Guy gritted his teeth. "Just make it quick."

Richard positioned the last bag over Guy's head, loaded Marguerite's bicycle on top, and helped her into the cab. "Let's get out of here."

She twisted her neck to see Guy out the rear window, but he was completely hidden. She prayed that all those potatoes and her bicycle would not press too heavily on his thigh. The truck engine was loud enough to muffle any sound he might make.

Richard drove to Perdu and parked at the tunnel entrance. Bérénice pulled the thicket gate open, and together they helped a sweating Guy into the Cave and laid him on a cot. Marguerite checked his bandages and the splint.

"Are you all right?" she asked.

"*Oui*," came his weak voice. "But I could use something to drink."

Richard pointed up the stairs. "Bérénice, there are cases of calvados upstairs. Grab a bottle and see if you can find a cup or a glass. I've got to go, but make sure Guy knows where the food supplies are hidden."

Guy tried to smile. "*Merci*, Red. I appreciate what you and the girls have done for me."

CHAPTER SIX
TRAINING FOR RÉSISTANCE

June 1941

Marguerite finished the climb up Perdu's hill and stuck her head in the kitchen. "Richard, are you in there?"

"*Oui*, I'm here."

She followed his voice to the office, where he sat behind her uncle's desk. "*Bonjour*, Marguerite. What can I do for you?"

She closed the door, sat down, and folded her hands. "Is Guy all right? I could check his leg if you wish."

He gave her an assessing look. "We had a doctor look at him, and he's recovering well. The doctor said you did a good job."

"*Bon.* I'm glad." She pushed herself to the edge of her chair. "If Guy is in the Cave, could I look in on him?"

Richard leaned forward and spread his big hands on the desk. "Marguerite, you cannot have a relationship with one of our guests. We have to keep our emotions out of this work."

She straightened up, indignant. "But…but…"

"It was unfortunate that Morel insisted on your being there. It would have been better if it had been someone Guy did not recognize. That way, if he is captured, he couldn't identify either his contact or those who helped him. Now he can identify three members of *Réfugié*."

"Three members? He knows only you and Bérénice."

"He knows you, as well."

"But Richard, I haven't agreed to join you."

"Join?" Richard tilted his head. "I don't think you understand. You've been part of *Réfugié* ever since you saved LeBel. You know too much *not* to be a member. As a matter of fact, it's time to go over some rules in case any of us are arrested."

Marguerite's stomach tightened. "Rules?"

"We keep track of each other. If you have an appointment with another member of *Réfugié* and they are late, you need to get word to the rest of us immediately. That way we can go underground and protect the organization. And if you learn that someone has been arrested, you must go into hiding until you're certain it's safe."

"What if I am the one arrested? I would never tell them anything."

"Really?" Richard leaned back in his chair. "What if they use the *baignoire* torture? They use it on women because it doesn't leave marks."

A chill went up her spine. "What's the *baignoire*?"

"The Gestapo purposely uses male interrogators to question women prisoners. They humiliate the suspect by making her strip naked in front of them. Then they bind her wrists behind her back, put her in a bathtub filled with ice water, and tie her ankles to a rope thrown over a rafter. They pull on the rope until her head goes under water, and then they wait while she struggles until she almost drowns. They haul her up out of the water by the ankles and let her hang there until she stops choking and coughing, and then they question her. If they don't like the answers, they lower her back into the tub. Sometimes they beat her while she's hanging upside down."

"*Mon Dieu.*" Marguerite couldn't suppress the shudder that tore through her.

"We ask for 24 hours," Red explained. "If you can hold out for 24 hours, you can save us. After 24 hours, tell them whatever you need to tell them to stay alive. We will do our best to free you, but those 24 hours are essential to protect as many lives as we can."

She ran a trembling hand through her hair. "W-why are you telling me this?"

"For your protection and ours," he said shortly. "Marguerite, think! If you and Guy are involved and either of you is arrested, the other is compromised. We would lose both of you. If you were arrested, Guy could not be trusted."

"Richard, stop! You're frightening me. I am not interested in Guy." She looked away, uncomfortable with the lie. *Was it really that obvious?*

"I'm not saying you are." He stood up, came around his desk, and patted her shoulder. "Try not to let it upset you. Let's talk about your nursing internship in Paris."

"My internship? What internship?"

"With the help of your Aunt Germaine, I've made arrangements for you to serve an internship at her hospital in Paris."

"Really? Oh, Richard, I'm so excited!"

"I have an ulterior motive. We need to equip the Cave like an emergency hospital clinic. During your internship, we want you to learn how the emergency unit is equipped and supplied. Make lists of what we will need to treat any downed Allied airmen we recover or members of *Réfugié* who may have been hurt." He studied her face.

Her head spun. "I'll do it, I promise. *Mon Dieu*!"

"When can you leave for Paris?"

"Soon. Tomorrow."

"*Bon*. Germaine has arranged your assignment to the emergency room. Keep a record of everything you use; British MI-9 has promised us whatever we need."

Marguerite blinked. *Réfugié* was in contact with British military intelligence? She stood up and began to pace across the carpeted floor. The more she thought about going to Paris the more excited she grew. She would be spending the summer with her favorite aunt and working as a nursing intern in a real hospital. And she was going to equip her own emergency room here at Perdu. She would do it for France! Her head swam, and she could not stop smiling.

"Don't mention your internship to your friends," Richard advised. "Tell them you're going to spend the summer with your aunt. We want to keep your medical training confidential. And Marguerite, while you're in Paris, I want you to work on your disguise as Patrice."

"What? I don't understand."

"You need to develop a different look for Patrice. You know, wear pumps when you are Patrice and flat shoes when you are Marguerite, that kind of thing. When you pose as Patrice, you must learn to transform yourself into Patrice."

She mulled the possibilities in her mind. "*Oui*, I'll think about that. Tomorrow, I need to go into town and talk to Dr. Morel. He expects me to help him this summer."

"Don't tell him what you'll be doing in Paris and when you talk to him, find out if the police have questioned him about Guy. We think there may be an informant inside *Réfugié.*"

* * *

The next afternoon, Marguerite bicycled to the animal clinic and waited for Dr. Morel to finish with his last patient, then followed him to his office and knocked on the door. "May I speak with you?"

"Certainly." He rose and pointed his pen at the door, indicating she should shut it. "Is this a social visit?"

"*Non*, Doctor. I'm going to spend the summer with my aunt in Paris. My friends in *Réfugié* want to know if you were questioned by the police about Guy Massu."

"I was, but I told them nothing. Only Guy and I knew about the meeting here at the clinic. If the police were tipped off, it had to have come from inside *Réfugié*." He tapped his pen on his desk. "Was Guy badly hurt?"

"He had a broken thigh bone and a bullet wound. They tell me he's fine."

"Where is he?"

"He's in hiding. They won't tell me where."

He tented his fingers under his chin. "Marguerite, I must be honest with you. The police think Guy came here to meet me. I cannot risk doing more work for *Réfugié*. Do you understand?"

"I understand." She took a deep breath. "I need go now."

Dr. Morel stood and gave her a hug. She would miss him.

That evening she reported to Richard. "Dr. Morel thinks that if there is an informant, it to be someone from *Réfugié*."

Richard thought for a moment. "He's probably right. The police are convinced Guy is in the area and they're asking questions. He's become a symbol of resistance, and now the Gestapo is involved. They're not close to finding him, but it's getting uncomfortable for us. We must find the informant."

Marguerite fought down a feeling of fear. Sooner or later the Nazis could discover their secret organization.

* * *

Before leaving for Paris, Marguerite rode her bicycle into town one last time. When she finished her errands, she was supposed to meet Bérénice at the small park dedicated to fallen Ville de Pommes soldiers from the Great War, but Bérénice wasn't there yet. While she waited for her cousin she traced the names of her two uncles engraved on the marble monument.

She was disappointed that Guy had not contacted her, but she understood the danger of a romantic entanglement. Still, she had saved his life and she had to admit she would like to see him again.

Another fifteen minutes passed, and all at once Richard's words came to her. Bérénice was late. Too late. Alarmed, she mounted her bicycle and started toward home, taking a short cut down an alley that led to the main road out of the village.

Suddenly a man in a black overcoat stepped out of a building and flagged her down. Something about him frightened her, so she tried to steer away from him, but he grabbed her handlebars. Another man, dressed in a similar black coat, yanked her off the bicycle. She screamed and tried to fight him off,

"Marguerite Auriol, you're under arrest! Come with us."

She tried to twist free, but his grip was too strong. He shook her hard. "Do not struggle, *Mademoiselle*."

Her heart pounded wildly. Again she tried to wrench free, but he stepped behind her and pinned her arms. "Stop! We've been looking for you. Come with us."

He pushed her roughly toward a steel door leading into an abandoned building; the second man followed with her bicycle. The first man shoved her inside past an armed German soldier in a black uniform. She glimpsed a skull and crossbones on his cloth cap and the double lightning bolts of the SS on his collar.

Her abductor gripped her arms and forced her down a dimly lit hallway toward a dark staircase that led down into a dank, moldy-smelling basement. At the bottom of the steps he opened a door to a brightly lit chamber and shoved her down onto a straight-backed chair in the center of the room.

Marguerite squinted into blinding lights, but she could make out only dark forms shifting behind a table. She tried to shield her eyes, but rough hands held her arms down at her sides. Fear choked her.

Off to the side stood a full bathtub, and over one end, a rope hung from a pulley attached to the ceiling. The wall behind the tub was wet and there was a large puddle on the floor surrounding the tub. She could scarcely breathe. *The baignoire*. She balled her fists. *They're going to drown me. How can I going to hold out for 24 hours?*

She ripped her right arm free and put her hand over her eyes, but whoever was behind her muscled her arm back to her side. "Sit still!" She clenched her hands in her lap and compulsively kneaded her skirt.

Even when squinting directly into the lights she could not distinguish the faces at the table. Her breath came in short gasps and her heart felt as if it would leap out of her chest. She could see the shadow of a man in civilian clothes at the center of the table; two shadowy figures on either side of him wore German military uniforms. More dark shapes moved behind the figures at the table.

Her dread turned to terror. *Oh, God, help me. Whatever happens, I must hold out.*

A demanding voice with a German accent snapped out a question. "You are Marguerite Auriol? And you use the name Patrice Cerne?"

She was stunned. *How could they know this?* She tried to think.

The interrogator's voice rose. "I asked you a question. Are you Marguerite Auriol and have you used the name Patrice Cerne?"

"*J. . . Ja.*" she stammered. *Maybe that was wrong. Maybe she should deny using Patrice.*

"I am Colonel Klaphauten of the Gestapo. We have information that you participated in the escape of the criminal Guy Massu. What have you to say for yourself?"

Her whole body shook. She was trapped.

"Marguerite Auriol," demanded one man at the table, "what have you to say for yourself?"

Silence.

"I asked you a question, *Mademoiselle*."

"I don't know. I don't know anything about any Guy Massu."

"Do you see that bathtub?"

"*J. . . Ja.*"

"We have enough information to execute you as a terrorist. Convince us that you are on the side of the German occupying forces."

Her mind spun. "I have nothing to say," she blurted. Then she closed her eyes and braced for the worst.

"That is unfortunate," the man said slowly. "Give us something, anything that would convince us we should let you go."

Silence

"We have arrested your cousin, Bérénice Auriol. She has already enjoyed a little bath, and she has given us quite a bit of information. We only need you to corroborate what she has already told us."

Marguerite imagined her cousin dangling helpless over the bathtub, sputtering and choking. They must have done a lot to her to get her to talk. She began to sob.

"We are in the process of arresting the other members of your *Réfugié* organization. What can you tell us about *Réfugié*? Who are the other members? We could spare both you and your cousin if you cooperate. What can you tell me?"

Marguerite couldn't bear to think about Bérénice's torture. She drew in a long breath. "*N...nein*, nothing," she stammered.

"Tell us something about *Réfugié,* anything to keep you alive. Convince me we should not execute both of you."

She didn't answer. She kept her head down and shook her head. Again she choked out a sob.

The questioning went on and on, but Marguerite said nothing. She was terrified that the questioning would end and her torture would begin.

"For the last time, *Mademoiselle* Auriol, it's up to you. Save yourself and your cousin."

She squeezed her eyes shut and shook her head.

"Stand up," he ordered. "Unbutton your dress."

Mon Dieu, she couldn't do it. She couldn't make her fingers move.

Another voice murmured, "She's pretty. This will be fun."

Instantly she felt dirty. She remained seated, clutching her skirt, and kept her eyes shut.

"STAND UP!" he shouted.

She jerked, then slowly got to her feet. Her breath came in choking gasps and perspiration slicked her neck.

"Once again, tell us something."

Silence

"UNBUTTON!"

Slowly she moved her hands to the top button of her dress. Her fingers fumbled and she took as long as she could to slip it free, then stopped.

"Keep going."

Her hands shook on the second button. Then a different voice said in a conversational tone, "What do you think?"

One of the dark forms standing behind the blinding lights moved forward so Marguerite could see him. *Richard!* Confusion and anger flooded her. She bolted forward and pounded on his chest. "What are you doing?"

"Calm yourself," came a woman's voice from the darkness. A second figure moved into the light. It was Bérénice.

"What is happening?"

"Marguerite," her cousin said. "Marguerite, it's all right."

Her legs buckled. Richard caught her and eased her back to the chair where Bérénice put her arms around her. "It's all right," she whispered. "This isn't the Gestapo. We needed to know that you weren't the informer. They did the same thing to me this morning, and I was terrified. You did well."

Marguerite tried to stand, and all at once she wet herself. Her face burned.

"How could you do this to me?" she cried. "I wanted no part of this, and yet you did this to me. How *could* you! I'm sick of all of you."

"We had to know," Richard said. "We were worried that you and Bérénice were too young, that you could have been compromised. We need to do this again, Marguerite; please keep this to yourself until we examine the others."

Marguerite stared at him.

"My father did this in Spain," Bérénice explained, "and it worked. We flushed out a traitor."

Richard folded his arms and nodded toward the exit. "Bérénice, you'd better get her home."

Marguerite shook her fist at him. "How could you do this to me?" She wiped tears from her eyes. "You knew you could trust me!"

"I do now. But I needed to be sure. Bérénice, take her home."

Her cousin helped her to her feet and slowly walked her up the stairs. Her underwear was cold and damp and moving up the steps was mortifying. She couldn't control her trembling. At the top of the stairs she stopped. "Did you wet yourself, Bérénice?"

"*Non,* but I cried, and I never cry. I didn't suspect a thing. I was terrified, Marguerite. They told me you had already confessed." She wrapped her arm around Marguerite's shoulders. "Don't be ashamed. Now you know what is like to have a half an hour with the Gestapo, and they didn't even touch you. Imagine weeks or months."

Marguerite closed her eyes. "Half an hour! Was that all it was?"

"*Oui.* Are you all right?"

"I…I think so." She moved forward another step and stopped. "I need to go to Paris. I need to get away from Ville de Pommes. From . . . all of this."

CHAPTER SEVEN
PATRICE

Nothing seemed to stop the Nazis. Late in June 1941, Hitler invaded his staunchest ally, the Soviet Union, and by July Marshal Pètain, named Chief of State of the Unoccupied Zone, had established his capital in Vichy. Hitler offered peace to Britain but, despite the bombing of London, the English chose to fight on and later declared victory in the Battle of Britain.

In November, Parisian students demonstrated, and the police responded with riot batons, an action that galvanized French resistance to the Nazis. Clandestine publications began to surface and resistance movements sprang up all over German-occupied Europe; the center of these movements was Paris.

* * *

Maman pressed a rosary into Marguerite's hand. "I have intended to give you this for some time, *chou-chou*. My mother gave it to me when I was a child, and it has been blessed by the Pope. Come back to us, *cherie*. And do not, *do not* fall in love with a partisan while you in Paris. Promise me, Marguerite."

"I promise," Marguerite said, her voice tearful.

Maman wept and Papa held her tight, his voice thick when he spoke. "Be safe my daughter. We-- I love you dearly."

She kissed her parents one last time and slid into the truck next to Bérénice while José loaded her suitcase and duffel bag. At the train station in Creully,

Marguerite had a moment of doubt. *I am leaving my home. My family.* Then she straightened her spine and clambered out of the vehicle.

Bérénice brushed a speck of lint off Marguerite's fitted green jacket. "Do you have everything? Your train ticket? Identification papers?"

"*Oui*. And stop fussing, Bérénice. It's exciting to be going at last." *Even if I am a little frightened.*

Her cousin hugged her. "Don't let them scare you. And," she added in an undertone, "I put two bottles of vintage Auriol calvados in your duffel bag. Tell Germaine to give them to Sister Hélène at the hospital, with thanks from Red."

José swept off his beret and smiled, his teeth white beneath his drooping mustache. She pecked him on both cheeks and he blushed. "*Adieu,* José. Look after Bérénice for me." She turned to go, and then changed her mind. "Oh! I have been wondering, have you found the informant yet?"

He replaced his hat and shook his head. "*Non*. But we will. Red wants to know if you've recovered from the questioning."

Marguerite caught her breath. Never, ever would she forget the terror she had felt on that black day. "Not yet, but I will. I still have nightmares."

He nodded, his face somber.

"One last question, José. Is Guy in London yet?"

"*Non*. He's still recuperating."

"He wishes you good luck in Paris," Bérénice added.

"He does? He said that?" She remembered how he had made her feel when they were at school together, all weak and shaky inside; a single look could reduce her to pudding.

Her cousin smiled. "*Oui*, but don't tell Red I told you."

She squeezed Bérénice's hand, took a deep breath, and climbed the narrow iron steps into the passenger car. The train lurched out of the station, and she waved at Bérénice and José through the window until she could no longer see them.

Aunt Germaine met her at the station in Paris, dressed in a dark blue suit with a matching wide-brimmed hat and a feather in the band. Her stylish aunt hugged her and then hailed a taxi.

Inside her aunt's apartment, Marguerite dropped her suitcase and duffel in the spare room, unpacked the bottles of calvados, and carried them to the kitchenette where her aunt had fixed a plate of bread and cheese. "These are for Sister Hélène. Richard sent them."

Germaine nodded and accepted them, then sent her a quick look. "Red told me about the Gestapo trick they pulled on you. Was it terrible?"

Marguerite sucked in her breath. "*Oui*, it was. I am still angry with him."

"Don't be angry with him, Marguerite. Red carries heavy responsibilities. Lives depend on him, and he must be able to sacrifice someone to save the rest of us. I sometimes worry that he'll get so obsessed with the Résistance he'll go too far. Be careful around him."

Marguerite nodded, and Germaine folded her slender, work-worn hands on top of the table. "Now, let's discuss your apprenticeship. While you are in Paris, you must not call yourself Marguerite Auriol."

"Richard already explained. I will be Patrice for the summer."

"*Bon.* I will call you Patrice at the hospital, and even when we're alone so I won't make a mistake. And you must call me Germaine, not Aunt Germaine, agreed?"

"*Oui*. What will I be doing at the hospital?"

"You'll work with my friend Janet Ranquet in the acute care department. But, Marguerite, I haven't told her you are my niece."

"Aunt Germaine, there's something else you can help me with. Richard wants me to develop a disguise for being Patrice. I thought I would put my hair up and wear makeup and pumps."

"It's more important that we talk about what you can and cannot say. The Germans know there is a Résistance organization operating around the hospital, and they are aware that Auriol calvados is a part of the Résistance currency. It's important that you hide your real identity from everyone here. If the Nazis connect you with Auriol calvados, they'll take you in for questioning and, well, you've already had a taste of that."

Marguerite's mouth went dry. Germaine touched her hand. "Do you understand?"

"*Oui*, Aunt, I understand.

* * *

The next morning Marguerite dressed in a dark gray blouse and matching skirt. She rolled up the waistband on her skirt to shorten the hemline. Then she piled her hair on top of her head, undid the top three buttons of her blouse, and went into the kitchenette. Her aunt was already dressed in her grey nurse's uniform, including a white cap with a small red cross on the front.

"*Mon Dieu*," Germaine exclaimed, looking up from her coffee. "Just look at you. You're really a beautiful young woman, Marguerite."

"*Merci*." Marguerite blushed at the compliment. "After work, I need to shop for Patrice's wardrobe. It's different choosing clothes for someone you're not, trying to think what Patrice would wear."

"It's going to be even more difficult than you think. The Germans have seized cotton to use for their uniforms and bandages, leather for combat boots, and silk and nylon for parachutes. The French clothing industry is growing desperate, but I know a few shop owners, and if you're patient they can get what you want by bartering and then altering used garments. They have a network, at least the ones still in business do."

After her breakfast of coffee and croissants, they walked the kilometer to the hospital along narrow brick side streets with small shops on the ground floor of apartment buildings. The morning was cloudy and cool but promised summer heat.

The largest building on the St. Jeanne d'Arc Hospital campus was a six-story brick structure with smaller buildings surrounding it. At the entrance, rose bushes and pink and red flowers grew around a life-sized white marble sculpture of a young girl chained to a stake. She held aloft a crucifix and gazed heavenward.

Marguerite nudged Germaine and nodded toward the statue. "I know just how she feels."

Germaine frowned. "How *does* she feel?"

"As if she has worked to free France and they're going to execute her for it."

Her aunt laughed. "Before you're off to liberate France, you'll spend the morning filling out paperwork." She led Marguerite through a staff entrance marked *Employes seulement*.

"After work," her aunt continued, "we'll register you for ration cards. That's really important if we want to eat. Did you see the vegetables planted on all those apartment balconies? We're growing food, but it's not nearly enough. The Germans are systematically looting everything, bed linen, machinery, surgical instruments, milk, mutton, wine, champagne, even calvados. We have become a nation of liars and cheats in order to survive."

Marguerite gasped. "I had no idea things were so bad. I was only aware of our struggles in Ville de Pommes, but things seem much worse here." She remembered something Dr. Morel had often said: "When you think things are bad for you, look around."

"The Germans ration everything," Germaine continued. "Whatever they don't take for themselves, they ration, and the food ration for the citizens is not enough. Even if we had the money, we can't buy what we need. Parisians are starving.

"Oh, Aunt, I had no idea."

"That's why *Réfugié* has so much success on the black market. The more liquor is rationed, the higher the price we can charge for Auriol calvados and the better we can fund our Résistance activities."

We are all turning into cheaters, Marguerite thought. *Will we ever recover our morality?*

They entered the hospital administrator's office. "*Bonjour,* Sister Barbara," Germaine said. "May I introduce Patrice Cerne, our apprentice from Caumont? Patrice, this is Sister Barbara Robideau, our hospital administrator."

The Daughters of Charity wore blue-green habits and large, white, winged cornettes on their heads. With her pencil, Sister Barbara pointed to a chair. "*Mademoiselle* Cerne, I understand you have an aptitude for treating animals, and Germaine tells us you work well under stress."

Marguerite smiled. "*Merci.* I hope so. Sister, may I ask why we're speaking French? I thought German was required."

Sister Barbara blinked. "How is your German?"

"*Fort bien.* I spent my last year of *lycée* learning to read, write, and speak German."

"We don't have the advantage of school to learn German," the nun said. "We're learning on the fly, but you could help us. We want you to work in the emergency room. I hope that is acceptable?"

Marguerite nodded. "*Oui.* I want to be an acute care nurse."

The nun pursed her lips. "You have a good attitude. About speaking German," she continued with a slight smile. "In emergencies we speak French."

Marguerite tilted her head. "How do I know when to speak German and when to speak French?"

"Our first duty is to our patients," Sister Barbara said quietly. "It is essential that we treat their medical needs and not spend our time stumbling over translations. The Germans tolerate it. For now."

Marguerite spent the remainder of the morning filling out papers, selecting her uniforms, and finding her locker. At noon, she located the cafeteria and spotted her aunt at a table with another nurse. Germaine introduced her. "Janet, this is my friend Patrice Cerne. She's been assigned to you. Patrice, meet Janet Ranquet."

Janet was heavy, in her forties, and was thoroughly enjoying a cigarette. Marguerite shook her hand and sat down. "*Bonjour, Madame* Ranquet."

"Call me Janet, please. Now, tell me about yourself."

"I worked with a veterinarian in Caumont after school and during the summers. I like acute care work, and I want to learn more."

"Is this the girl you were telling me about, Germaine? The one who walked out of Paris with you and who treated that old man?"

"*Oui*. Patrice and my sister were with me that day."

Janet studied her. "I am impressed."

"That's not the best part," Germaine added. "Patrice patched up an escaped French prisoner of war, right under the noses of the police who were searching for him. She had a friend contact the Résistance and they are now hiding him while he recuperates."

Janet nodded. "I am truly impressed, but let me offer a word of warning. Keep your stories about the Résistance to yourself while you're here. Most Parisians think the Résistance is the reason Pètain can't get the Nazis to ease up on us. Many of them will report anyone they suspect is working with the Résistance. You don't want to be arrested and questioned."

"I understand." But she was disappointed. She had looked forward to her internship as a way to escape being constantly on her guard about what she said or did. She wanted to concentrate on medicine. Instead, she would have to watch every word she uttered.

"We will keep each other's secrets, agreed?" Janet said.

Marguerite nodded and tried to return her smile.

After lunch, Janet took her to the emergency room. "You need to stay out of my way in here. You may ask questions, but if someone snaps at you, don't take it personally. And don't be too persistent, understand?"

"I understand."

Janet introduced her to the staff as Patrice, the student apprentice who would help them with their German, and then an aide interrupted. "Excuse me, *Madame* Ranquet. They're unloading a patient."

"*Bon*. Patrice, let's get to work."

* * *

After their shift, Aunt Germaine treated her to dinner at *Restaurant Giovanni.* The café was two steps up on a street too narrow for motor vehicles, squeezed between a second-hand furniture shop and a bakery. The dining room contained 14 tables, half of which were occupied by uniformed German soldiers. Marguerite pushed down her fear and tried to act unconcerned, but her heart hammered beneath her blouse.

The waiter, an older man, wore a white shirt with a black bowtie and black trousers; a white apron encircled his waist. To calm her nerves Marguerite took a cigarette from her purse, and instantly the waiter appeared to light it for her.

Civilians occupied the tables closest to them; their conversations were in fluent German with no hint of a French accent. She leaned across the table toward her aunt. "Do only Germans patronize this restaurant?" she whispered.

"*Nein*, but most of the customers are German. Berlin has set the exchange rate of 20 French francs to 1 German *reichsmark*. Germans with *reichsmarks* can afford to eat at places like this. For the French, it's too expensive."

"How can we afford this?"

"This is a special treat for both of us, Patrice. Don't ask how, just enjoy."

She shot a glance at Germaine's face but could read nothing there. "*Danke*, Germaine."

"How did it go at the hospital today?"

Marguerite leaned back in her chair and flicked her cigarette in the ashtray. "It was difficult. When I'm working with patients, I can think clearly and I know I can handle it. But it feels odd, as if I am starting a new life as Patrice." Again she tapped her cigarette on the ashtray. "I can't imagine what Papa would do if he saw me smoking," she murmured.

"He would sputter, as he always does when you surprise him," Germaine said with a laugh. "It's an hour until curfew; when we're finished eating let's go for a walk along the Seine."

They made their way to the tree-lined boulevard that led to the river, strolled across a bridge, and stopped mid-span to watch the boats float beneath them. It was beautiful, but she missed Ville de Pommes with its tiny cafés and quiet streets. Pedestrian traffic was light and Marguerite leaned her back against the concrete guard and rested her elbows on top of it.

"Did you give Sister Hélène the calvados Richard sent?" she asked.

"Hush!" Germaine motioned to the bridge behind her. She turned her head to see two SS officers strolling toward them, chatting with another man in civilian clothes. The Gestapo! Marguerite casually looked away and waited for them to pass.

Her aunt bent close to her. "You should know that my Résistance work did not begin with *Réfugié*," she murmured. "I actually started with the Daughters of Charity."

"What? The nuns are running a Résistance organization?"

"*Réfugié* and the Daughters of Charity are working together. The sisters smuggle Jewish families away from the Nazis, especially children. Red had to get one of his people out of Paris and I asked Sister Hélène to help. The calvados was a thank-you gift. Twenty-year-old calvados is like gold on the black market. The nuns use it to barter for whatever they need."

Marguerite glanced in both directions and stood aside to let another group of civilians pass by. "Let me understand this, Germaine. The nuns risk their lives to protect Jews from the Nazis and *Réfugié* pays them in liquor so they can trade it on the black market?"

Germaine rubbed her chin. "*Oui*," she said shortly, "That's about right."

Marguerite looked her aunt in the eye. "*Mon Dieu!* Our world is truly upside down."

Then she noticed a German soldier watching them. He was too far away to hear them, but he might be able to read their lips. She turned to lean over the concrete guard and study a barge on the river below. When she glanced back in the soldier's direction, he was gone.

She swallowed hard. *Am I getting over-suspicious?*

CHAPTER EIGHT
LOUIS

August 1941

All that summer Marguerite saw broken bones, bloody wounds, injured children, shock, and cardiac arrest, but late in August they brought in a taxi-driver with his left eyeball hanging from its socket, the result of an automobile collision. It repelled her. She could not look at the man's face, and even though she tried to be composed, as a nurse was required to be, she had to steel herself to touch his wound.

She numbed her mind to his suffering and focused on treating him. As long as she was on her feet and moving, she could cope with her unease around the eyeball, and while she waited for the surgeon she forced herself to look at the mutilation more closely. The eye socket was bloody, but the orbital bones seemed to be intact; still, the man was in terrible pain. His hands opened and closed convulsively, and Marguerite struggled to hold them away from his face. When the nurse finally gave him a shot of morphine, tears of gratitude streamed from his good eye.

Near the end of her apprenticeship, she thought she was prepared for anything until a hysterical mother carried in an unconscious boy coughing up blood. He was perhaps six-years old. Marguerite told her to lay the child on the treatment table and called for Janet, who looked the boy over.

"Is this your son?" she asked the woman.

"It is."

Janet sat her down and gave her a glass of water. "Tell us what happened."

The woman looked at the child, then back to Janet, unsure of what to say.

"You must tell us," Marguerite implored. "We need to know how to treat him."

"One of the German soldiers hit him with his rifle," she sobbed. "He hit him in the chest!"

Marguerite's body went cold. "Soldiers?"

The woman glanced around the room with a terrified look. "I…I don't know what to tell you."

Janet lowered her voice to a whisper. "*Madame*, calm down. You are among friends. Please tell us what happened."

"German soldiers came to arrest us," she murmured. "They took my husband, but my son tried to fight them. One of the soldiers slammed the butt of his rifle against his ribs. I-- I dragged him out of the way and escaped out the back door."

"What is his name?" Marguerite asked gently.

"Alain. My name is Miriam Cevert. We— we are Jews."

"Miriam," Janet said, "we will do all we can for your son. Marguerite will take you to the registration desk and help you with the admission forms." She looked at Marguerite. "Patrice, have admissions fill out the paperwork for young Lucas Rousseau here. Tell them that his mother, Victoire Rousseau, forgot their identification papers and will bring them later. Then take Victoire to Sister Barbara. Do you understand?"

"*Oui.*"

Janet then called for the emergency room physician and Marguerite guided the young mother to an empty office and closed the door. "Do you have your real identity papers with you?"

"*Oui*. I have both mine and Alain's."

Marguerite took the papers and thrust them into an empty desk drawer. Then she escorted *Madame* Cevert out to the registration desk, where she explained that "Victoire" had left the proper papers at home.

The clerk threw up her hands in frustration. "Don't you know? You are required to have your identity papers with you at all times. I can't process you without your papers."

"I'm sorry," said *Madame* Cevert. "I forgot."

"I'll take her to up to Sister Barbara's office and see if we can straighten this out," Marguerite volunteered. The clerk waved her toward the stairs.

Upstairs, Sister Barbara stood in the doorway of her office. "Is there a problem?"

"Sister, we need your help." Marguerite closed the door and explained what had happened.

"Marguerite, take Victoire back downstairs. When they finish treating Alain, keep him in the emergency room until I can get there."

Janet met them at the emergency room door. "*Madame* Cevert, please step into the office with me."

Marguerite's stomach twisted. *Mon Dieu, something has happened.*

"Why? What's wrong?"

"Please, just come with me." She escorted the woman into the empty office and closed the door. Marguerite took a seat outside the office and waited.

Suddenly, a piercing scream rose from behind the door, and she went numb. Her mind spun. The boy must be dead. *Oh, the poor woman, losing her husband and her son in the same day.* She felt sick. All at once she thought of Guy. How she wished she could talk to him, about what was happening in Paris.

* * *

By the end of her apprenticeship, the endless parade of mutilated bodies and the agonies of the victims were giving her nightmares. On duty, she made medical decisions with detachment, and she honed her focus and the discipline required for trauma work. She was proud of herself for not giving up. But at night, the horror of what was happening overwhelmed her. For weeks, she slept badly and got up exhausted every morning.

Finally summer drew to a close, and one morning at breakfast Germaine announced that the Auriol truck would come for Marguerite the next day. "Red has permission from Stephan Mann to transport the Auriol calvados quota directly to Paris. He will be here tomorrow."

"Who is Stephan Mann?"

"The Nazi *Weinführer*. He's in charge of setting prices and production quotas for French liquor."

Marguerite caught her breath. "The Nazis *tell* us what we can charge for our calvados? Why should we transport our calvados to Paris to help him?"

"Under the new Vichy regulations, we cannot make, sell, or ship our calvados without Nazi permits. Mann issues us legitimate operating and shipping permits and Red uses them to truck the legitimate calvados to Paris. That way Mann makes more profit and we get legal permits to allow us to go back and forth to Ville de Pommes."

Marguerite tilted her head. "How does that help us?"

"With the proper permits and counterfeit bills of material, we can move both legal and black market stock. And if a truck is stopped at a Nazi roadblock, we have a legitimate reason to be on the road."

Marguerite's breath hissed in. "Roadblock! Do you think they'll stop us?"

Germaine grasped her hand. "There is something else you should know, Marguerite. We use the truck to smuggle people. On the trip back to Ville de Pommes, you will be carrying two refugees Sister Hélène has rescued from the Nazis."

She began to perspire. "Where are we taking them?"

"To Perdu. They will be safe there until Red can make arrangements to get them out of France."

Marguerite stared at her aunt for a long moment. *So much is going on that I know nothing about. I should ask more questions.*

The white, slat-sided delivery truck arrived the next morning. Marguerite hugged Aunt Germaine and watched José load her duffel and suitcase behind the seat.

"Do you have your identification papers and travel pass?" he asked.

She patted her purse.

"And your other papers? For Patrice?"

"Sewed into my duffel lining. Where are we picking up our passengers?"

"In the warehouse district on the way to Ville de Pommes."

They rumbled west into an industrial area where José pulled up to a nondescript cinderblock building with no windows and a roll-up door big enough to admit the truck. He honked three times and a man peeked out. Then the roll-up door opened, José drove inside, and the door rattled down behind them.

Marguerite got out and watched two men climb into the truck bed and move the empty barrels around. Next to the warehouse wall stood two casks, identical to the ones on the truck except that the tops had been removed.

Beside them a clean-shaven young man in a suit waited with a slim blonde woman in a blue dress. They squeezed themselves into the barrels and the men nailed down the tops. An overhead crane lifted the two casks into place on the truck, and four men reloaded the empty casks to cover them.

José pointed to the truck cab. "Get in, Marguerite. We have to get out of here."

Marguerite slammed her door shut behind her. "Will those two be all right in there?"

"They'll be more comfortable when we get to Perdu." He carefully backed the truck into the street.

They drove out of Paris and soon reached lush green pastures of grazing livestock and vineyards, the vines heavy with grapes. Oh, how wonderful it all looked! She hadn't realized how much she had missed the countryside.

Suddenly, José's voice rose above the roar of the engine. "Roadblock ahead." She could see German soldiers manning a military checkpoint in the distance.

Marguerite shifted in her seat. *Would the refugees understand what was happening?* She couldn't think about it. She counted six automobiles in line and another truck that had been pulled out of line and off the road. Uniformed guards were unloading wooden barrels while three soldiers stood by, their rifles trained on the driver. One of the guards waved José to the shoulder, and a knot tightened her chest.

"Is this normal?" she whispered.

"*Oui*, just stay calm."

She took a deep breath and watched a helmeted soldier with a rifle slung across his back stride up to José's door. "Papers, *bitte*. Turn off the engine."

José turned the key in the ignition and the engine went silent. The soldier carefully studied each document, then strode around back to inspect the barrels. After a long minute, he returned to the driver's side and yanked the door open. "Get out."

"Is there a problem, Corporal?" José asked, his voice polite.

The soldier eyed Marguerite. "Who is she? What is she doing with you?"

Marguerite froze.

"Show him your papers," José muttered.

She dug into her purse and reached across José to hand her identity papers and travel permit to the guard. "I spent the summer in Paris with my aunt, and now I am going home. My father owns Auriol Farms." She clenched her jaw.

The soldier snorted. "Get out! Both of you."

She swallowed hard, climbed out, and stood next to José.

"Dieter, check those barrels," the guard shouted. "Make sure they're empty."

The soldiers began to remove the slat sides of the truck and Marguerite's heart started to pound. *What if they find the refugees? Would they all be arrested?*

Two soldiers climbed up onto the truck bed and began tossing down casks.

Marguerite edged closer to José and waited, feeling perspiration dampen her underarms. The corporal began rooting around inside the truck cab. "What's this?" he yelled, peering over the seat.

"That's my luggage," she responded, struggling to keep her voice steady. "I told you, I am returning home from a summer in Paris."

The soldier stared at her. She could not look him in the face.

"Open your bags, *Mademoiselle*. I need to inspect them."

She reached into the cab and pulled her duffel from behind the seat. The soldier grabbed it, dumped her clothes onto the ground, and began sifting through them. Other men were rolling casks off the truck bed. Terrified they would discover the refugees, Marguerite thought desperately. *What could she do?*

She had to create a diversion.

She advanced on the soldier. "How dare you touch my undergarments!" she snapped. She snatched a pair of panties from the corporal's hand and stuffed them back in her duffel. "Did you find any contraband in my underwear?" Even though she was cringing inside, she forced herself to look directly into his eyes.

Red-faced, the soldier stared at her, then shook his head. "Another false alarm," he muttered. "Come on, re-load those barrels and get them out of here," he yelled to the soldiers.

Marguerite glared at him while she stuffed her clothes back in her duffel. Her entire body was shaking.

"Is there anything else, Corporal?" José asked.

"*Nein*. Get that truck out of here." He waved them through the checkpoint.

José started the engine and drove back onto the road and through the roadblock. Marguerite couldn't stop her hands from shaking.

After an hour, he arrived in the Perdu farmyard and honked the horn. Miguel emerged from the barn, turned on his heel, and pushed the sliding door open wide enough to admit the truck. José drove in and Miguel slid the door shut behind them.

"Welcome home," the dark Portuguese man said. "Any trouble?"

"*Non*," José responded. "We ran into a roadblock, but Marguerite distracted them."

Marguerite clambered down and watched the men pry off the tops of two barrels.

The young man climbed out, stretching his muscles. His suit was creased, and he paced anxiously while they pried the top off the second barrel. The young blonde woman popped out, her blue dress rumpled. José helped her off the truck.

"How are you doing," Marguerite asked in German.

"*Ich bin gut.*"

The couple threw their arms around each other and began massaging their back muscles. "I cannot tell you how grateful my wife and I are," the man said. "I am-- "

"Please don't tell us your names," Miguel interrupted. "It's to protect us. And you. Are you all right?"

"*Ja*, a little stiff." The woman smoothed her dress and leaned her head against her husband's shoulder.

Marguerite turned to Miguel. "Where do they go from here?"

"We have food in the house."

She beckoned to the refugees. "Come with me." She led them into Perdu House where cheese and fruit waited on the dining table. A woman Marguerite did not know was kneading bread in the kitchen.

"Where are we?" the man asked.

"We cannot reveal this location," Miguel said.

Marguerite pushed the plate of food toward the couple. "We hope you understand."

At that moment, Uncle Pierre and Richard walked in the back door. "How are our guests?" her uncle asked.

"They are well, just hungry," Marguerite answered. "What will you do with them?"

"We're hiring help for the harvest," Richard said. "We'll use him as a field hand for a week or two until we can make arrangements to smuggle them both to Spain." He picked up a slice of apple and popped it into his mouth. "We have another farmhand you should meet, Marguerite. His name is Louis. He's working out pretty well."

Marguerite stared him. "Why should I meet a farmhand?"

The big Irishman grinned and changed the subject. "Your aunt says you did well at the hospital. Do you have the list of medical equipment and supplies for the Cave? To get us started, I've ordered a combat medical kit from the British."

She nodded and withdrew piece of paper from her skirt pocket. "That makes sense. That should give us the basics."

Richard scanned her list and walked her out of the room. "I'll contact MI-9 tomorrow," he said quietly. Louis is in the Cave. Go down and see if there are other changes you think necessary right away. And, Marguerite, when someone is staying with us, we don't want them to know your real name. Use Patrice."

"I understand."

Back in the kitchen Marguerite apologized to the German refugees. "*Bitte*, excuse us. We are rude speaking French. How is the food?"

"*Das gut*. What will we do here?"

"You will work in the fields," Richard said. "And your wife will work as our housekeeper."

Marguerite translated, then picked up her duffel and suitcase. "I need to go home and see my parents."

Richard nodded. "Before you leave, go find Louis and have him note any changes you think necessary."

She slipped down the hill and entered the Cave through the thicket gate. Someone was pounding something upstairs, and she called out, "*Bonjour*. Is anyone here?"

The pounding stopped and a young man appeared at the top of the staircase, the sleeves of his linen shirt rolled up. "Well, look who finally showed up," he said with a broad smile.

"Guy!"

He started down the stairs, a hammer in his hands. "Louis, remember?"

"*Non*. To me you are Guy. Especially when we are alone," she purred. A smile reached his eyes, and something in her chest lifted.

He reached the bottom step. "Tell me about Paris, Marguerite. Was it what you wanted?"

She hesitated, watching him turn the hammer over and over in his hand. His forearm looked tanned and muscular.

"Marguerite?"

"*Oui,* Paris was what I wanted. And also…what I didn't want." She tightened her jaw. "Yesterday there was a boy, a child. He—," her voice broke.

Guy dropped the hammer and touched her arm. "Tell me."

She gulped a shuddery breath. "It was horrible. A soldier had hit him with his rifle, crushed his chest, and killed him. And his mother—*Mon Dieu*, his mother screamed and screamed."

"The boy died?" Guy asked, his voice quiet.

She nodded. "I wanted to run away. I wanted to kill that Nazi soldier!"

"*Oui*," he breathed. "Of course you did. Anyone would. We all do."

"They can't all be unfeeling monsters, can they? They are human beings after all. At least they used to be."

"Don't underestimate soldiers. They are trained to obey orders."

"Nobody ordered that soldier to crush that boy's chest."

He pressed his lips together. "The Nazis are thugs. They need to be driven out of France."

She looked into his face and saw tears glisten in his eyes. *How expressive his eyes are, and so green, like fresh mint leaves.*

"The first time something like that happened to me, I was standing in line at a *tabac* in Lyon. A German soldier arrested the man next to me. Called him a Jew and a traitor. They loaded him into a van and drove off and I just stood there like a fool."

"Oh, Guy, you couldn't have done anything."

"If I'd had a gun I could have— "

She cut him off. "*Non*! They would have shot you, and for what? You could not have saved him. Here, working for *Réfugié,* we can save many. We need to stand for life, not death. We must to stand for France."

He tried to smile, but she could see it was forced. "Let's list the changes we need to turn this place into a medical facility. *That* is the way to help, Guy. We must offer life to those escaping death."

From his shirt pocket he pulled out a pencil and piece of paper and smoothed it out. "I am glad you're back, Marguerite. Very glad."

"*Moi aussi*," she murmured. "I…I thought of you often." Her voice shook and she didn't understand why. She disguised her embarrassment by walking through the Cave, dictating. "First, we need white linens and bandages, clean and sterile if possible." She felt the nap of a blanket folded on the end of a cot. "It's cold down here, and these aren't heavy enough. We need heavier blankets, and we're also going to need better light and more heat."

Guy jotted everything down.

"Richard ordered a combat medical kit," she continued. "I need to see what's in it to compare it with the list I gave him. Then I'll order whatever is missing." She sat on the edge of a cot and looked up at him.

"Why did you come back to Ville de Pommes? Why didn't you join de Gaulle in London? You're a soldier. Shouldn't you be with the Free French?"

He took the chair near her. "After I escaped from the prisoner of war camp, I was determined to make it back home, to Ville de Pommes and my father. Once I was home, I tried staying on our farm, but the police came there looking for me. So I contacted *Réfugié* and decided to join so I could fight for France and be near my father."

They shared their concerns about their families and friends and fears about the cost of resistance. An hour later, Guy folded the list and put it in his shirt pocket and Marguerite climbed the hill back to Perdu to look for Bérénice. She found her in her bedroom.

“Marguerite!” Her cousin hugged her. “Welcome home.”

“I need to talk to you.”

“What’s the matter?”

“I spoke to Guy. He says he’s going to stay and work for *Réfugié*.”

“Marguerite, you must convince him to go to England.”

“*Non*, he’s right. He needs to stay and fight. He’s a trained soldier. I’m sure Richard will need him.”

“Maybe you’re right. Marguerite, there’s a parachute drop tomorrow night at eight. Red wants him to lead it.”

Marguerite caught her breath. “Is it safe?”

“Red uses words like ‘relatively safe’, but to be honest these drops are never safe. He ordered a combat medical kit for you, and it’s supposed to be included. You should come along and help.”

Come along and help? The idea of retrieving supplies parachuted from a plane into a deserted field in the middle of the night terrified her. *But I should go with them. I must try to help.*

CHAPTER NINE
THE DROP

Late October 1941

The afternoon before the parachute drop, Marguerite asked José to drive her into town, where she met Simone, Yvonne, and Yvette at *Café Angéle*. Simone jumped up from the table and hugged her. "Welcome home, Marguerite. How was your summer in Paris?"

Marguerite smiled at her friends, all fashionably dressed in wide-shouldered linen jackets over pastel summer dresses, wide-brimmed hats, and real silk stockings. *Collaboration has its privileges, even in Ville de Pommes,* she thought. In Paris, silk stockings were so rare women painted lines up the backs of their legs to simulate seams. She hid her annoyance.

"*Bonjour, mes amies*. Paris was very busy." She signaled the waiter and ordered a sandwich and what passed for coffee, then turned to Yvonne. "How is construction coming on the beach defenses?"

Yvonne leaned forward on her elbows. "This is the largest contract my father has ever received, but it's only for concrete structures. It's a huge project, and the Germans are having trouble finding help. We use surplus farm labor, but it's not nearly enough."

"Don't the Germans use prisoners from the work camps?" Marguerite asked. She had wondered about the construction crews on the beach; she would ask Richard how many prison camp laborers *Réfugié* had liberated.

Marguerite's sandwich arrived. When the waiter left, she turned to Simone. "How are things at Nazi headquarters?" she asked in a low voice.

"It's pretty quiet." Simone flicked an ash from cigarette. "They consider the area pacified except for some trouble here and there. We just got word that the German military commander in Nantes was assassinated, and in retaliation the Gestapo shot fifty citizens."

Marguerite gasped. "Why, that's awful!"

"Not only that," Simone continued. "Berlin wants Nantes to be the model for military response to assassinations in France. If we're absorbed into the Reich peacefully, it will be better for everyone in Ville de Pommes."

Marguerite bit her lip. *How can they not see how destructive their collaboration is for the French? How can we lie prostrate at the feet of the Nazis?*

"And you, Yvette? How is your father's law practice doing?"

"Not as well as Callion Construction." Yvette took a sip of her coffee and wrinkled her nose. "I'll be so glad when we can get back to normal and enjoy real coffee." She replaced her cup on the saucer. "Most of Papa's work is transferring property from people arrested by the Nazis to other family members, but the Gestapo keeps coming in and making notes from our records. They're supposed to be confidential. When we can't find any relatives, or they don't come forward, the property reverts to the Germans. Sometimes they sell it, sometimes they just keep it."

Marguerite related the problems with the annual harvest, the turnover in labor, the rush to collect the apples and pears at just the right time, and her father's concern that this year's yield might be low. Then Simone spoke up.

"Have you heard about Germany invading Russia? Pétain is urging the French to conquer the resistance of those who oppose order." Marguerite merely nodded. By 'resistance,' Petain meant the activities of people like Richard and Uncle Pierre and Guy. And herself.

She left the café, found José, and climbed into the pickup truck, where she sat in silence as he drove out of town and into the country.

"What is wrong, Marguerite? Did you enjoy lunch with your friends?"

"*Non*," she muttered. "José, could you drop me at Perdu? I need to talk to Bérénice."

He pulled into the farmyard and her cousin came out of the house to meet her. "How was your afternoon with the collaborators?"

Marguerite groaned. "I need to do something to scrape the slime off my soul."

Bérénice laughed. “Then I assume that means you’re ready for the parachute drop tonight.”

“*Oui*, I am ready. After an hour with those three, I feel like I want to shoot something.”

“You? You’re going to shoot something?” Bérénice laughed again. “That’ll be the day.”

Marguerite ignored her. “What time should I be here tonight?’

“Be here by eight. Wear something dark and a hat to cover those golden locks of yours.”

* * *

That night, as she headed out the door after supper, her father stopped her. “Marguerite, wait. Where are you going at this hour?”

“To Bérénice’s for the night, Papa.” She held up her duffel. “I told you, remember?”

“*Non*, you did not tell me. What’s going on over at Perdu?”

“Nothing special. We’re just going to listen to the radio.” She hated to lie to him, but it was better that he know nothing about the parachute drop.

He stared at her for a long moment and she managed to hold his gaze without dropping her eyes. He looked at *Maman*, who simply shrugged.

“Just be back early in the morning,” he grumbled. “We have work to do.”

“*Oui*, Papa.” She kissed his cheek and escaped out the back door. She disliked deceiving her parents, but confiding in them would be worse. Even dangerous. She hiked the back way to Perdu and joined Bérénice, José, Miguel, Guy, and Richard in the farmyard. The men wore dark sweaters and trousers with black knit caps pulled down over their ears.

The pickup truck was already running and loaded with four bicycles; Richard stood beside it with two black metal boxes at his feet. His face was grim.

“It’s eight-fifteen. Guy will position you in the drop zone, and at eleven-thirty the plane will fly over. If you’re not back at Perdu by one, we’ll assume you’ve been captured.”

Captured! Marguerite caught her breath. *Surely so late at night no one would notice . . . But of course the Germans might be watching.* Suddenly she felt cold all over.

Richard picked up one of the black boxes. “Marguerite, Bérénice, you will use these signal lamps. When you hear a slow plane from the north flying very low, slide the front cover up and the light will automatically switch on." He demonstrated, and the strong light nearly blinded her.

"The pilot will fly between the lights and release the parachute. After the canisters hit the ground, Guy, José, and Miguel, disconnect the parachute and hide the canisters. Marguerite and Bérénice will hide the signal lamps and then help dispose of the parachute."

Marguerite's stomach tightened. She realized she was frightened, *really* frightened. Could she actually do this?

Richard paused and scanned their faces. "When you've finished, scatter. If you hear an automobile engine, leave everything and get away any way you can. Nothing in the canisters is important enough to risk getting arrested. Use your *Réfugié* names. Are there any questions?"

He studied each of them again. The only sound was the chugging of the truck engine. "Then let's go!"

Bérénice and Marguerite crowded into the front seat with Miguel. José and Guy clambered in back with the bicycles. For thirty minutes Miguel drove slowly through the hedgerows, then turned into a grassy cow pasture. Marguerite could see why they had chosen this field; dense hedges bordered it on all sides. It was a crisp, clear night with a bracing sea breeze, and the landscape was illuminated by a three-quarter moon. She could taste the salty sea air on the tip of her tongue.

José, Miguel, and Guy quietly unloaded the bicycles and the signal lamps, and Miguel climbed back into the truck and put it in gear. "*Viva la France*," he whispered as he pulled away.

Guy gave last-minute instructions. "Girls, take the lamps across the road into that field and go about a hundred meters up each side. When you hear the plane, switch the signal lamps on. The pilot will see them and return the signal by turning his landing lights on and off three times. Once you see his lights flash, turn the lamps off and push them into the hedges. Then come back here. We'll hide everything, and then leave on the bicycles in pairs. Is that clear?"

No one said anything. Marguerite was so apprehensive she felt nauseated.

Guy held out a tin of black grease. "Cover any exposed part of your face and hands."

They each dipped their fingers into the grease and smeared it on their skin. It smelled of soot.

"How long before the plane arrives?" Bérénice asked, her voice tense.

"About ninety minutes. Find your hiding places and make yourselves comfortable. I'll warn you at eleven-fifteen."

Marguerite and Bérénice picked up the signal lamps and darted across the road. The lamp was heavier than it looked. Her cousin moved up the left side of the field, Marguerite took the right. She was warm enough when she was moving, but when she settled down to wait, she grew chilly. She hunkered down, pulled her sweater around her, and shoved her hands deep in her trouser pockets. To keep her mind off the cold, she thought about Guy. She wished he would go to England and join de Gaulle. Here in France he was in constant danger. She decided to talk him into going to London.

Someone touched her shoulder and she yelped.

"Shhh, I didn't mean to frighten you."

"Guy! You scared me to death. How did you manage to sneak up on me like that?"

"I'm a soldier. I'm trained to move quietly. Are you all right?"

"Is it time yet?"

"*Non*, another hour at least. I wanted to check on you."

"I'll be fine when my heart slows down. I'm just cold."

He moved behind her, sat down, and wrapped his arms around her. Then he gently pulled her back against him so she could curl up between his legs.

"Are you hungry? I brought a sandwich." He reached in his jacket pocket and offered her half.

"*Non*." She snuggled closer to the warmth of his body. His skin smelled of grease and something faintly spicy. Carefully he broke the sandwich in half. "Here. You should eat." He lifted her hand and folded her fingers around the bread.

"*Merci*," she whispered.

"It's chicken. From your farm."

"*My* farm! Don't you keep chickens at Perdu?"

"Not anymore. We killed the last one yesterday."

She pushed her half of the sandwich back at him. "Guy, it's *you* who are hungry."

He chuckled softly. "Not that hungry. For a sandwich, anyway."

Her cheeks grew hot, but she could not think of anything to say. They sat together eating in silence. When she swallowed her last bite she turned her head and found him looking at her, an odd expression on his face.

"Guy, what's wrong?"

He shrugged his broad shoulders. "This. The war. The drop. You and me. It's all wrong."

"I know. But it can't last forever, can it? This is why we're here tonight, to help put an end to it. Surely things will be normal when this is over."

"I don't think so, no. I think we'll all be changed in some way. Scarred."

"Oh, Guy." Tears slipped down her cheeks. "I don't want things to be different. I want . . ." She swiped the moisture off her face with her hand.

"Marguerite, don't cry. I can't stand it when you cry." He turned her toward him and pulled her tight.

"Guy..."

"Don't say anything, Marguerite. Just let me hold you for a moment."

She slipped her arm around his back and clung to his hard chest. Her heartbeat stuttered and then thumped in her ears. She wanted to stay in his arms forever.

Finally he released her and stood up. He wouldn't look at her. "I need to check on the others," he said, his voice low and hoarse. He turned and silently made his way back through the hedge.

All at once she heard a faint buzzing sound. As it got closer, it became a high-pitched whine. She jumped up and slid the cover off her lamp and saw Bérénice's light stab the darkness across the field.

The plane flashed its lights three times. She turned off her lamp, pushed it into the bushes, and worked her way back to the break in the hedgerow to wait for Bérénice. Just as she arrived at the opening, two dark forms on bicycles with rifles slung across their backs pedaled into view.

German soldiers! An icy hand gripped her insides. Frantically she signaled Bérénice to keep quiet.

Her cousin crawled near. "What is it?" she whispered. Marguerite pointed to the two soldiers. Bérénice moved in front of her and drew her revolver from under her jacket.

The soldiers had stopped and were looking up, watching the ghostly parachute descend. They quietly dropped their bicycles, unslung their rifles, and crept through the opening in the hedgerow across the road.

Bérénice whispered, "Follow me."

"What are you going to do?" Marguerite hissed.

"Shush!"

Making no sound they followed the soldiers into the field. As soon as the canisters clanked onto the ground, two shadowy figures emerged from the hedges and ran toward the chute.

The soldiers stood and raised their rifles. "*Halt.*"

José and Guy froze, then turned toward them, their hands in the air. Bérénice silently passed her revolver to Marguerite. She pulled the hair out of her face, folded her hands around the butt, and slid her forefinger onto the trigger.

The soldiers advanced toward the men. "Don't move."

Bérénice inched closer. When the Germans were only steps from Guy and José, she took two quick steps, launched her body into the air, and planted both feet in one man's back. His rifle toppled to the ground. The second soldier swung his weapon toward Bérénice, but José caught him with a kick in the face, followed by his fist. The first German recovered his rifle and swung it toward José.

Marguerite squeezed her eyes shut and pulled the trigger. Her hand jerked, and she glanced down at the gun. *God in heaven, what have I done?*

The soldier crumpled to the ground. She stared at the still form and her stomach clenched. She had killed a man! God forgive her, she had committed murder.

Bérénice snatched the revolver away from her while José and Guy collected the soldiers' rifles.

"Patrice," her cousin hissed. "We need to get out of here. Come on."

Marguerite hesitated, then knelt and felt the soldier's pulse. "We can't leave them here."

Someone, José or Guy, grasped her arm and yanked her up, forcing her to move. Just as she turned away she heard another shot. She couldn't look.

"We had to kill them both." José's voice was matter of fact. "We'll hide the bodies and come back later to bury them."

Guy thrust his face into hers. "Patrice, come with me." He tugged her hand and led her away. She looked back only once to see Bérénice and José walking the canisters out of the field. When they reached the road, they both mounted bicycles and pedaled off.

Guy halted and turned to look at her. "Patrice, are you all right?"

She could only nod. His voice sharpened. "Patrice?"

"*Oui*. *Oui*, I'm all right." Her voice sounded strange. Detached.

They mounted their bicycles and took a roundabout route back to Perdu. When they arrived, Richard was pacing in the dark farmyard, his hands behind his back.

"Where are Bérénice and José?" Guy asked.

"In the barn, hiding the bicycles."

"Did they tell you what happened?" Marguerite's voice was unsteady. "About th-the two soldiers?"

"*Oui*. You did the right thing, Marguerite. It was the only thing you could do. Otherwise…" His voice trailed off.

"*Oui*, perhaps, but . . . I feel sick about it."

"One thing for sure," Richard continued. "Two German soldiers have been killed. There is sure to be retaliation."

Marguerite shuddered. Guy slid his arm around her shoulders and squeezed, then released her to roll both their bicycles into the barn.

CHAPTER TEN
SELECTION

Late October 1941

Marguerite had just finished washing the supper dishes when she glanced out the window to see Bérénice climbing the hill to Charentais. She dried her hands and met her at the kitchen door. "What are you doing here? Have you had supper?"

"I've eaten, *merci*. Can we talk privately?"

Marguerite peeked into the living room. *Maman* was knitting a sweater and Papa was reading the newspaper. "Let's go outside."

They stepped through the door and sat on the grassy hill overlooking the orchards. "Marguerite, I need to tell you something. Red sent a couple of men to bury those two German soldiers, but they found only one body and one of the canisters.

"I don't understand. The two soldiers were together. What happened to the other body?"

"Apparently we only wounded one of them, and he must have crawled away after we left. Richard and José searched the area, but they found no sign of him. One of the canisters was missing, too. The one with your medical supplies in it."

Marguerite stared at her. "What does that mean?"

Bérénice drew in a long breath. "It means the Germans probably have the wounded soldier and he is telling them everything he saw and heard."

Her heart stopped.

"The men retrieved the other canister and the signal lamps and hid them in the Cave. But we have to assume the Germans have the other canister. London will send another drop later this week, so that's not the main problem."

"What is the main problem?"

Her cousin looked away. "Red wants to know if your Auxiliary is meeting soon."

Marguerite nodded. "The day after tomorrow. Why?"

"Simone is working as a secretary at Nazi headquarters, and she may know something. Red wants you to have lunch with your friends and report back to him."

Marguerite pulled up a few blades of grass and tossed them in the breeze, watching as they swirled and drifted. *What will happen to all of us? We have no control over anything, just like these bits of grass. We can only hope and pray and do the best we can.*

"And, there's another thing, Marguerite. Guy has gone. He packed his things yesterday and left for Caen."

"He left? But why?"

"He wanted to join the OCM, the *Organisation Civil et Militaire*. That is the main Résistance organization operating around Caen. They're mostly French soldiers who escaped from prison camps. They collect information for the Allies."

Marguerite was stunned. "Did Guy say anything before he left?"

"*Non*. Red asked if you knew why he left so suddenly."

Marguerite studied her hands. "*Non*, I don't know." *Why would he leave? He wanted . . . she didn't really know what he wanted. And he didn't even say goodbye. It hurt.*

* * *

Simone arrived late for lunch at *Cafe Angéle*, hung her new leather purse on the back of her chair, and sat down. "*Bonjour, mes amies*." She leaned forward. "Have you heard?" she whispered. "Two German soldiers were attacked by the Résistance right outside Ville de Pommes. One of the soldiers was killed and the other was wounded, but they killed three of the partisans."

Marguerite clamped her lips together. *That wasn't true.* "They said they killed *three* terrorists?" she ventured. "Were there more than that?"

"*Oui.* They won't say how many, but the wounded soldier claims he can identify the leader. A woman named Patrice."

Marguerite's stomach lurched. She fought to keep her expression blank. *They think I'm the leader?* She resisted an impulse to laugh. "What are the Germans going to do?" she asked, working to keep her voice even.

"They've called in the Gestapo," Simone replied. "The wounded soldier is making excuses for himself—it was too dark, there were too many of them, they wore disguises, that sort of thing. Colonel von Wilk's people don't believe he really saw much of anything. They think he's covering for himself. The Gestapo will be here tomorrow."

Marguerite jerked and her coffee slopped onto the tablecloth. Her hands shaking, she sopped up the dark liquid with her napkin. "What will the Gestapo do?"

"No one knows," Simone said. "They have their own methods."

A choking sensation closed Marguerite's throat. As soon as she could, she claimed she had a headache and fled. She found José near the police station and they raced back to Perdu.

"They know my name," she cried to Richard. "What should I do?"

Richard rubbed his chin. "They don't know your real name, Marguerite. They only have your Résistance code name, and they don't know who that is."

"Richard, I'm frightened."

"Marguerite, listen. That soldier has no idea what you look like. All he heard was the name Patrice."

"Maybe you should send me to Spain?"

"*Non*. You can't just disappear, it would attract suspicion."

"I can't stay. I just can't." She twisted her fingers together until they ached.

He caught her arm. "*Oui*, you can. You have to. That soldier cannot identify you. Just carry on normally. No matter what you do, don't give yourself away."

Brave talk, she thought. She clenched and unclenched her fists. But he was right, she must carry on. She could do this. She *must* do this.

That night she lay awake thinking about Guy. How could he leave without telling her? She needed his strength. His quiet courage. *But perhaps he doesn't need me.*

When the sun came up, she dressed and dragged herself downstairs for breakfast. Her mother studied her, narrowing her eyes. "Marguerite, are you feeling all right?"

"*Oui, Maman*. I'm just tired from . . . from yesterday. We harvested all the apples from the western orchards." She wished her mother's eyes weren't so sharp. To escape them she went to the front window and looked out.

Her heart nearly leaped out of her chest. Two German transport trucks with canvas stretched over the back end were parked in the yard. Three soldiers marched toward the house, and more jumped out the back of one of the transports and spread out in the farmyard.

"Papa," she called over her shoulder. "There are soldiers in the yard!"

Her father opened the door before the soldiers got to the porch. "What is going on?" he demanded.

"We have come for Marguerite Auriol."

Her father looked at her, then at the German. "Is she under arrest?"

"*Nein*. But she must come with us for questioning." He looked at her. "*Fraulein,* you must come with us."

"But I have done nothing wrong," Marguerite protested.

Her father stepped in front of her, but the soldier shoved him aside with his rifle. "Do not interfere."

"Where are you taking her?" he snapped. She had never heard Papa so angry.

"She has been ordered to Ville de Pommes."

They walked her under guard to the back of a transport truck. Inside, Bérénice and two other girls from nearby farms huddled on a bench. The soldier pushed her up into the truck and climbed in behind her.

She sat down across from her cousin. "What is this about?" Marguerite asked. She could not stop shaking.

Bérénice sent her a quelling look, and the other two shook their heads. "Keep quiet!" the guard ordered.

I must stay calm. No matter what happens, I must stay calm. Oh, God, what if they interrogate me? What if they—

She couldn't think about it.

The truck convoy stopped at two other farms and collected three more girls. When they arrived in town, 40 or 50 young women stood behind a line of military transports in the open field behind the *lycée*. A ring of armed soldiers separated them from the townspeople. In front of them loomed a newly constructed wooden platform where half a dozen chairs were lined up facing the crowd. Marguerite wanted to throw up.

Two armed soldiers took positions at both ends of the platform, and a single line of men, including a German officer followed by an SS officer and a tall, handsome man in civilian clothing, climbed the stairs and occupied the chairs. The agitated townspeople shouted encouragement to the girls.

"*Achtung*!" one of the guards shouted. "Military Prefect Colonel von Wilk wishes to address you."

The crowd quieted and the tall, stiffly erect colonel stalked to the front of the platform. *"Meine Damen und Herren . . ."* He paced across the front edge of the stage, his hands clasped behind him. "It is unfortunate that we have had to inconvenience you and these young women this afternoon." He stopped and propped his hands on his hips. "A few days ago, our soldiers discovered a cache of terrorist medical supplies and weapons near Ville de Pommes. The terrorists then ambushed our men. We know that a young woman by the name of Patrice led the attack."

Marguerite breath stopped.

"We cannot have this," the colonel continued. "Our brave men held off the criminals and killed three of them, but one of our men sacrificed his life and another was wounded."

Mon Dieu, what lies. She shook the thought out of her head and concentrated on keeping her face expressionless.

"That soldier," the colonel pronounced distinctly, "can now identify the leader of this unprovoked attack, a woman named Patrice. We have gathered these young women so that our man can identify this Patrice. The young ladies will be taken inside the *lycée* and questioned."

Marguerite began to tremble. She and Bérénice stood near Simone and Yvette, who looked terrified. The women were herded into the *lycée* assembly area where rows of chairs were lined up facing the stage. Armed guards closed the doors and stood in front of them. Then the well-dressed civilian strode onto the stage, followed by a Wehrmacht soldier with his right arm in a sling.

Marguerite sucked in her breath. She recognized him! Inside she felt sick.

"*Achtung, bitte*. I am Captain Ritter of the Gestapo." He wore a black fedora at a rakish angle, which emphasized his sharply chiseled features. Slowly he removed his coat and hat, revealing short blond hair and broad shoulders. He folded his coat over a nearby chair and carefully positioned his hat on top. Then he sat down and crossed his legs.

"*Guten Tag.*" He smiled.

Silence.

He raised his voice. "*Guten Tag*," he said again.

Scattered voices responded. "*Guten Tag*."

He nodded. "*Danke*. Now, as Colonel von Wilk has explained, we have had an unfortunate terrorist incident. Corporal Bleckenschmit here was ambushed and wounded. He believes he can identify the leader of the terrorists, one called Patrice. We are looking for a girl, small and blonde. She could be quite young. Do any of you here know a person who matches this description?"

Marguerite, seated near the center of the room, mimicked the other girls as they stared at each other.

Ritter stood and paced across the stage. His boot heels sounded like gunshots. "We will see if Corporal Bleckenschmit can identify her. Correct, Corporal?" Bleckenschmit nodded.

The silence thundered in her ears and her palms began to sweat. Desperately she tried to calm herself by thinking about Papa and their farm and yesterday's apple harvest.

"You." Ritter pointed to Simone in the front row. "Stand and repeat these words: 'We can't leave them here.' Use French, if you please." He resumed his seat.

Simone stood and repeated the phrase in a seductive tone. She glanced at Bleckenschmit and smiled. Marguerite turned her head and met Bérénice's eyes.

Ritter looked at Bleckenschmit, who shook his head. He pointed to another young woman. "You. Please stand and repeat the line."

"We can't leave them here," one of the farm girls recited. Again, the corporal shook his head.

Ritter pointed to another young woman. "If you please."

Marguerite saw that he was picking the blondes. She clenched her jaw and fought for control.

Suddenly Ritter pointed to her. Her hands began to shake. She gripped her skirt to disguise their trembling and slowly stood up. Her knees felt wobbly. She repeated the line in the same monotone as the others. "We can't leave them here." She forced herself to casually glance at Corporal Bleckenschmit. He paused, lifted his chin, then looked at Ritter and shook his head.

Marguerite steeled herself not to collapse onto her chair; instead, she carefully lowered herself onto the seat and studied the floor. Ritter pointed to the last blonde, and then began selecting brunettes. Still Bleckenschmit shook his head. Finally, Ritter slapped his knees with both hands and stood erect.

"Well, we had to try," he said. "Please rejoin your townspeople outside. We have an announcement."

Thank you, God. Merci beaucoup! She couldn't believe her luck. With Bérénice and the others she made her way back to the open field, where her father, José, Miguel, and Richard were standing together. She and Bérénice fought their way through the crowd to reach them.

Her father's face was pale and strained. "Marguerite?" His voice was unsteady.

"I'm all right, Papa," she whispered.

Richard leaned toward her. "You had us worried," he murmured. "When they came for Bérénice, I telephoned Guy in Caen. He's waiting for you at Perdu."

Guy is here! Already she felt better. She could hardly wait to see him.

Colonel von Wilk led a procession of officers and civilians onto the platform where they took seats. More soldiers gathered at the edge of the crowd, and all at once an uneasy feeling bloomed in the pit of Marguerite's stomach.

"We must make a short announcement," von Wilk said. "A soldier of the Reich has been murdered. This criminal act has brought Captain Ritter of the Gestapo from Paris. We cannot have these atrocities. Captain Ritter will now address you."

The Gestapo captain rose and strolled to the center of the platform. "This community has been identified as harboring terrorists. We ask you to come forward with any information you have regarding the identity of these criminals and their ringleader. When we identify this Patrice and her partisan group, your community will again be safe."

He paused and cleared his throat. "We will provide an additional incentive. We are detaining three of your citizens, and we will hold them until we identify the culprits. *Heil Hitler*." He snapped his right hand in the air and clicked his heels together.

Pairs of German soldiers began moving through the crowd. One group headed straight for Marguerite where she stood with her father and Richard. Suddenly they seized her father.

"Papa!" She lurched toward him, but Richard gripped her shoulder.

"Non," he muttered.

Horrified, Marguerite watched the soldiers prod her father toward one of the trucks with their rifles. She gripped Richard's arm. "Do something! They can't take my father!"

He caught her shoulder. She tried to wrench free, but he tightened his fingers and turned to Miguel. "Get her out of here."

"Where?" Miguel murmured.

"Wait!" she shouted. "Richard, listen to me!"

"Take her to Perdu. Keep her there until I can find out more."

Miguel clamped his hands on her upper arms. She tried to pull away, but he shook her, hard. "Stop struggling." He yanked her to the pickup truck and pushed her in. Numb, she sat beside the swarthy Spaniard until they reached Perdu. He parked in front of the house and Guy bounded out the door.

"Guy!" She stumbled out of the truck and threw herself against him. He wrapped his arm around her shoulders and guided her into the parlor.

"What happened?" he asked over her head. Before Miguel could explain, Richard strolled in, a stricken look on his sunburned face.

Marguerite tore herself out of Guy's arms and lunged at him. "What is happening?" She grabbed the front of his shirt. "Tell me!"

He hesitated. "We have seventy-two hours to produce the attackers. If we don't, they will shoot the hostages."

"*Non!* They can't!"

"Calm down," he ordered. He reached for her arm but she batted his hand away. When he reached for her again she slapped him across the face.

Guy pulled her away, but she shook him off. "Richard, you have to do something." She glared at the big Irishman. "Don't you understand? You have to!"

Richard massaged his cheek. "We'll think of something."

Tears clogged her throat. "I have to tell them I'm Patrice."

"You can't tell them anything," he warned.

"But, my father. . . "

"What do you think they'll do after you tell them?" Richard shouted. "They'll interrogate you until you tell them everything you know. Then when they're finished with you, they'll execute both you *and* your father. After that, they'll hunt down the rest of us."

She turned into Guy's arms. "It's my fault," she wept. "I should never have shot that soldier."

"*Non*, Marguerite, it's not your fault," Richard said, his voice harsh. "You don't know if it was you who killed that soldier. And if you hadn't fired, one of us would be dead."

She couldn't think. Her brain felt as if it were stuffed with cotton. "There must be something we can do."

"*Oui*, there is. But with only seventy-two hours, it's going to be tough. Miguel, I need you to drive to Le Havre, find Pierre, and explain what has happened." He touched Marguerite's shoulder. "Don't give up, Marguerite. We still have some time."

She swallowed back sobs and forced herself to think rationally. "*Maman! Mon Dieu,* how am I going to tell her?"

"I'll go with you," Guy volunteered.

Richard nodded. "We'll drive you to Charentais, and Bérénice and Guy can stay with you and your mother tonight. I'll telephone Paris and ask Germaine to come. And Marguerite, I want you to call your friends in the Auxiliary and arrange to meet for lunch tomorrow. Tell them you need to be with friends. Maybe you can learn something."

Marguerite nodded. "I can do that."

Guy walked her to the truck and climbed in beside her. Bérénice sat in the driver's seat and started the engine. All the way to Charentais Guy held her, and when she could no longer suppress her tears, he unfolded his handkerchief and pressed it into her hand.

What could she say to *Maman?* She could reveal nothing about *Réfugié*; it was better that her mother knew nothing. *I must to do this. But how?*

Bérénice parked in the yard, and Marguerite sat for a long moment staring at the front door. Guy took her hand and led her into the house.

"*Maman*?"

Her mother stepped out of the kitchen, drying her hands on a dish towel. "*Oui? Chou-chou*, what is the matter? You are pale as milk."

Marguerite took the towel from her mother and tossed it onto the dining room table. "*Maman,* come and sit down." She led her to the couch and took her thin, work-worn hand in her own. Guy and Bérénice took chairs across the room.

"*Maman*, I have something to tell you."

"*Oui?*" she said warily.

"There's been some trouble."

"What kind of trouble?"

Marguerite steeled herself. "Some German soldiers were ambushed near Ville de Pommes, and one of them was killed. The Germans seized three men from the village, and they will hold them until the ones responsible come forward." She swallowed hard. "One of the men seized was Papa."

Her mother's eyes clouded in confusion. "I don't understand. Why Antoine?"

"The Germans picked men at random," Bérénice explained.

"Is he safe?" Her mother's blue eyes were huge and frightened, but she did not weep.

"*Oui*, he is safe. The Germans think they know the name of the . . . of the leader, so — " She broke off. *Mon Dieu,* she couldn't do this. She couldn't lie to her mother. Across the room she caught Guy's somber gaze. Almost imperceptibly he shook his head.

Maman clasped her hands in her lap. "How long before the Germans find those men?"

Marguerite's stomach roiled. "I don't know, *Maman*. I don't know."

But she *did* know. She tightened her jaw until it ached. She knew, and she could say nothing. She could *do* nothing.

"Come." She took her mother's hand. "Let's go upstairs. This has been a bad shock, and you need to rest."

When she returned to the parlor, Bérénice looked up. "Did you tell her about the seventy-two hour deadline?"

"*Non.* I couldn't, I just couldn't. It's best if she doesn't know. In seventy-two hours either my father will be shot . . . or— " Her voice broke. She felt like screaming.

In an instant Guy was beside her.

"Richard will come up with something," he murmured.

Marguerite drew in a shaky breath. "He has to," she wept. "There has to be a way to save my father."

CHAPTER ELEVEN
THE PLAN

In the morning, after a sleepless night, Marguerite went downstairs to the parlor to wait for some word. Her head ached. Too fidgety to sit still, she paced between the kitchen and Papa's office until Richard drove into the farmyard. She met him as he emerged from the truck. "Is there any news?" she asked.

His eyes looked tired and his skin was grey with fatigue. "*Non*," he said shortly.

"I'm having lunch in town today with Simone and my other friends. What do you want me to find out?"

"The Germans are sitting on their hands, waiting for someone to come forward. See if that Nazi secretary, Simone, knows anything."

Marguerite nodded, and when Richard left she told *Maman* she was going into town and waited for José to pick her up. He dropped her off near *Café Angéle* in a thick fog, laced with rain. "I'm going to the *tabac* for cigarettes. I'll wait for you across the street. Good luck."

"*Merci*, José." She was heartened by the Spaniard's effort on her behalf; at the same time she dreaded trying to pry information out of Simone.

She pulled her coat about her and hurried past the empty sidewalk tables into the packed café. She saw Simone sitting at a table in the back, but before she could fight through the crush, a woman grasped her hand. "Our prayers are with your father, *Mademoiselle*—I mean *Fraulein*."

Marguerite didn't recognize her, but the sentiment from a stranger touched her. "*Danke*, I appreciate it. Please excuse me, I see my friends."

Simone sat sipping coffee with Yvette and Yvonne Callion; Marguerite hung her purse on the empty chair and draped her rain-spotted coat over the back. When she sat down Simone leaned toward her. "We're sorry about your father, Marguerite. Everyone is working hard to find the partisans."

Marguerite began to cry. *God in heaven, she could not bear this.* Simone rubbed her shoulders and Marguerite had to stop herself from recoiling at her touch. She fished a handkerchief out of her purse and dabbed at her eyes. "What is the Gestapo doing to find the attackers?"

"They are following a lead. They are looking for an informer."

Marguerite went still. "An informer?" *Mon Dieu, there is an informer inside Réfugié!*

"Once they find him," Simone said in an undertone, "they will find and arrest that Patrice woman and release your father."

"An informer?" Marguerite repeated, keeping her voice steady. "Do they know who the informer is?"

Yvonne shook her head. "He's been leaving envelopes addressed to Police Sergeant Boulot at our beach construction office. My father delivers the messages to him."

Marguerite's head spun. She had to get to Richard immediately. "Please, all of you, you must excuse me; I don't feel well. Could we meet for lunch tomorrow?"

"Of course," said Simone. All three women embraced, but Marguerite could scarcely stand their touch. She bolted out into what was now a gusty rain and ran across the street and along the slippery sidewalk to find José.

"We have to go back to Perdu," she gasped, "I know how to find the traitor inside *Réfugié*." They raced to the truck and José jammed it in gear. She gripped the dashboard while he careened through the rain, and when they burst into the Perdu parlor, Richard and Uncle Pierre were deep in conversation.

"I know how to find the traitor inside *Réfugié*!" Marguerite announced.

The men stared at her.

"How?" Richard shot.

"A man leaves messages at the Callion Construction office. Yvonne's father passes them on to Sergeant Boulot."

Richard frowned. "Miguel coordinates our laborers with Callion."

"It can't be Miguel," her uncle said.

Richard agreed. "Miguel's been with me since before Spain. I trust him with my life."

"Here's what we know," Uncle Pierre said slowly. "Information apparently goes from the Callion office to Yvonne's father and on to Boulot, and then to the Nazis. The weak link is somewhere in that chain."

The men stared at each other in silence. Finally Richard jolted to his feet. "I need to talk to Miguel." He nodded to Marguerite. "Go home. Tell your mother we're working on something, but don't give her any details."

Marguerite slogged through the rain back to Charentais, where she stripped off her wet garments while her mother brewed a pot of tea. They sat in the kitchen without talking, waiting for some word. Marguerite couldn't stand the inactivity. She tapped her fingernails, then stepped into the parlor to turn on the radio and paced back and forth across the carpet.

At eight o'clock that evening, Richard arrived, looking exhausted. Her mother jumped up from her knitting on the sofa. "Is Antoine all right? Is he coming home?"

"He is all right, *Madame* Auriol. We're working hard to get him freed." He glanced at Marguerite, then cut his eyes toward the front porch. "In private," he murmured.

She nodded and they stepped outside. "What's going on?" she whispered.

"We caught the informer. It was the orchard foreman who works for Miguel. *Réfugié* had helped him escape from the Vernet refugee camp, so it's disappointing that he turned on us. We had to get a little rough with him, but he admitted he's been trading information to get the rest of his family released from Vernet."

Marguerite shook her head. "How awful for him. For us."

"Should we tell your mother?"

"*Non*. If *Maman* knows too much... She is frightened enough already. I would spare her that."

"There's more," Richard muttered. "We called the OCM in Caen for help. We're going to kidnap Gerard Callion and use him as a hostage."

Marguerite blinked. "Why Callion?"

"We need to hold someone the Nazis value. Gerard Callion is the most prominent local man to collaborate openly with the Germans. They will have to protect Callion to show that if you support the Nazis, they will protect you."

"How is all this going to end?"

"God only knows," Richard said quietly. "Tomorrow morning they'll grab Callion. They will use OCM members who are not known in Ville de Pommes, so the family will report that the kidnappers were strangers. We hope the Nazis will conclude that the partisans they're looking for are not from this area. It's a long shot, but we're going to try."

"How does this help my father?"

"We'll offer to exchange Callion and their informer for the hostages."

Marguerite frowned. "Why include the informer as part of the exchange? He will give us all away."

Richard hesitated. "I committed to exchanging the hostages for both Callion and the informer, Marguerite. I didn't commit to exchanging a *live* informer."

"*Mon Dieu*," she gasped. "Do you think it will work?"

"It will be tricky. We'll know tomorrow."

It has to work, she thought desperately. *It must*. She couldn't bear it if... She caught herself and went back into the house.

"*Maman*, the negotiations to release Papa are still going on. It may take a couple more days." Her mother looked at her with tears in her eyes and Marguerite had to look away. Later she climbed the stairs to her bedroom and began to undress. She knew the hostage exchange would be dangerous. Too many things could go wrong.

Again she couldn't sleep. At dawn she dragged herself down to the kitchen to find Richard and Aunt Germaine seated at the table, drinking tea. "*Bonjour*, Aunt Germaine. How did you get here?"

"Red brought me in the delivery truck."

"Where is *Maman*?"

"Still in bed," Germaine answered. "Let her sleep."

An hour later they heard a sharp knock at the front door. Marguerite stiffened.

Richard stepped out on the porch with Marguerite right behind him. He spoke in whispers to a man she did not recognize, then turned to her. "The kidnappers have Callion. They are demanding release of the hostages. We'll know soon if this is going to work."

Hope for her father began to rise. "This has to work," she whispered. "You are gambling with my father's life."

"Go back into town tomorrow, Marguerite. Have lunch with the Nazi secretary and the Callion girl. Find out if the Nazis are interested in the trade. If they are, it will take a few hours to work out the details." He hesitated. "I think now is the time to tell your mother what's going on."

At that moment her mother stepped out on the porch.

"*Bonjour, Madame* Auriol," Richard said. "Are you well?"

Maman looked pale, her eyes red and swollen. "Is there any word about

Antoine?"

"*Non*," Richard said, "not yet. But we hope for good news soon. We have a plan to rescue him."

"You do?" Her mother's blue eyes narrowed. "What plan is that?"

Richard pursed his lips. "It's complicated. Marguerite can explain. Now I need to get back to Perdu."

Marguerite watched the big Irishman leave, and then told her mother about Uncle Pierre's Résistance cell and the work *Réfugié* was doing. She explained about the medical supplies the British parachuted in, and she confessed her involvement in the shooting of the two soldiers the night of the drop. Finally, she outlined the trade Uncle Pierre and Richard were trying to arrange.

"Why did you not tell me this before?" her mother said, her voice surprisingly steady.

"We didn't want you to worry."

Maman snorted. "I am not a child, Marguerite. My Antoine was wounded fighting for France in the Great War. Do you think because I am old that I do not care about my country?" She sent Marguerite a penetrating look. "One does what one must."

Tears came to Marguerite's eyes. Her mother was stronger than she imagined.

In mid-afternoon Richard arrived in the truck and asked if she was meeting with her friends. "*Oui*, I am."

She kissed her mother and climbed into the orange pickup. Half an hour later, Richard dropped her at the café.

Simone arrived first, her face white.

Marguerite half-rose from her chair. "Simone! What is the matter?"

"Three men broke into Yvonne's house and kidnapped her father right in front of her! They left a note saying they had a Nazi informer and they would execute him and *Monsieur* Callion if the hostages were not released."

Marguerite sat down suddenly.

"Marguerite, Yvonne is hysterical and her family is scared to death."

She leaned toward Simone. "Where is your Pètain now, Simone? No one is protecting us. The Nazis are taking hostages, the Résistance is taking hostages, and all we can do is sit here." Instantly she realized she'd said too much. "I'm sorry," she said quickly. "It's just that I'm worried about my father."

Simone squeezed her hand. "It's all right, Marguerite. The Germans are only trying to protect us from terrorists. I am sure your father will be released."

Marguerite's control slipped. "I am sure my father doesn't feel as optimistic." She lowered her voice. "Forgive me, Simone, I'm just on edge." She excused herself, left the café, and found Richard.

"Take me home. I couldn't bear one more minute with Simone saying the Germans are protecting us. How can she be so blind?"

"She's justifying the collaboration of her own father, Jean LaVaque. If she keeps saying it, maybe she will believe it."

At Charentais, they found Bérénice in the kitchen with Uncle Pierre and Germaine. Her mother had gone upstairs to rest. "Is there any news?" Marguerite asked.

Her uncle stood and pulled on his jacket, concealing his black leather holster. "*Non*," he said, resignation in his voice. "If the OCM can't make any progress by three o'clock tomorrow afternoon, the seventy-two hours will be up and …"

Marguerite wrung her hands together. *Please God, please.* It will all be resolved by tomorrow, but oh, God, what then?

CHAPTER TWELVE
TURNING POINT

Marguerite watched the black sky slowly lighten until red clouds streaked the horizon. She hoped it wasn't a bad omen. She dressed and went down to the kitchen to make tea, then sat at the wooden kitchen table sipping the hot brew, unable to stop thinking about the looming 72-hour deadline.

When the sky lightened, Aunt Germaine and Bérénice joined her, but no one felt like talking. Just after noon, Richard and Guy drove up in the Peugeot sedan with her uncle following in the orange Perdu pickup truck. After an interminable silence, Uncle Pierre pursed his lips and nodded to Germaine. "Will you stay here with Annelle?"

"Non!" Maman shouted from the kitchen. "I will not sit at home to wait and wonder. I will not. I am going with you."

"Marguerite?" her uncle said. "What about you? Will you stay? It could be dangerous in town."

"We are both coming," her mother insisted. "My daughter is not a coward."

Pierre heaved a sigh. "Bring your identity cards. We'll probably be stopped on the way. And . . ." He leveled a look at Marguerite. "Leave behind anything that could get you in trouble."

In silence they filed out of the house and piled into the vehicles. Richard and Pierre drove the truck; José brought the sedan with *Maman*, Aunt Germaine, Bérénice, Guy, and Marguerite. At the edge of town, a line of vehicles was halted, their engines still running. “It’s a roadblock,” José muttered.

Marguerite leaned forward. “We cannot stop! We will be too late.” She fidgeted while two German soldiers checked their identification cards and searched both vehicles. After what seemed like hours, they drove on into town and parked near the *lyçée.*

Soldiers in combat helmets with rifles slung over their shoulders swarmed over the adjacent field. It was bitter cold. The icy wind cut through her wool coat like a razor and Marguerite shuddered. All at once she stopped short. Three roughhewn posts had been erected in the center of the field. Guy took her hand, and she trudged on.

Townspeople were gathering, and a ring of armed soldiers surrounded the field. Marguerite and her mother moved closer. The crowd around them began to mutter and shout, but a hundred armed guards kept them outside cordoned-off area.

“Stop,” her uncle murmured. “I’ll telephone the OCM one last time to ask about the negotiations.” He moved off toward town. Marguerite stared after him, afraid to hope for a reprieve.

Six German soldiers armed with rifles emerged from the *lycée,* leading the three blindfolded hostages, hands tied behind their backs. Papa was the last man. Six more soldiers followed the prisoners; last in line was Colonel von Wilk.

Maman stood beside her without moving. Marguerite felt like hitting something.

Soldiers prodded the hostages forward toward the poles while guards shoved back the unruly crowd. The colonel directed an aide to place a chair on the ground, then stepped up onto the seat. Soldiers began lashing the blindfolded men to the poles.

“*Meine Damen und Herren,*” von Wilk shouted. “We have not yet learned the identity of the terrorist leader, Patrice, or her terrorist friends. The German Army does not bluff. Is anyone willing to come forward?”

Marguerite ground her teeth. She could confess and save Papa’s life. *Ah, no,* she acknowledged. She could not betray *Réfugié*. She wanted to, but she could not.

“Let them go,” shouted a man from the crowd. The mob buzzed and pressed forward against the ring of guards. Von Wilk drew his pistol, raised his arm, and fired into the air. Instantly the crowd froze into silence.

“If we do not have order, we will seize three more hostages and execute them immediately."

Papa stood erect, his chin raised.

"This is murder," a man yelled.

"We will have quiet!" von Wilk shouted. "Now, will any one of you confess to the attack on our soldiers?"

A hoarse cry came from Marguerite's right. "René," a woman called out. "René, I love you." One of the blindfolded men turned his head toward the voice. "*Je t'aime*, Giselle." A German drove the butt of his rifle into the man's belly, and other soldiers fought their way to the weeping woman and dragged her off to the *lycée*. The man tied to the post began to whimper.

Marguerite clenched her hands at her sides. She could save her father; all she had to do was speak up. She ached to do it, but she knew she could not. She would endanger all of *Réfugié*. *God in heaven, what should I do? Give me an answer.*

The wind picked up and drove freezing rain into her face. Tears of frustration chilled her cheeks. She turned into Guy's chest and clutched his lapels. "I must do something," she said through her teeth. She turned her head and stared at her father, then lunged toward the Nazi colonel, but Guy held her fast. She began to tremble.

"What, no one speaks?" von Wilk said. "Very well." He lifted one hand. At once a block of nine soldiers, three abreast, goose-stepped into the field, rifles at their sides. They separated into three squadrons that fanned out in front of each hostage.

An ominous quiet fell. *Maman* stood rigid, her eyes staring straight ahead. Shaking, Marguerite moved forward to touch her shoulder.

"*Achtung*." The firing squads came to attention. Marguerite gripped her mother's sleeve. A strange humming sounded in her ears.

"*Zeil*." The soldiers aimed their weapons, and she shut her eyes.

"*Feuer*!"

She jerked at the sound of gunshots. Guy grasped her shoulders, but she pushed away from him to see her father. He was bent forward, his head hanging at an odd angle, blood spreading on his shirt. She screamed.

Two soldiers moved toward her, and Guy thrust her behind him. Richard and Pierre stepped into their path. "We will take care of her," Richard said angrily. He pushed one of soldiers away. "You just shot her father."

"We have our orders," the man returned.

"Get her out of here," Richard called to Guy.

He pulled her away; Richard and Pierre moved to flank her mother.

Marguerite had one final glimpse of *Maman*, a slight woman standing perfectly still, her hands clenched at her sides, her head raised defiantly.

Guy drove Marguerite to Dr. Morel's office at the animal clinic, where she collapsed into a chair.

"Marguerite," the doctor said. "I am sorry. So sorry. Are you all right?"

She couldn't answer.

Minutes later, Richard, Pierre, and Bérénice arrived, their faces ashen. Richard folded his arms and leaned heavily against the wall. "They won't release the bodies. And they will allow no memorial service, not even a Requiem Mass. They're afraid it could spark an uprising. That's why so many soldiers were in town today."

Numb, Marguerite could only nod. His words seemed to come from far away. "Where is *Maman*?"

"She's with Germaine. They will be here soon."

"How is she?"

"Braver than I would be under the circumstances," Richard replied. "She is an amazing woman."

"What will happen to the informer?" Bérénice asked. "And Gerard Callion?"

"The informer is dead," Richard answered. "I don't know what the OCM will do with Callion. They hate French collaborators. The hostages were executed publically as a message to the people, and the OCM will feel they need to answer. None of this will be good for Callion."

Marguerite felt cold all over. *Papa was dead.* She reached for Guy's hand.

When Germaine and her mother arrived, Dr. Morel offered them all cups of strong coffee. No one spoke. Finally Richard thanked the doctor and opened the clinic door.

Without speaking they climbed back into their vehicles and worked their way slowly through the traffic clogging the town streets and out onto the road to Perdu. Marguerite felt dead inside, as if her body had turned to stone. Papa's death was her fault. Over and over she prayed that he would have understood.

When the Peugeot pulled into the Perdu farmyard, she asked Guy to walk with her to the Cave. When they reached the quiet refuge she turned into his arms and at last allowed herself to weep. He said nothing while she raged against the Gestapo, the Nazis, the police, Simone, Yvonne, collaborators, the entire Third Reich. He simply kept quiet and listened.

After a long while, she pushed away from him. "I can save lives, but it's not enough," she said, her voice shaky. "I want to do more. I *must* do more. I know Papa would want me to."

When she looked up at Guy, there were tears in his eyes.

* * *

The next morning the telephone rang in her father's office; Guy answered it. "Marguerite, it's Simone."

"*Guten Tag*, Simone."

"Marguerite, I wanted you to know what has happened. Gerald Callion's body was found this morning hanging from a lamppost."

Marguerite put her head down on her father's desk and closed her eyes.

"Marguerite, are you there? Are you all right?"

"*Oui*, I'm here," she said dully. "Is there more?"

"There was a note pinned to his shirt. It said, 'Collaborators Beware'."

Marguerite felt sick inside. Wooden. "How is Yvonne?" she asked in a lifeless voice.

"She is beside herself. Perhaps you could call her?"

"I will. *Danke*, for the news. *Auf Wiedersehen*, Simone."

"*Auf Wiedersehen*, Marguerite."

Slowly she replaced the receiver and sat for a long time, staring at nothing. *This can't be happening. It's like a terrible dream, but I can't wake up.*

She forced herself to stand up and walk into the parlor where Guy was pacing back and forth, his jaw tight. She laid her hand on his arm. "Gerald Callion is dead. I want you to find me a gun."

CHAPTER THIRTEEN
THE ANGEL OF THE CALVADOS

February 1942

In the winter of 1942 the Vichy government created the *Milice Francaise*, the French Militia, modeled on the German SS and the Gestapo and specifically organized to round up Jews and to infiltrate and expose members of the French Résistance. The *Milice*, like the SS and the Gestapo, used torture, execution, and assassination to control the French, and Richard and Pierre felt it was more dangerous than either the Gestapo or the SS. They curtailed *Réfugié* activities until they could strengthen security.

Outside France, Hitler had turned on his ally, Stalin, and attacked the Soviet Union; the Japanese had bombed Pearl Harbor; and both Hitler and Mussolini declared war on America. To add to the misery in France, the British began bombing civilian non-military targets in both Germany and France.

One brisk spring afternoon Marguerite joined *Maman*, Richard, and Uncle Pierre in the parlor to share some bread and cheese. They talked about work in the apple orchards, the latest news from London, even the refugees housed in the Cave, and then suddenly Marguerite stiffened. "I just remembered the missing canister, the one the Germans didn't find that night."

"It's in the Cave," Richard said. "Why are you asking about it now?"

"Did the British send guns with the medical supplies?"

"*Oui*.

"And ammunition?"

"*Oui*," answered Richard warily.

"I want one of the pistols."

The room fell silent. She sensed everyone's eyes on her, and then her uncle raised his eyebrows. "You want a gun?"

"*Oui, oui*, with bullets and everything," she said impatiently. His question irritated her. "I want to know how to handle a pistol."

Richard stared at her. "What do you want to do with this pistol with the bullets in it? You already know how to fire it—you killed that soldier the night of the drop."

"And now I want to do more. I want to kill the bastards who killed my father!"

"Marguerite!" her mother admonished.

"Calm down," Richard snapped. "We operate with purpose, not with emotion. You need to concentrate on your role, and that role is not gunning down Nazis."

"I still want to learn to shoot," she said stubbornly.

Richard and Pierre exchanged exasperated looks. "Absolutely not," *Maman* announced. "I refuse to worry about you roaming around Normandy with a loaded gun. Red, you can count on Marguerite and me for food, hiding places, and alibis. Marguerite knows enough medicine to patch up your refugees, but the Auriol women do not carry guns. No guns, *chou-chou*."

"Your mother is right," Pierre added.

Marguerite sniffed. "She is *not* right." She stomped upstairs to her bedroom, followed by Bérénice.

"Have you lost your mind?" her cousin accused. Her usually placid expression was belligerent, her face flushed with anger.

"Why can't I have a gun? You have one."

"*Et bien*. Right in front of your mother Red is going to say, 'Tomorrow I'll teach you how to shoot, and then I'm going to drive you into town so you can kill a couple of Nazis.' Marguerite, be sensible. Don't ask, *do*. Ask Guy to get you a gun, one that's small and easy to hide. He'll show you how to use it."

Marguerite dropped her head and ran her fingers through her hair. "Of course it was foolish to ask for a gun in front of *Maman*. I don't know what I was thinking. She is probably worried to death about me."

"Not quite," Bérénice said. "The Auriol women are *trés formidable*. After all . . ." She opened her arms and grinned. "Look at me!"

Marguerite laughed. She expelled a long breath and went downstairs to reassure her mother.

But it wasn't such a crazy idea. And later, she found Guy.

* * *

Marguerite finished her chores and walked down the hill to Perdu to meet Guy. A cold wind was blowing the last leaves from the apple and pear trees, and the chill penetrated her wool jacket. She pulled it tighter around her shivering body and spied Guy's tall form in the Perdu yard.

"I have something for you," he said with a smile. He stepped into the bunkhouse and returned with a package wrapped in blue paper and tied with red yarn.

"What is it?"

"Let's drive up to the coast and I'll show you." He helped her into the pickup truck and started the engine.

"Can I open it?"

"*Oui*, go ahead." He put the truck in gear and steered north and then west along the seacoast road high above the English Channel. She stripped off her gloves, untied the yarn, and tore off the paper. "Oh! Oh, Guy, *merci*!"

"What do you think? Do you like it?"

She ran her hand over the bluish metal gun barrel and the hard rubber grip. "What kind of gun is this?"

"It's a pocket gun, like the *Le Francais* police service revolver except with a shorter barrel. It fires eight shots."

She leaned over and brushed her lips across his cheek. "*Merci*, Guy." She turned the weapon over and over in her hands. She liked the feel of it. "Will you show me how to use it?"

"*Oui*. There's a remote field up here that we can use to practice; the waves on the rocks below will cover the sound of gunshots.

He parked on an isolated patch of land at the edge of the cliffs overlooking the sea. No buildings were in sight and only a few stunted bushes grew in the stiff breeze blowing off the Channel. Marguerite swung her legs out of the cab, and when the icy wind hit her, she found her leather gloves and pulled them on.

She walked to the edge of the cliff, faced into the wind, and sucked in deep breath of fresh sea air. Down below she could see the German beach defenses stretching in both directions along the sandy beaches.

"Why do the Germans build along here? No ships could land, it's too rocky." She stepped away from the cliff edge.

Guy found a smooth, medium-sized black stone, walked to a wind-bent tree, and balanced it on a dead branch. "Have you ever shot a gun like this before?"

"*Non*," she shouted above the surf. "The first time was at the parachute drop, and I used Bérénice's gun. I don't know what kind it was."

"Show me how you aimed her gun."

She brought the pistol up with both hands, aimed it, and squeezed her eyes shut. She pulled the trigger and the gun exploded. "This gun doesn't jerk as much as Bérénice's did."

"Hers is a .38 caliber. This is only a .25 caliber. It's less powerful, but it's smaller and easier to hide. Now, try again. Extend your arm, and this time keep your eyes open. It's a wonder you didn't kill one of us that night." He stepped behind her, pulled her hands apart, and held her right hand straight out, away from her body.

She gripped the pistol, then swung it from side to side, aiming at imaginary targets.

"Be careful, it's loaded! I doubt that you'll ever need all eight shots, but it was the smallest pistol I could find."

She looked up at him and grinned, then sighted down the barrel. "Where did you get this?"

"Don't ask."

She sent him a quick glance, then aimed just below the black stone and fired. A large chip of wood flew off the branch. "Missed again."

"Aim a little higher."

She tried once more, and this time the stone shattered. "I like it! Does Richard know I have this? Or Uncle Pierre?"

"*Oui*, but your uncle isn't happy about it."

"That's too bad." She slipped the pistol into her coat pocket.

* * *

Sunday evening, Marguerite and her cousin sat in the Perdu living room listening to Radio London. Ten minutes into the broadcast, two words jumped out at her: "Patrice" and "Calvados." Her heart stopped. "Did you hear that?"

"*Oui*," Bérénice said with a frown. They leaned toward the radio.

"There is a heroic young woman serving with the Résistance. She is known as Patrice, the Guardian Angel of the Calvados. This model of French patriotism smuggles medical supplies to refugees in Normandy."

Her cousin gaped at her. "Marguerite, they're talking about you!"

"Me?" A fist squeezed her heart.

"In an attempt to flush her out, the Nazis shot three hostages. They neither understand nor deserve French womanhood. Such women are bold, courageous, and merciful."

Marguerite caught her breath. "*Mon Dieu*. They are talking about someone else. Another Patrice."

"But it has to be you! What of the part about shooting three hostages?"

"*Non*," Marguerite said more forcefully. "It has to be someone else."

Her cousin sent her an admiring look. "London understands that we need heroes and heroines. They're always reporting stories about Nazi resistance. Someone from Ville de Pommes must have talked about what happened, and it got back to England."

A knot tightened in her chest. "What am I going to do?"

"I don't know. We should ask Red." They pulled on their coats, raced out to the bunkhouse, and pounded on the door.

The big Irishman loomed in the doorway. "What is the matter?"

"Come up to the house, Red, please," Marguerite begged. "I need to talk to you."

"Why? What has happened?"

"Just come. I'll tell you at the house. Hurry!"

They waited in the living room until Richard walked in, his shoulders tense. Marguerite scooted to the edge of the couch. "Radio London just broadcast a story about someone called Patrice who is smuggling medical supplies into France. They mentioned that the Nazis had shot three hostages because of her. Could they be talking about me?"

Richard gave her a long look. "*Oui*." He rubbed his chin. "I think the smartest way to handle it would be to change your Résistance code name."

"You're right. I feel less like a target already." *Patrice would simply evaporate. Let the Nazis chase a phantom.*

As the weeks passed, Radio London continued to broadcast propaganda stories about Patrice, the Angel of the Calvados. But as her supposed exploits became more farfetched, Marguerite's relief faded. Patrice was not evaporating; she was growing more and more important to the cause.

She bit her lip. Perhaps it didn't matter. After all, she wasn't carrying out any more missions for *Réfugié*.

For Easter, Aunt Germaine took the train from Paris and on a sunny afternoon in April, Richard met her at the station in Creully and drove her to

Charentais. When they entered the house, Pierre and José rose from the couch; Bérénice and *Maman* came in from the kitchen, dusting flour from their hands.

Germaine dropped her suitcase, unbuttoned her winter coat, and hugged each of them. "*Bonjour*, everyone."

"*Bonjour*, Germaine," Pierre said. "How are things in Paris?"

The tall woman in the faded green dress shook her head. "Things are bad in Paris. The Nazis are deporting huge numbers of Jews to the work camps in Germany and Poland. So many doctors and nurses at the hospital ask for our help escaping that we're overwhelmed."

Richard folded his hands into fists. "I'm worried about the *Milice*. We must expand operations and start taking more chances."

Germaine pursed her lips and nodded to Marguerite. "I have more bad news. You cannot come to the hospital next summer."

"Why? I was looking forward to it."

"A Gestapo captain was questioning the hospital staff and someone told him about a summer intern named Patrice Cerne who matches the description of the Patrice from the German soldier shooting. The more he searches for Patrice from Caumont, the more he's convinced he's on the right track. If you show up in Paris, you will be arrested and interrogated by the Gestapo."

Marguerite wiped her hand across her cheek. "I knew that broadcast was going to be trouble."

"There's more," her aunt said.

She sucked in her breath. "More?"

"This Guardian Angel thing is taking on a life of its own. It has inspired the nurses, the nuns, and other female staff to become more active in the Résistance." Germaine pulled out a folded wad of paper and slowly smoothed it open. "Here's a copy of *Combat*, a Parisian Résistance circular. There's an article in it about Patrice."

She handed it to Marguerite, who scanned it, passed it to Pierre, and then buried her face in her hands. "All I wanted to do is help people who need medical attention."

No one spoke until Germaine broke the silence. "At least they're looking for Patrice in Caumont."

Marguerite stared at her hands. "That won't last long. What am I going to do?"

"This Gestapo captain is rounding up Jews in the northwestern sector of Paris. He's too busy to spend time looking for someone who doesn't exist."

"If things get too dangerous for you," Uncle Pierre said quietly, "we'll get you to Spain."

"What do I do this summer, just wait for the net to close in? I'll go mad."

"Work in the orchards with Miguel and José," her uncle replied. "We can protect you in the fields. We have a good warning system in place here and at Perdu. If our lookouts see the police or Nazis in the area, we warn the field workers and they can hide until we know what's going on."

"But I want to be of real help, not work as a field hand."

"I have an idea," Germaine said suddenly. "One of the Jewish doctors at the hospital needs to escape. You could hide him here on the farm. He could work with Marguerite, teach her more about medicine."

Richard thought for a moment. "We can smuggle him out of Paris in the calvados barrels."

"*Bon*," Germaine said with a tired smile. "It's a good plan. He will be grateful."

After Easter dinner on Sunday, Germaine took the train back to Paris to arrange things, and Marguerite prepared to go to work in the fields.

* * *

"Marguerite, there's a telephone call for you."

"Oui, Maman." She picked up the receiver in her father's office.

"Can you come to Perdu?" Richard asked. "We have something to discuss with you."

"*Oui*, I can be there in five minutes." She hung up, put on her blue wool coat, and stepped out the back door. She couldn't shake the feeling that something was wrong.

She found Richard, Uncle Pierre, and Bérénice in the Perdu living room. "Please sit down and listen," Richard said. "MI-9 wants us to establish a medical aid station in Caen."

"In Caen, why?"

"They didn't say, but we suspect they're planning a military operation somewhere in northern France.

A surge of excitement went through her. "You mean we might be liberated?"

"*Non*, I don't think so, not yet. But they have their reasons. As it happens, we know a *Monsieur* St. Jacques and his wife who own a liquor distribution warehouse in Caen. Both are Jewish and they want to sell the business and have us smuggle them to Spain. Their warehouse has a basement where we could hide refugees and treat injuries. It would be perfect for us."

Marguerite tried to suppress a smile.

"MI-9 has agreed to send us the money to buy out St. Jacques. Then Dr. Katz, from St. Jeanne's hospital in Paris, will join us in Caen. We'll put him in charge of the medical aid station and he can pose as the general manager for Auriol Distributors."

Marguerite looked from Richard to Uncle Pierre and back. "Why are you telling me this?"

"We need a, um, a secretary," Richard answered carefully. "Someone who can double as a nurse. You can commute from Charentais with José; he goes back and forth to Caen on a regular basis. Are you willing?"

She thought about a long, hot summer working in the fields and the decision was easy. "*Oui*, I will go." Her spirits soared. Something positive was going to happen, she could feel it. Something big. *Would there be an Allied invasion? Mon Dieu, if there were, it would mean casualties and death and destruction and . . .*

Suddenly she wanted to hide from everything ugly that threatened her and those she cared about.

Guy. Where was Guy? She needed to talk to him. *Now. Tonight.* She stood up and pulled on her coat. "I'm going to out to the bunkhouse."

Bérénice caught her hand. "What, now? It's cold out there."

"I don't care."

"Wait, I'll go with you."

"*Non*. I know the way."

Then she was out the door and racing down the hill.

CHAPTER FOURTEEN
DANGER

June 1942

The new Auriol Distributors warehouse was a nondescript two-story cinderblock rectangle with a flat roof in the largely uninhabited industrial section of Caen. Second-floor windows faced the street and graffiti marred the walls. José shook his head at the black-painted swastikas and the word "*Juden*" scrawled on the wall. The old Jewish couple living here must have been terrified. She wondered if they were safe in Spain yet.

The tiny office on the second floor smelled of mildew and cigarette smoke. Four battered, mismatched wooden desks sat in a tight square in the center and file cabinets lined one wall.

The sole occupant rose, his brown eyes widening behind round framed glasses.

"*Mon Dieu*. Aren't you Patrice Cerne?"

"*Bonjour*, Dr. Katz." She extended her hand to the surprised physician. "I am glad to see you again."

Richard introduced Bérénice, then reminded Marguerite to avoid using Dr. Katz's name. "Use the name Alfred Renier."

The doctor shook Bérénice's hand, then surveyed Marguerite with interest. "You caused quite a stir at St. Jeanne's after the Radio London broadcasts and Résistance circulars about you. Is it true the Nazis are after you for smuggling medical supplies into France?"

"*Non*. That is only partly true."

"Then I am honored to be working with the Angel of the Calvados!"

Marguerite wasn't sure how to react. His attention was flattering, but it made her uncomfortable; she had done nothing special. "When did you arrive?"

"Just this morning. The Gestapo appeared at the hospital last week and started arresting some of the staff. Germaine helped me escape and hid me in her apartment until I caught an uncomfortable ride to Caen in a calvados barrel."

Marguerite smiled. "I look forward to working with you, Dr. Ka—Alfred."

Richard leaned back in one of the desk chairs, his big hands clasped behind his head. "José and our staff are repainting the basement inside and out; that will be our secret aid station. We will take direction from you on stocking the medical clinic. Any questions?"

* * *

Marguerite and Bérénice began commuting to Caen every day to work as clerks at Auriol Distributors. José supervised the new warehouse crew of transient immigrants and *Réfugié* agents, and Dr. Renier worked on the secret basement medical clinic. Marguerite thought their progress agonizingly slow; she wanted to save lives, not tally shipping numbers.

One afternoon Uncle Pierre telephoned her. "Marguerite, could you come to Perdu this evening?"

"*Oui*, I can be there. Is there some special reason?"

Her uncle hesitated. "I'll explain when you're here."

When she arrived, her uncle took her aside. "MI-9 has contacted us. There will be an Allied raid somewhere along the north French coast."

Marguerite caught her breath. "An invasion?"

"*Non*. It will be a raid."

"A raid? What is the difference between a raid and an invasion?"

"In a raid, enemy territory is penetrated for some short-term purpose, like destroying a railroad line. When that is accomplished, the force withdraws. In an invasion, enemy territory is penetrated with the intention of occupying it. The difference is important."

"What will they do on this raid?"

"They want to capture and hold a French port for a short period of time. It is practice for a major invasion."

Marguerite was giddy. *The Allies are coming to France.* "How can we help?"

"Our medical aid station in Caen will be a help to them, and MI-9 wants us to cooperate with the OCM. Tomorrow morning, Red will drive you to Caen for a meeting he's going to set up with them."

"Me? Why me and not Bérénice or José?"

Pierre studied the floor for a long minute. "Because, Marguerite, the OCM people want to work with Patrice Cerne."

"But why?"

"De Gaulle wants to continue to exploit Patrice; they view this as a priority. They don't want her to simply vanish."

"Do I have anything to say about it? I feel so vulnerable."

"They think Patrice is an inspiration and an important propaganda tool. They want to keep up the radio broadcasts about her."

So, Patrice is back. "Bon, Uncle, I will be ready.

The next morning, the air was sweltering, so she chose a cool pink sundress with buttons down the front. After her quick breakfast of tea and toasted bread, Richard and Bérénice drove up in the orange truck. Her cousin wore a light print dress and, as usual, her ugly savate shoes. *Someday, I'm going to hide those shoes.*

On an isolated country road leading into Caen, a helmeted German private with an infantry rifle across his back stopped them. "Oh, no," Richard groaned. "A German roadblock." No other vehicles were in line at the roadblock, so he drove directly up to the sentry. The soldier approached the open window and stared inside at Marguerite and Bérénice.

"Do you want to see our papers?" Richard offered.

"*Nein,*" he growled.

"Then can we go?"

The soldier shook his head. Four other soldiers wandered up and stood in a semicircle around the truck, whispering among themselves. Their stares made Marguerite uneasy.

"Peter," one of the men shouted at the sentry. "Send them through there." He pointed to an opening in the hedgerow lining a pasture. "Willy and I want to, uh, question them about their activities." The other soldiers laughed.

The one called Peter shook his head. "Not now, Kurt. Leave it alone."

"I said send them through there!" Kurt demanded. "You." He pointed at Richard. "Drive into that field. Slow."

Richard opened his mouth to object, but Kurt shouted, "Now!" He trotted ahead of the truck and opened the gate into the pasture.

"We're on our way to work," Richard called out the truck window. "We don't want any trouble."

"Now!" the soldier barked again.

Richard slowly steered the truck over the berm into the field. Dairy cattle were scattered in the meadow. Kurt waited for them to pass, and then closed the gate behind them. Marguerite suddenly felt uneasy, as if they were locked in a room.

"Over there," Kurt demanded, pointing to another break in the hedgerows across the field. Richard eased the clutch out and crept toward the second opening. The two soldiers cradled their rifles and strode behind the pickup.

"I don't like this," Richard said in a low voice. "Do either of you have your pistols?"

"*Oui*," Marguerite whispered. "In my dress pocket."

"I have mine," muttered Bérénice. "I always carry mine."

Marguerite twisted to glance back at the two soldiers. "What do they want?" she whispered. The big Irishman didn't respond, but his jaw muscles flexed.

Kurt trotted past the truck and opened another gate that led into another, much smaller field, lined on all sides with tall, dense hedges. He motioned to Richard, and he drove past the gate. Marguerite noticed there was no other access to the field, and her anxiety rose. They were completely out of sight of the main road. The one called Willy left the gate open and tramped up to Richard's window, checking over his shoulder.

"Get out," Kurt demanded. "All of you."

Marguerite clutched her skirt and shot a look at Richard. His face was pale. Trembling, she slid out the passenger door. Kurt pointed his rifle at her. "You, over there. Move!"

The trio moved away from the truck, and Marguerite felt for her gun. Willy leered at her and motioned for her to step away from Richard and Bérénice. She removed her hand from her pocket and moved to the side, then looked back at her cousin and Richard. Kurt kept his rifle trained on them.

"Farther," Willy ordered.

Marguerite moved three more steps away from the truck and realized she was trembling.

Willy gave her a hooded look. "Unbutton."

"What?" she shouted, wide-eyed.

"Unbutton your dress."

"I…I don't know what you mean." *I must think. Should I grab for my gun?"*

Willy lowered his rifle, strode up to her, and ripped the top button off her dress. Her breath choked off.

"Unbutton," he ordered again.

Mon Dieu, he is going to rape me!

Richard bolted forward. "Wait a minute, you can't do this!"

"Stand back," Kurt shouted. He raised his rifle and Richard froze in place.

"Leave her alone!" Bérénice yelled.

"Quiet! Your turn will come soon enough," Kurt sneered.

Willy held Marguerite's gaze. "Now you," he snapped through clenched teeth. "I said to unbutton!"

Her heart pounded. She stared at Richard, but he was watching Bérénice. Her cousin shifted her eyes from Richard to Willy, rotated her hips, and softly kicked at the grass.

With quivering hands Marguerite felt for the second button and slowly undid it, breathing hard. She looked straight at Richard, whose blue eyes were studying Kurt, waiting for an opening. Her cousin was edging toward Willy.

Marguerite stepped back and sideways, forcing Kurt to turn away from Bérénice. Very deliberately she slipped the next button free and watched her cousin slide toward Willy. She could see what Bérénice had in mind, but what about Kurt?

Oh, God. What should I do? She undid the third button, then the fourth. Even though the day was scorching, her entire body felt cold. She freed the last button and stood unmoving, then slipped her right hand into her pocket and grasped the hard rubber grip of her pistol. She squared her shoulders and waited.

"Now, take off your dress."

She couldn't do it. She stood motionless, watching Bérénice. Her cousin's face was a blank mask devoid of emotion, her eyes cold and predatory. Richard's eyes bored into Kurt's back.

She removed her hand from her pocket and crossed both arms over her chest.

Willy licked his lips. "I said take your off dress!"

Marguerite hesitated. He stepped toward her and pulled her arms down to her sides. "Don't move." He thrust his hand down the front of her dress and cupped her breast. She stared straight ahead, breathing hard, and then he brushed the strap off her shoulder.

"Now!" he shouted, "Take it off!"

Richard mouthed, "Do it."

She thought about drawing her pistol. She ached to close her fingers around the butt of her gun, but Kurt raised his rifle and aimed it at her.

"I'll do it. I'll do it," she muttered.

Bérénice made an exaggerated turn and Richard gave her a nod. *I hope they know what they're doing. Does Richard have a gun hidden somewhere?*

She expelled a long breath and slipped the other strap off her shoulder. Richard lowered one hand and inched closer to Kurt. Bérénice looked deathly calm.

Kurt glanced in Richard's direction and raised his rifle. "Settle down, big man. Where do you think you're going?" Richard raised his hands but did not step back, and Marguerite knew he was waiting for her to distract the German soldier.

Willy suddenly jabbed his rifle toward her. "Let your dress drop!"

Her throat went dry. *I cannot do this*. She uncurled her fingers and let the smooth cotton garment slide to her waist, then immediately crossed her arms over her breasts. The hot sun seared her bare back. She was terrified. Pretending to sob, she dropped to her knees, her hand closer to her pistol.

Willy set down his rifle, took off his helmet, and began to unbutton his tunic. Bérénice edged closer, and in one motion stepped forward with her left foot and twisted her right hip away from him, as if coiling a spring. Then she landed a kick that lifted her completely off the ground. Willy half-turned toward her, but it was too late. Her thick-soled shoe smashed into his jaw. She pivoted away, changed direction, and attacked again.

Kurt swung his rifle toward Bérénice. "*Was die Hölle*?" he yelled, and in the next moment Richard was on him. The Irishman wrapped one arm around the German's neck, swung him violently from side to side until his rifle and helmet tumbled away, then tightened his grip. Spittle trickled from one corner of his mouth as the German kicked and scratched at Richard's arms. Slowly his body went limp.

Willy was down on his hands and knees and Bérénice delivered another kick to his head. He pushed himself up, but she drove her foot into his face and he flopped over, his body splayed on the ground.

Panting, Marguerite scrabbled for her pistol, then grabbed her dress and pulled it up. Richard's face was flushed, his breath coming in guttural gasps. Silently he signaled Bérénice, who raced to the break in the hedgerow. He took up station on the other side of the opening.

He held two fingers up to Marguerite, mouthed "two shots," and fired an imaginary gun in the air. Willy groaned on the ground in front of her. She clenched her jaw, looked down at Willy, lowered her pistol, and fired twice into his temple. His body convulsed and went still. Hiding the pistol behind her back, she walked to the center of the small field and knelt facing the hedgerow entrance.

The three other soldiers raced halfway through the first field, then saw her. She let her dress fall open and the confused soldiers instantly slowed down as they entered the second field. At that moment, Bérénice jumped out and fired three shots into the body of the closest soldier. Richard stepped forward, grabbed another's chin and yanked his head around with a crack.

Marguerite had her pistol up and took careful aim at the last soldier; rapidly she fired two rounds into the trunk of his body. Instantly she was up on her feet, running to the other bodies to check to be sure they were dead.

"Let's get out of here," Richard muttered.

Marguerite bent down to one victim and felt his neck for a pulse. He was still alive. She slapped his face, and when he moaned she brought her mouth close to his ear. "You will never again try to rape Patrice Cerne or any other French woman." Then she stood erect and fired one bullet into his forehead.

They collected the rifles. "Get their identity papers, we can use them," Richard shouted. They searched the uniforms and raced back to the truck. Bérénice climbed into the cab and Marguerite followed, re-buttoning her dress.

Richard jammed the vehicle in gear, roared out of the fields back onto the highway, and raced toward Caen. When he tried to tap a cigarette out of his pack, Marguerite noticed his hand was shaking. "Are you all right?"

He glanced at her sideways, then stared down at his hand. "I'm fine. How are you doing?"

"I need a shower. I feel so dirty. Did we have to kill them?"

"They were going to shoot all of us to cover up the rapes."

Marguerite nodded agreement. *Of course we had to shoot them.* She felt dead inside. When she killed the first soldier she felt nothing, no emotion, no remorse; she wondered how these assassinations were affecting her. The second soldier had been easier.

At the warehouse they climbed the stairs to find Alfred talking with José. The doctor took one look at them and Marguerite's torn dress and half rose from his chair. "What's happened?"

"The Germans stopped us at a roadblock outside of town," Richard panted.

"A soldier tried to rape Marguerite."

"*Mon Dieu*, are you all right?"

Marguerite flopped into the nearest desk chair and laid her head on her folded arms. "I will be all right. The damage is mostly to my nerves." She felt a hand on her back and looked up. Bérénice stood beside her, tears in her eyes.

"Truly, Bérénice, I am all right." She straightened and took her cousin's hand. "You saved my life. And Richard," she said, turning toward him, "I have never seen you like that."

The big Irishman tilted his head back and closed his eyes. "That's as close to losing control as I've ever come."

She stood up and touched his arm. "Don't tell Guy about this."

"For God's sake, Marguerite, why not?"

"Please. Just don't tell him."

He studied her for a long moment. "All right, we keep this to ourselves."

Suddenly she was so fatigued she couldn't think clearly. She had taken more human lives. *Oui, the soldiers were evil, but was killing justified? Would she do it again?*

Something deep within her felt satisfaction that she'd begun to avenge her father. She'd done it for Papa. For herself. If fighting to protect citizens and free France from the Nazis meant killing more German soldiers, then she would do it. She swallowed hard. Already the morning seemed unreal, as if it had happened to someone else. She shuddered at the memory, the hungry eyes on her body, the German's voice ordering her to…

She couldn't think about it anymore.

She would not tell *Maman*, she decided. And she would not tell Guy. Richard's somber gaze held hers and she tried to smile. "*Et alors*, there is more work to be done."

"You are right, Marguerite," he said, admiration in his voice.

She leveled a long look at him and sent him a nod. Patrice Cerne would reappear in Caen.

CHAPTER FIFTEEN
COMMITMENT

July 1942

In the weeks following Marguerite tried to occupy her mind with liquor shipments and transfers, but she couldn't rid herself of the image of the German soldiers she had shot. She stared out the window, twisting her hands until she could no longer concentrate.

"Excuse me, Alfred, I'm going for a walk around the warehouse."

The physician glanced up from his desk, a concerned look on his drawn face. "Are you all right?"

"*Oui.*" *But she was not all right at all. She couldn't shake the memory of that soldier's hungry eyes.*

She went downstairs and idly wandered through the warehouse section where the pallets of calvados boxes were stored, dodging forklifts unloading late harvest wines and cases of bottled calvados.

"Marguerite." Bérénice's voice startled her.

Her cousin stood on the stairway, her hands on her hips. Marguerite shook her head. "I'm sorry, did you say something?"

"You've been down here a long time. Are you all right?"

"Everybody keeps asking me that!" she snapped.

"We're worried about you," Bérénice said quietly.

"I am just . . . just trying to get my mind off things."

"Well, come back upstairs and help me get the shipping manifests done before the afternoon delivery trucks arrive."

Marguerite nodded and wearily climbed the stairs to the office, where she tried to concentrate on the paperwork. She worked distractedly until late afternoon when Richard returned from a meeting with the OCM.

"MI-9 has decided to do a broadcast about the assault on Patrice last month."

Marguerite was stunned. "Why? That will just stir up the Nazis."

"We have our reasons. First, the German Army command is still wondering why those soldiers we killed were found so far away from their post. Second, it's a message from the Résistance to the French people about the Nazis' weakening control."

"But that will make things worse for us!"

"Maybe. The Germans will intensify their search for Résistance members, and we will have to cut back on *Réfugié* activities until the Nazis get tired of investigating the incident."

She hated to admit it, but she was relieved.

"I found out something else even more important," he continued. "Whole families are being deported, even the children, to camps near Auschwitz and Buchenwald. Rumors are that these are not work camps, but something else. Something different. I hope the rumors are exaggerating."

He waited a full minute while she stared at him in horror, then suddenly asked, "Have you been to St. Lô or someplace near that area?"

"*Non*. Why do you ask?"

He fished a copy of *Combat* from his trouser pocket. "Read this."

She scanned the newspaper and looked up into his tired face. "I don't believe this. You know I haven't been anywhere near St. Lô."

"A woman near St. Lô helped some English fliers escape the *Milice*. She claimed she was Patrice Cerne, and now the Gestapo and the Vichy police are scouring the area looking for her."

Marguerite went cold. "God help her if she's caught."

He looked away. "Patrice is an inspiration, so London wants her to surface once in a while. The more often she appears and eludes capture, the more mythical, the more divinely protected she will seem. This is how the Résistance is legitimized."

"And, what if I *don't* elude capture?" she asked in an unsteady voice.

"We have contacted other Résistance organizations. They will have a Patrice appear in different places. But you need to be very careful."

All the way back to Perdu that evening Marguerite thought about Radio London. *I had to strip in front of a Nazi soldier, and now my shame will be broadcast all over France. The world is sick.*

Uncle Pierre met them in the parlor. "Sit down, all of you. I have news."

Richard came to immediate attention. "What news?"

"According to MI-9, the Allies are about to launch their raid on France. They can't tell us where or when it will take place, but we are instructed to stand by and assist if needed."

Marguerite leaned forward in her chair. "How are we supposed to assist, exactly?"

"The Allies don't have much faith in the Résistance as a fighting force, so our job is support. If we find any Allied soldiers marooned behind enemy lines, we are to hide them and get them out."

"We can do more than that," Bérénice protested.

Pierre shook his head. "*Non*. We follow orders."

Richard paced back and forth a few steps. "Did they say anything else? Anything more specific?"

"*Non*. Be patient."

The Irishman released an exasperated breath. "Fine." He focused his gaze on Marguerite. "Tomorrow afternoon I want you and Bérénice to come with me to an OCM meeting. They will enjoy meeting the famous Patrice Cerne."

All of a sudden she felt trapped, pinned and wriggling like a butterfly specimen. She hated this war. *Hated it.*

The next afternoon Richard drove them across Caen to an older, run-down industrial part of the city and parked the truck on a side street. Then they walked to a narrow medieval alley paved with large flat cobblestones and raised sidewalks made of smaller stones. Marguerite liked the gloomy streets and the old stone buildings. They reminded her of French endurance throughout its long history; she prayed her country would emerge strong once more. She wanted to be part its rebirth.

She shivered at the lack of sunlight; the narrow four-story buildings lining the streets had a feeling of foreboding. They stopped at a nondescript storefront with the name *Christien's* painted over the entrance. Old books filled the front window.

A small bell tinkled when they entered, and Marguerite wrinkled her nose at the smell of dust and mildew. A young boy was sweeping the aisles toward the back, and an overweight, balding man with reading glasses looked up from the counter.

"I'm looking for *Herr* Schmitzendorf," Richard announced.

"He is not here, but I can help." He climbed off his stool, rose up on his toes, and called to the boy. "Rob, please conduct these visitors to *Herr* Schmitzendorf."

Without a word the youth leaned his broom against the wall and led them out the entrance and across the alley to the main thoroughfare. They hiked a kilometer in a circuitous route to an ancient building with boarded-up windows. Checking over his shoulder to be sure that they weren't followed, Rob knocked twice on the scarred door, then rapped once more.

The door swung open, and over the boy's shoulder Marguerite saw five young men sitting around a well-used wooden table. When she and Bérénice entered, they rose in unison. The tall, attractive man standing at the head of the table spoke first.

"Welcome, Red. Please take a seat." He introduced the others, and Marguerite was struck by how young they were.

Richard introduced Bérénice and then her. "This is Patrice Cerne." At the mention of her name, the men around the table stared.

"Red told us we would meet the famous Patrice Cerne," the tall man said. "Could that truly be you, *Mademoiselle?"*

"It is," she breathed. Slowly she eased herself into a vacant chair, took a cigarette out of her purse, and struck a match. Richard glanced at her out of the corner of his eye, then shot a look at Bérénice, who shrugged.

"You are so…so petite," one of the men exclaimed. She narrowed her eyes at him.

"Big things come in small packages," Richard said.

The tall man resumed his seat. "Yesterday a Caen police officer who was collaborating with the Nazis was shot. A woman in our organization found him and bandaged his wound. The officer was grateful, and when he asked her name, she told him *she* was Patrice Cerne."

Marguerite inhaled on her cigarette. "I appreciate your people taking risks pretending to be me."

The leader chuckled, then continued. "MI-9 wants us to merge with *Réfugié*. The OCM is an intelligence organization; we collect data on German troop movements, fortifications, and beach construction. We do not have a network to smuggle people or move them around. We have our hands full hiding our own people."

Richard cleared his throat. "*Réfugié* was organized before the Occupation. We have medical facilities to care for injuries, and Patrice has medical training." He glanced at the men around the table. "With the Allied raid imminent, we'll have plenty of opportunities to work together."

For the next hour Marguerite and her cousin listened in silence as the men worked out logistics and operational details. She was impressed at the thoroughness of their plans.

The next evening Richard, Uncle Pierre, Bérénice, Guy, and José gathered at Charentais, listening to the radio. Marguerite was preparing bread and cheese in the kitchen with *Maman* when Bérénice shouted, "Listen! The Allies have invaded Dieppe!" Marguerite banged the tea kettle onto the stove and joined everyone in the parlor, where they huddled around the radio.

"The Allies are here?" *Maman* asked, her face shining.

"Vichy's Radio Paris is saying the Germans have repelled an invasion at Dieppe," Pierre said.

"How far away is Dieppe?" Marguerite asked.

"About 140 kilometers northeast. Wait. . ." He cocked his head toward the radio.

"*The forces of France, supported by our allies in the Third Reich, have repelled an invasion at the port of Dieppe. Units on every front report that the invading forces were thrown back into the sea. The great French Republic has been saved.*"

Marguerite felt sick.

"Switch on Radio London," *Maman* said. "Let us hear what they're saying."

Bérénice spun the dial, but they heard nothing but uninterrupted regular programming for the next half hour. "The BBC is saying nothing," Richard said at last. "That's not good."

Deflated, Marguerite returned to the kitchen and rescued the boiling tea kettle. At least the Allies had *tried* to land in France.

* * *

At nine the following morning, Marguerite was in her bedroom when she heard someone pounding on the front door. She slipped her gun in her dress pocket and went downstairs. Richard stood before her, his face grim.

"Anything more about the raid?" she asked in a monotone.

"It started yesterday before dawn using Canadian troops, and it was over by noon, but many soldiers were left behind. We need to find as many as we can and hide them until we can get them out of France."

He ushered her to the Peugeot where Bérénice was waiting. "Are we going to Dieppe?" she asked.

"*Non*," Richard answered shortly. "This morning an OCM runner arrived from Caen. They have found two Canadians, but one is wounded. I want you and Bérénice to go to Caen, to Christien's book shop. They'll take you to OCM headquarters. I'll send Guy and José with you for protection."

"*Merci*, Richard. It makes me nervous traveling alone."

He put the car in gear and drove out of the yard toward Perdu. "When we get to the Cave, put together a field medical kit. I don't know how badly the Canadian is hurt. José will drive the truck to avoid roadblocks."

"*Oui*, of course." Excitement warred with fear inside her, and she tried to keep her voice neutral.

"The OCM escorting the Canadians will meet you outside Caen. Bring the Canadians back to the Cave," Richard instructed. "We're hiding only one other refugee, so there's plenty of room. Understand?"

"Who is in the Cave now?" she asked.

"A woman. She was passing out *Combat* circulars in Paris, and when they tried to arrest her, she killed a Gestapo agent. Be sure to yell before you go in so she doesn't shoot you."

José drove the Peugeot with Bérénice, Marguerite, and Guy down to the Cave entrance and waited while Guy opened the entrance.

"Coming in!" Bérénice called.

A woman stood at the top of the stairs, aiming a Luger at them. She lowered the gun. "What's going on?" She was in her early thirties, thin and elegant with unkempt short brunette hair, wearing a wrinkled dark blue traveling suit.

"The Allies have raided Dieppe," Bérénice said, her voice excited. "Two Canadians are lost somewhere around Caen, and one is wounded. Marguerite and I will bring them here."

"Are we being liberated?"

"*Non*," Marguerite answered. "The raid failed."

Marguerite assembled her medical kit and stowed it in the Peugeot. Bérénice slid into the back seat next to Marguerite and Guy climbed in the front. José put the automobile in gear, backed out of the hidden lane, and drove the 40 kilometers southeast to Caen.

At Christien's book shop they found the boy, Rob, who took them to another meeting place, this time in an abandoned warehouse. The OCM leader greeted them.

"We have two Canadians, one with a bullet in his leg. They'll meet you here, south of Caen." He pointed to a map. "Use this route to avoid the police and the Germans."

José and Guy bent to study the map.

"The meeting place is a sunken road between this steep hill and a hedgerow," the leader explained. "Drive your car here…" He tapped his forefinger at a black X on the map. "Hide it behind these hedges. Our people will meet you at sunset so you can take back roads to Ville de Pommes under cover of darkness. After you pick up the Canadians, go this way." He pointed. "We're throwing this together on the fly, so be careful. Take this map with you. Any questions?"

"*Non*," said José and Guy together. Marguerite noticed that Guy gnawed his lower lip. They left the warehouse and drove to the rendezvous, where José hid the car. They climbed out and Guy unfolded the small map.

"Marguerite and Bérénice, climb up that hill about fifty meters. If you see anyone coming, signal with your flashlight."

They jogged across the road and up the hill while José and Guy waited with the Peugeot. An hour passed with no sign of anyone. The sun sank lower in the sky and her cousin touched her shoulder. "It'll be dark soon," she muttered. "Where are they?"

"I don't know. Perhaps something has gone wrong."

"There's a moon tonight. We can't afford to wait, we'll be seen."

"We have to wait," Marguerite whispered. "We cannot abandon a wounded man."

Another hour dragged by. Marguerite's nerves were taut as piano wire. *Where are they? Has something happened?*

Just as she was ready to give up, she heard a car engine.

CHAPTER SIXTEEN THE CANADIANS

A black Peugeot approached from the north. As the automobile slowed and turned into the field, Bérénice jumped to her feet and waved her flashlight at José and Guy. Through the hedges, Marguerite watched the men from the OCM car help two uniformed soldiers out of the Peugeot and into the *Réfugié* vehicle; one of the men limped and his trouser leg was bloody.

Suddenly she spied an approaching Citroen with red emergency lights flashing. "Police," she shouted.

The men ducked behind their cars, and she and Bérénice hunkered down between some bushes. If the police went on by, they would all be safe, but Marguerite felt exposed. Her blouse dampened with perspiration.

The police car slowed but drove past the break in the hedgerows. *Thank God, they hadn't seen anything*. But then the brake lights flashed; the car stopped and backed up to the opening in the hedgerow. Two officers emerged, guns drawn.

Marguerite's heart beat so furiously she could hardly think. "What should we do?" she whispered. She reached in her pocket and gripped her pistol.

"Get ready, but don't fire," Bérénice murmured. "These police may be sympathetic to the Résistance." Marguerite held her pistol down at her side. *Mon Dieu, not more killing!*

The officers advanced through the opening in the hedge. "We see you," one yelled. "Get out from behind those cars." They aimed their weapons.

"You're under arrest."

"Now," Bérénice shouted. She stood up and fired her revolver. One policeman turned and fired wildly up the hill at them; the men at the OCM vehicle exchanged fire and scattered. Marguerite fired to distract the police.

One police officer fell instantly and an OCM man was hit. Then a bullet caught José and he crumpled to the ground.

"José!" Bérénice cried. She worked her way down the hill, firing at the police, and the second policeman scrambled into the police car and roared away.

The gunfire ceased. Blood thundered in Marguerite's ears and her hands shook. She raced toward the body of the police officer lying beside the lifeless form of the OCM agent. Bérénice knelt next to José, helped him to a sitting position, and leaned him up against the *Réfugié* Peugeot. "I'm all right," he panted.

"Patrice, check him over," her cousin begged. Marguerite tore open his bloody jacket and inspected his bleeding chest wound.

"We need to get him home."

The uninjured OCM agent stood over his dead comrade, shaking his head. "We know this can happen, but you're never ready for it," he said in a low voice. "He had a family." He carefully pulled his dead comrade's body into his car.

"Let's get out of here," Guy yelled. He and Bérénice helped José and the two remaining Canadians into the Peugeot. Marguerite retrieved her medical kit from the trunk and crawled into the back seat with José and the other wounded man; Bérénice climbed into the front seat with the other Canadian and twisted to face them. "José, how are you feeling?"

"Light-headed. And my shoulder feels like it's on fire."

Guy followed the OCM car out of the field and headed toward Ville de Pommes; the OCM car sped in the opposite direction. Each time the Peugeot hit a bump, José yelped. Marguerite rummaged through her kit for a morphine syrette, broke the seal, and slipped the needle into his arm. "This will help."

Half an hour later they rolled quietly up to the hidden entrance to the Cave. Guy stopped the car, opened the outer and inner doors, and helped Bérénice carry the unconscious José in and lay him on a cot. The woman occupying the Cave met them. "What happened?" she asked.

"The exchange went badly," explained Marguerite. "José's been shot."

Guy directed the wounded Canadian to another cot. Marguerite barked at Bérénice, "Help me get José's shirt off." They stripped the garment off over his head and Marguerite poured alcohol onto a sterile cloth to clean the wound in his chest.

"He's lucky. The bullet just missed his lung. He's going to be all right, but he'll hurt in the morning."

Guy touched her arm. "I need to report to Red."

"Go." She waved him away without looking up, and he disappeared through the tunnel inner door.

The makeshift bandage on the Canadian's thigh was caked with dried blood. Carefully she cut it off, and when she removed it, blood and pus oozed up. The area around the wound was red and swollen. "I'll have to get a poultice on this today. Right now, all of you men need rest."

"I'll stay with them," Bérénice volunteered.

"You need sleep, too," Marguerite reminded her.

Her cousin shot her a belligerent look. "*Non*, I'm staying." She settled herself on the floor beside José's cot.

Marguerite took a deep breath and slowly blew it out. "*Mon Dieu*," she exclaimed to no one in particular. "I hope all our refugee rescues won't be this exciting." She turned to leave, but the uninjured Canadian grabbed her hand.

"I cannot tell you how much we appreciate what you've done for us. We are so very grateful." He spoke such rapid English it was hard to understand him, but she smiled.

"You are welcome," she said in her heavily accented English.

In the Perdu kitchen she found Richard and Guy sitting at the table sipping calvados. Richard motioned for her to sit down. "Guy told me what happened. How are José and the Canadian?"

"José will be all right, but the Canadian's thigh wound is infected. It will be at least a week before he can travel." She heated milk on the stove for a poultice, then spooned hot, milk-soaked bread into a cheesecloth square and plopped it in a ceramic bowl. "I need to get this on his wound now. I'll be right back."

She went back down to the Cave and slapped the poultice onto the Canadian's wound. When she was finished, she returned to Perdu, so exhausted she ached all over.

"Care for a glass of calvados?" Richard asked.

"*Oui*, I would." She needed something to calm her nerves. "*Merci*."

He filled a tall glass and she took a small sip, then a larger one. Warmth spread through her chest. She continued sipping until she reached the bottom of the glass. She looked at the men and realized she could no longer focus on their conversation, and she let her head droop toward the tabletop.

Guy leaned toward her and slipped his arm around her shoulders. "I'm taking you upstairs." He helped her stand, then walked her up the stairs and laid her on the bed in Bérénice's room.

"Stay with me," she murmured. She tugged on his hand, and after a slight hesitation he lay down beside her until she fell asleep.

The next morning when she awoke the sun was already up, and the light hurt her eyes. Her brain felt swollen. She rolled over, and Bérénice let out a muffled cry.

"Oh, I'm sorry." Her head pounded, but she steeled herself to crawl out of bed. "I need to go down to the Cave and check on José and the Canadian."

"They're all right," her cousin said in a groggy voice. "I've been there most of the night."

"I must start another milk poultice. I don't want the Canadian's infection to get any worse."

"I'll help," Bérénice volunteered. She rolled off the bed and tried to smooth the wrinkles from her dress, then picked up her hair brush, and swiped at her hair a couple of times before giving up. She tossed the brush back onto her dressing table and went down to the kitchen.

Marguerite poured water from the pitcher into the wash bowl, splashed some on her face, and inspected herself in the mirror. She looked exhausted, with dark circles under her eyes. She made no attempt comb her hair. Once back at Charentais, she would change her dress and pull herself back together.

Downstairs, Bérénice stood at the kitchen stove with her back to Marguerite. Richard and Guy were eating breakfast at the table, and a strange woman was washing dishes. A full plate of eggs and toast sat at an empty chair.

"You look terrible," Guy said. "Did you sleep?" She nodded, then absentmindedly smoothed her hair, sat down in the empty chair, and picked up a fork.

"Hey, that's mine," Bérénice objected. "Get your own breakfast."

Marguerite didn't look up. "When will that poultice be ready?"

"In a minute, in a minute," her cousin snapped. She waved an unspoken apology. She covered the ceramic bowl and tossed the spoon onto the counter. "There, it's ready."

Marguerite sent her a searching look. Why was her cousin so out of sorts? She rose, found two potholders, and carried the poultice bowl to the door. Bérénice held the door and the two cousins made their way down the hill, Marguerite carefully keeping the bowl level. Bérénice went ahead to open the

Cave entrance.

Inside, Marguerite gently cut the bandage off the Canadian's thigh, cleaned his wound, and applied the fresh poultice. José was awake, trying to sit up. "How do you feel?" she asked.

"It hurts when I breathe or when I try to move."

Bérénice gently pushed him flat and took his hand. "Then don't move, silly. Try to hold still when you breathe."

* * *

Over the next three days, after the woman with the Luger was escorted out of the Cave on the next leg of her escape, both the Caen medical facility and the Cave filled with Canadian military refugees. Marguerite went back and forth, working long hours in both places. As the number of wounded men multiplied, she grew more and more tired. It was a relief to come home to Charentais at night where she could sleep in her own bed.

One morning before she left for the Cave two black police Citroens stopped in front of the house. Three policemen and two uniformed Germans fanned out in teams. Richard, who had spent the night on the living room sofa, saw them from the front window and walked out onto the porch.

Lieutenant Lastrange made a beeline for him, followed by Sergeant Boulot. Marguerite went out the front door and stood next to Richard.

"*Guten Abend*, Lieutenant. Why are you here today?"

"*Guten Abend*, Richard." Lastrange fished out a pack of cigarettes and offered one to Richard, then lit it for him.

"*Danke*, Lieutenant."

Lastrange returned the lighter to his pocket. "I have a question for both of you. We are looking for a man. He speaks with a Spanish or Portuguese accent. Does that describe any of your farm workers?"

"Sure. We have many workers from Spain and Portugal. Do you have any more information?"

"He will have a bullet wound."

"Well, that narrows it down, but we have no one wounded here. Why did you shoot him?"

Lastrange bristled. "*I* did not shoot him! The Caen police shot him. This man was helping some Allied soldiers. The police killed one of the terrorists."

"Who were they? Are they from around here?"

"*Nein.* But the officer heard the name José, and also Patrice. We want to check your driver, José Castello, to see if he has a bullet wound. We think he may be working with Patrice Cerne."

Richard looked beyond Lastrange to where two soldiers were emerging from the barn. "Do you have a description?"

"*Nein*. We're checking all the farms in the area. Where is this José?"

"He works at Perdu, but he's in Portugal right now, on family business. He's been gone for a week."

"We will search the farmyard buildings, is that all right?"

"Of course." Casually Richard flicked ash off the end of his cigarette.

Lastrange and the soldiers carefully searched every building at Charentais. When they found nothing, they climbed back into their vehicles and drove away.

"How can they be sure it's José?" Marguerite asked when the noise faded.

"They can't. But if they pick him up, he won't be able to explain his gunshot wound."

"Why? His shoulder will heal."

"He'll still have a scar months from now, so he's finished here." Richard hesitated. "And there's another problem. Whenever they take a man in for questioning, they check to see if he is circumcised."

"I don't understand. Why would José be circumcised?"

Richard stared at her for a long moment. "Because he's a Jew."

Marguerite's eyebrows went up. "Oh, I didn't know."

He paced to the edge of the porch. "I'd like to know who told the police about the Canadians we picked up that night. It had to have come from the OCM. We had no idea where the pickup would take place until they told us."

The thought of an informer among the OCM gave her pause. Anyone could be an informer, she realized suddenly. *Anyone.*

She hiked the back way to Perdu and went down to the Cave, where she found Bérénice at José's side, wiping away tears on her cheeks.

Her breath caught. "Bérénice, what is wrong?"

"Richard just telephoned to warn us about the police search."

"I wouldn't worry," Marguerite said. "The Cave is well hidden."

Her cousin sent her a disgusted look. "It's not that, Marguerite. It's that—" Her voice broke. "Jose has to leave. Richard says it's dangerous for him to be here, so he's sending him back to Spain on a special mission."

"José is extremely capable," Marguerite assured her. "He is a good *Réfugié* agent. He will be all right."

"You don't understand," Bérénice said, her voice turning hard. "That's not the problem. The problem is that Spain is hundreds of miles from here."

"Ah." Marguerite understood more than her cousin guessed. If Guy were sent away, she would be heartsick, just as she'd been when he suddenly left for Caen without telling her. Later he confessed he'd done so because it was getting hard to be around her, but it had still hurt.

All at once she had to talk to him.

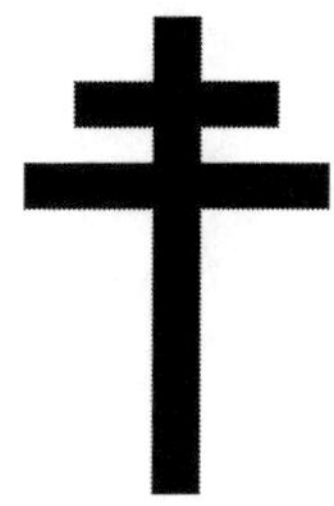

CHAPTER SEVENTEEN
WORKING IN THE OCM

In August 1942 the British Eighth Air Force bombed the Rouen-Sotteville railroad marshalling yards east of Caen. Six months later, three major Résistance organizations united into the MUR, *Mouvements Unis de la Resistance*, which eventually merged with five other Résistance movements, including the OCM and *Réfugié.* At the same time, organized guerrilla fighting units called *maquis* developed in the hills of southern France and in Brittany.

During the week, Marguerite occupied a spare room at Auriol Distributors, returning to Charentais each Friday. She couldn't avoid the daily bombing of Caen, but at least on weekends she could be safe at home at Charentais. Seeing less of Guy led to her missing him in unexpected ways. His warm, quiet regard for her made her feel special. She knew she liked him more than she should.

One Tuesday morning Alfred took her aside. "The OCM has a problem, Marguerite. One of their contacts was delivering information about German fortification construction along Normandy's beaches, but he was killed in a *Milice* raid. Now his fiancée wants to continue gathering this information, but she needs someone new to receive the reports. The OCM thinks it would be less suspicious if the contact were another woman. Are you interested?"

"Who is she?"

"They call her Babette. For obvious reasons, they don't want you to know her real name. If you're willing, an OCM agent will take you to meet her at lunch today. She will be wearing a black hat with a red feather."

"What if I say no?" Marguerite kept her relationships in Caen at arm's length; she did not want to be friends with anyone who might be killed or, worse, captured.

"In that case, MI-9 will not receive vital information."

She hesitated. She wanted to help those who had been injured and Canadian and British airmen stranded in France. Then she thought about the risks taken every day by those in *Réfugié*, harboring refugees and smuggling them to safety in Spain. She wanted to help, she decided. She nodded once. "I'll do it."

At five minutes before noon, she headed downstairs to meet Peter, her OCM contact. They stepped out into an overcast spring day with a cold wind blowing from the north. She pulled her blue wool coat around her as he walked her to the café.

It was packed with diners. Marguerite couldn't help wondering how many of them were collaborators.

"There she is," Peter said. He directed her attention to a table at the back.

The woman wore a black hat that shielded her eyes, but below the brim Marguerite could see her bright red lipstick that matched the small red feather in the hat band. She was well dressed in a black suit with padded shoulders and an ornate brooch pinned to her lapel. One white-gloved hand held a cigarette, and her elbow rested on the table.

Peter led Marguerite to the table. "*Guten Tag*, Babette."

Yvonne Callion looked up. "Marguerite!" She stared at her and clapped her hand over her mouth.

Marguerite sucked in her breath. *What was Yvonne doing here? Surely*. . . Quickly she assumed a blank expression and scanned the café to see if anyone had noticed Yvonne's slip. Then she took off her coat, folded it over an empty chair, and sat down.

"*Guten Tag*, Babette," she said, her voice neutral. "My name is Patrice."

Yvonne looked away, but stole furtive glances at her until the waiter arrived to take their order. During lunch they made small talk. When they finished eating, they walked out the front door together, and a car pulled up. Marguerite recognized the driver as Rob, the boy from Christien's Book Shop. Surely he was too young to drive? But in wartime, people did what they had to do.

She slid in next to Yvonne, and Peter gave directions to Auriol Distributors. When the car joined traffic, Marguerite leaned close to her friend. "Do you have something for me?"

Without a word, Yvonne pulled a folded manila envelope out of her purse and handed it over.

"*Merci.*" Then she laughed and the two friends embraced.

In the front seat Peter craned his neck to stare at them. "Do you know each other?"

"That is none of your business," Marguerite said. When they reached the warehouse, she turned to Yvonne. "Do you have time to come in and talk?" Yvonne nodded and they climbed out and entered the building.

Upstairs, Alfred looked up from behind his desk. "Alfred, this is Babette." She gestured at the physician. "Meet Alfred Renier."

Alfred inclined his head. "*Mademoiselle.*" Yvonne offered her hand.

"Will you excuse us?" Marguerite asked. "Babette and I are going for a walk."

In a protected corner of the warehouse Marguerite turned to Yvonne and hugged her tight for a moment, then drew away, her eyes brimming with tears. "Yvonne, you are the last person I would expect to be with the OCM."

Yvonne looked down for a moment. "I know. After we graduated from the *lycée* and I started working at my father's construction business, I met a man. I liked him very much. We talked about the Occupation and how the Nazis were treating us. I told him about my father's death and he told me he was with the OCM. I wanted to help, so I started passing him copies of technical details from the German construction plans. Then…" Her voice faltered. "Then he was killed in a Résistance operation."

Marguerite touched her hand. "Oh, Yvonne, I am so sorry. First your father and now him. It must be hard."

Yvonne furtively brushed one hand over her eyes. "Vichy is bringing forced labor from all over France, and the Nazis are pressuring us to speed up construction. There are no sleeping quarters for most of the laborers and there's not enough food. When the British and the Americans bomb the beaches, the laborers are left in the open. It's horrible."

"*Oui*, I can imagine. Bérénice and I…"

"Bérénice? Does Bérénice work with you?"

"Sometimes. She works mostly at Perdu Farm. What about Simone and Yvette, do you see them?"

"I have lunch with them often. It helps me maintain my cover to be seen with collaborators. We don't talk about the Occupation. I have no other friends in Ville de Pommes; collaborators are pariahs, especially since the Dieppe raid."

"Dieppe was a disaster. We are still picking up stranded Canadians. People all over France are helping."

"*Oui,* I've heard that. There's one woman, Patrice Cerne, who is-- " Yvonne suddenly stared at her and her hands flew to her cheeks. "*Mon Dieu, you* must be Patrice!"

Marguerite rolled her eyes. "Someday, God will deliver me from Patrice Cerne!"

Yvonne shook her head in disbelief. "When those men kidnapped my father, it was *you* the Gestapo was after! Oh, Marguerite, that must have been terrible for you when your father was shot."

She swallowed. "*Oui*, it was. But I couldn't speak out and compromise other Résistance workers. And it must have been terrible for you when your father was . . . " She stopped at the look on Yvonne's face.

"I always suspected Bérénice was with the Résistance," Yvonne said with a strained laugh. "I never dreamed that you might be."

"And I never dreamed that *you* were. The Germans had better watch out," Marguerite exclaimed. "We will drive them out of France, I swear it!"

* * *

Throughout the summer, Vichy's forced labor laws drove young men underground and swelled the ranks of fighting *maquis* units in France. *Réfugié* developed a special pipeline to guide young men to the *maquis* in Brittany, but with increased Résistance activity came increased Nazi retribution. The *Milice* and the French police ruthlessly hunted down and arrested escaped laborers; the Gestapo then interrogated them.

One beautiful late spring day, Marguerite waited impatiently while the warehouse crew unloaded the orange pickup truck from Perdu and reloaded flattened cardboard boxes to be filled with watered-down calvados for the Germans. Some workers were new to her. Charles was an Irishman Richard knew from his days in Spain; he had reddish-blond hair and a plump body, and Marguerite guessed he was in his early forties. He was talkative and always had a permanent smile on his chubby face. Richard said his innocent looks disguised a cunning nature and killer instincts.

The other man, Roland, was a *maquisard* from southern France who fought with the *maquis* outside Marseille. When the *Milice* had infiltrated his unit and the Gestapo began arresting members, Roland escaped to Paris where Germaine recruited him for *Réfugié*. He was thin, almost emaciated, with olive skin and slits for eyes. He had short black hair and a receding hairline, which made his age hard to determine.

Charles now drove Marguerite to Charentais on weekends; Roland rode in the passenger seat. For security reasons, the men always worked in pairs. Charles's blarney got them through roadblocks. Roland avoided making eye contact with the soldiers because he always looked guilty.

She would never be as comfortable with Charles and Roland as she had been with José, but Richard kept sending his Portuguese friend off to Spain on special missions to keep him away from the Ville de Pommes police. As summer wore on, she realized how lonely she was, and she clung to Bérénice, *Maman*, and Uncle Pierre. Sometimes she felt so detached she was numb.

One morning after she hid her handgun in her room she announced she was going to Perdu to see Bérénice.

"Wait, *chou-chou*! I must talk to you about— "

"I can't wait, *Maman*. I have to see Bérénice." *And Guy.* But *Maman* didn't need to know that.

Maman propped her veined hand on her hips. "Marguerite!"

She stared at her mother. Not since she was a child had *Maman* used that tone of voice. "We will talk later, *Maman*. I promise."

Her mother said nothing, and Marguerite escaped out the back door.

The air smelled of apple blossoms, so sweet and heady she closed her eyes and imagined there was no war, no bombs falling, and that life was like it had always been, peaceful and happy. It made her chest ache to think about it.

She found her cousin in the Perdu kitchen. "You're earlier than I expected," Bérénice said with a frown.

"Tomorrow I have a date in town to see Simone and the others. Will you join us?"

"*Non*. And neither should you! They are lepers in Ville de Pommes. They grovel to the Nazis, and Simone lords it over everyone in town. She must be sleeping with a Nazi officer because she can get whatever she wants and everyone knows it. It's dangerous to spend time with them."

Ever since her return from Spain, her cousin exhibited an over-refined sense of justice. Things were either black or white. "Oh, Bérénice, they're just trying to survive as best they can."

"Stay away from them, Marguerite. They are not your friends."

Marguerite glanced away from her cousin's accusing look. "Please come with me, Bérénice."

"*Non!*" She stormed out the kitchen door, slamming it so hard it bounced back open.

Marguerite shook her head, went to Richard's office, and knocked on the door. "May I speak with you?"

The big Irishman looked up but did not smile.

"I have to ask you something. I have learned something about a friend of ours from the *lycée*. I want to tell Bérénice, but should I?"

"I need more information, more specific details." He surveyed her with somber blue eyes. Except for that day outside Caen when she was assaulted, Richard never showed any emotion, but he was always available to talk with her and he was always kind. She trusted him.

"One of our old friends is a member of the Résistance, but Bérénice thinks she's a collaborator. Can I tell her the truth?"

"Marguerite, I'm surprised you are even asking the question. Why would you want to put your friend at risk?"

Of course. He was right, as always. But still . . . She left the house, her nerves jangled and feeling a bit off-balance, and slipped away to the Cave. She hoped Guy would be there.

He was, but so was a new refugee, sprawled on one of the cots, asleep.

"Marguerite! I was hoping you would come. It's been more than a week since I saw you."

"It has been exactly five days, Guy," she said with a laugh.

He drew her outside into the warm, apple-scented air and closed the door behind him. "We have a guest." He tipped his head toward the Cave. "He's one of the OCM agents from near Dieppe. He's on his way to Spain."

"Is he injured?"

"*Non*. Just exhausted. They all are."

"We are all tired, I think," she said. "The Occupation, the war . . . it's wearing."

He tipped her chin up with his forefinger. "You don't look tired, Marguerite. You look wonderful. You always do." His green eyes held hers with such intensity she had to look away.

Her heart skipped two beats. She longed to tell him about that awful day and the German soldier, but somehow she couldn't, not yet. "Guy, have I changed?"

He hesitated. "In a way, *oui*. You seem . . . distant. Preoccupied."

Marguerite nodded. "*Oui*, I suppose I am. I'm . . . I'm working hard in Caen, treating wounded fliers and refugees in our basement medical facility, and soon I'll be working for the OCM, as well."

His dark eyebrows rose. “Doing what?”

“Collecting information from an OCM agent about German beach fortifications. It’s not dangerous. We meet over lunch.”

“A man?”

“What? Oh, *non*. It’s-- Guy, can I trust you?”

He huffed out a breath. “How can you ask that? Of course you can trust me.” He closed his hands around her shoulders and gave her a little shake. “What is it?”

“My contact . . .” She swallowed. “Richard said I shouldn’t tell anyone, but I have to tell someone or I’ll burst.”

“Tell me. We’re friends, aren’t we?”

“*Oui.*” *Liar. Guy is more than a friend.* She drew in a steadying gulp of air. “My OCM contact is Yvonne Callion.”

His eyes widened and then he whistled. “Yvonne Callion? Well, that is a surprise! Are you sure you can trust her?”

“Guy, the only people I trust completely are *Maman* and Bérénice. And you,” she added. “But I can’t tell them. I risk exposing Yvonne if I do.”

His quick grin surprised her. “*Bon*,” he said softly, holding her gaze. He folded his arms around her and pressed his lips against her forehead. “*Trés bon*.”

She looked up at him, and he bent his head and brushed his mouth over hers. “Marguerite,” he murmured. “I-- You can always trust me. Always.”

* * *

The next afternoon she asked for a ride to *Café Angéle* to meet with Yvonne, Yvette, and Simone. She was the first to arrive and as she shed her light jacket she noticed something odd. Uniformed Germans were sitting at tables with women who were nicely dressed. It was the first time she had seen French women who were openly friendly to the Nazis. Usually, the German soldiers met with the women surreptitiously; only the most brazen would be seen in public with them, but now many young women openly met with the Germans in restaurants.

When Simone entered the dining room, she gave a demure wave to a table of German officers. They smiled at her and touched two fingers to their foreheads. Then Yvette came in and casually laid her hand on the shoulder of a Nazi lieutenant at another table. He looked up and smiled broadly without saying a word.

Marguerite’s attention then strayed to two ragged-looking men whispering to each other outside the front window. One man spat on the ground and slowly shook his head. She thought she recognized them, but they looked so unkempt she couldn't be sure.

Yvonne arrived, and the women embraced. All three wore gay spring dresses, high-heeled shoes, and silk stockings. Marguerite knew how difficult it was to get silk stockings; a woman who could afford them didn't wear them for fear she would be thought a collaborator. But there were all those women sitting with the Germans . . . *Mon Dieu*, the world was upside down.

Simone looked up from the menu. "My father has finally joined the Nazi Party. He avoided it for years, but they threatened to close our bank if he didn't join. Ever since Berlin approved his membership, everyone treats him with more respect."

Marguerite clenched her fists in her lap. *Respect.* She wondered who 'everyone' was. German soldiers? The Gestapo? It certainly wasn't anyone French in Ville de Pommes.

"I'm seeing a man from Paris," Yvette announced. "He's with the *Milice*."

"Ah, the *Milice,"* Simone said. They're making France safe for all of us. I wish everyone could see them up close the way we do."

Yvonne tried to catch Marguerite's eye, but she refused to look at her.

"In Caen," Yvonne said quietly, "the locals working for the Germans are treated shabbily."

"What do they know?" Simone blurted. "If anyone in Ville de Pommes complains they'd better be careful. I can make trouble for anyone with a big mouth."

"Do you make trouble very often?" Marguerite asked, keeping her tone mild.

"Not often. I don't understand why people are so dissatisfied."

After lunch, which Simone insisted on paying for, Marguerite and Yvonne walked into town where they met Roland and Charles, who had come to pick up Marguerite. She hugged Yvonne, climbed into the car, and waved.

Charles started the engine, then twisted toward her and frowned. "You spend too much time with that crowd. They're going to get hurt, and you don't want to get caught in the crossfire."

Marguerite shot him a glance. "Do you know something?"

"Not exactly. But a lot of people want to hurt collaborators. When Liberation comes, I don't know where they're going to hide."

On the ride back to Charentais Marguerite remained silent. Things were getting more complicated and more dangerous.

CHAPTER EIGHTEEN
THE COST OF LIBERATION

March 1944

Sirens wailed in a continuous whine that rose and fell, a sound Marguerite knew she would never get used to. *Never.*

"Alfred," she called. "It's another air raid. Let's get down to the basement." She tossed her pencil on the stack of reports on her desk, grabbed her purse, and ran down the stairs. Under her feet she could feel the thump of distant explosions. *Mon Dieu, they are obliterating everything! Liberation may be coming, but the cost is dreadful.*

All at once the sirens went silent and she closed her eyes. *When this is over, I hope there will be something left to liberate.*

That night she listened to the broadcast of war news from Radio London. The Soviets had turned back the German army at Stalingrad. Mussolini was dead, and the new Italian government had surrendered to the Allies. Best of all, the British and the Americans were fighting their way up the Italian peninsula toward southern France.

Liberation *was* coming, but her beloved country was paying a terrible price. Strategic bombing was destroying entire sections of Normandy, and as more requests for sabotage on the ground came in from MI-9, the Résistance was growing increasingly bold. The Nazis responded by launching Gestapo and *Milice* terror campaigns against anyone even suspected of resistance. If someone was on their list, they destroyed their business, arrested and interrogated employees, and then burned homes and businesses to the ground. Dr. Morel had been arrested and later released, but his clinic had been partially destroyed.

When the all-clear finally sounded, Marguerite and the others ventured outside to see the damage. She gazed around her in disbelief. The warehouse next to Auriol Distributors lay in charred ruins, and the streets were covered with rubble. A column of black smoke rose from the direction of the northern Orne River bridges. The air smelled metallic.

She didn't want to see any more. Caen had survived another bombing, but all she wanted to do was escape to the safety of Ville de Pommes. She prayed the town and both Auriol farms had been spared.

She spoke to *Maman* on the phone, and then talked Charles and Roland into driving her home. On the way they passed fields and roads pocked with bomb craters, and near Ville de Pommes she saw the blackened ruins of two barns. *So close to home*. She gripped her hands in her lap and swore she would not let Charles see her cry.

When she arrived at Charentais she fell into her mother's arms. "It is terrible, *Maman,* all the destruction everywhere and people hurt," she wept. Her mother said nothing, just rocked her to and fro as if she were a child.

The next morning she crawled out of bed and lit a fire in the parlor fireplace while *Maman* brewed wartime tea, made of chicory. "Liberation cannot be far off, can it?" Marguerite asked.

Her mother sipped her tea in silence, her face tight. "Perhaps. One wonders what the cost will be."

"Caen is being destroyed building by building. The roads, the bridges, even whole buildings." She had to work to keep her voice steady.

"Could you spend more time here at home, *chou-chou*? I worry about you."

"*Non, Maman*. There are so many wounded now, not just Allied soldiers but Résistance workers, too. I am needed more than ever. I can't abandon Alfred and the medical clinic."

"Ah." Her mother said nothing for a long minute, then cleared her throat. "It is as I thought. You are a young woman now, Marguerite. You have a life of your own. I managed the farm during the Great War, when your father was away fighting, and I can do it now. I *shall* do it now."

Marguerite often wondered at the steel in her delicate-looking mother's spine. They finished their tea in silence, and she waited until late afternoon to go to Perdu. She wanted to see Guy, needed to be with him. She wanted to confess her fears about the cost of liberation.

She chose a yellow dress with thin straps and a low neckline. She liked it because it was a little too short, and she wanted to elicit a male reaction from him. And she had bartered for a pair of silk stockings on the Caen black market and couldn't wait to wear them.

Charles drove her to Perdu. When they got out of the car he pointed to the sky where waves of airplanes were flying overhead in neatly ordered V formations. "Southeast," he muttered. "Every day there are more bombers. Listen! You can hear the engines."

The low droning sound reminded her of honeybees in the summertime. "Where are they headed?"

"Rouen, maybe. Or Beauvais."

She clenched her jaw. "I wonder how many will die tonight?" she whispered. Charles shrugged and when Bérénice came out onto the porch, he drove off to park the car.

Her cousin propped her hands on her hips. "You're all dressed up!" She looked her over. "You look nice, Marguerite. Really beautiful."

Marguerite's cheeks grew warm. "I hope Guy will think so."

Bérénice just looked at her. "You are an idiot, do you know that? But then I am an idiot, too." When Guy stepped up on the porch, her cousin melted back into the house without a word, and later she slipped off to the Cave.

Guy took both her hands in his. "I will never forget how you look tonight." His words made her blush even more. She felt alive and supremely feminine. She closed her eyes, hoping he would kiss her. He did, but it was a mere brush of his mouth against hers.

"I have missed you," he said. He led her inside to the dining room and pulled out a chair.

"And I have a surprise for you."

"A surprise? What is it?"

"I made supper for you tonight!" He disappeared into the kitchen and returned with a bottle of calvados. "There is also baked camembert and fresh bread."

"Are you serious?"

He shrugged and poured two glasses of apple brandy. "I have many secrets," he said with a grin. "More surprises are coming."

While Guy fussed in the kitchen she savored the heat spreading through her chest, and when he returned with the cheese and a knife to spread it,

Marguerite began to wonder. He wouldn't go to all this trouble unless something important was on his mind.

Supper was rabbit stew with onions and garlic and a salad. "Charles provided the rabbit," Guy explained. "Trust me, it was a lucky shot. I was with him. Since rationing began, the rabbit population has thinned."

He poured two glasses of claret and watched her take her first bite. As they ate they talked about the war. "Tell me more about your work in Caen," he said. "I understand lots of the injured men are with the Résistance."

She told him everything, her long, exhausting hours in the medical facility, the scream of the air-raid sirens, the endless bombs falling and the ground shaking under her feet. "Tell me about the bombing here at home," she said at last.

"It's not so bad here," he said quietly. "The Cave is always full, but none of the injuries are serious enough to send for you. It is worse on the beaches, so we stay away from the coast."

To her astonishment he presented an apple tart for dessert. "*Mon Dieu*, do you bake, too?"

"Ah, *non*. Bérénice made this. It's a bribe for not revealing . . . Well, I cannot reveal it, can I?" He cut a piece of the tart and slid it onto her plate.

"Guy, what a surprising man you are! A most unusual man."

He looked suddenly uncomfortable, fished out a cigarette, and offered one to her. She shook her head and sipped her calvados while she watched him smoke in silence. She sensed some sort of tension in him. Even his face, normally tan and relaxed, was somber, and his eyes sometimes looked as if his mind were miles away.

At last he leaned forward on his elbows. "We need to talk." His voice sounded odd and Marguerite's breath caught. He took her hand. "I need to tell you something."

"*Oui*? Tell me, then," she said more sharply than she intended. "I don't like suspense."

"Marguerite, you know you mean a great deal to me."

"*Oui*, I know that and it makes me happy."

"It makes me happy, too. But . . . " He tightened his fingers about hers. "I am going to Brittany. There's a fighting *maquis* unit operating around Saint-Marcel. I'm going to join them."

She felt as if a black pit had opened up and swallowed her. "*Non!*"

"I have to."

"Don't you want to stay here and protect your father? Won't it be easier to do that here?"

"It would, but I'm not looking for easy. I can do more fighting with the *maquis* than here at Perdu, sneaking people out of Normandy one at a time."

She sat back and stared at him. "You are important to me, Guy. I rely on you. Please, please, don't leave. It is dangerous fighting in Brittany."

He looked her straight in the eye. "I am a French soldier," he said in a gentle but firm voice. "And a soldier fights for his country."

"*Non!*"

"Marguerite . . . Marguerite, when the war is over. . . "

"When the war is over you might be dead," she snapped. "I might never see you again. You should fight here with us." Her throat ached with the need to cry. Guy was leaving, and her heart was cracking in two.

But she would not cry. *She would not.* She gathered her emotions. "When are you planning to leave?"

He hesitated. "Tomorrow. They are expecting me."

She stood up and escaped to the front porch. She clenched her fists, then heard his voice behind her.

"It is hard to leave you," he murmured.

She turned her face into his chest. He put his arms around her, and they warmed her against the night air. She felt safe. *Don't go.* She wanted to scream it in his ear. *Don't leave me.*

"Marguerite, look over there!" She turned and looked to the southwest sky where dim flashes exploded like flowers in the blackness. "Can you feel it?" he asked.

She couldn't tell if it was her own trembling body or the tremors rumbling beneath her feet. "*Oui*, I feel it."

"The Allies are bombing Caen," he said softly. "See the spotlights searching for the planes? Those tiny fireflies going up are tracers from the anti-aircraft guns."

"*Oui*," she said dully. "I see them."

"Oh God," he whispered, watching the sky. "I have to go to Brittany. Liberation starts there."

She turned back to him and held him tight. "Tomorrow you go to Brittany, Guy. But now, tonight, you go upstairs. With me."

She heard him suck in his breath. She no longer needed to cry. She needed to smile at him, lie in his arms and . . . and love him.

"Marguerite, wait. There is something else I want to say." He cupped her shoulders in his hands and looked into her eyes. "I love you. I knew I loved you from the moment you shoved me into that cabinet at Dr. Morel's clinic. When the war is over . . ."

She bit her lip to keep from sobbing. "When the war is over, Guy, I will cook you the most spectacular dinner you have ever eaten." She could scarcely get the words out.

He kissed her for a long time, then lifted her into his arms and carried her into the house.

CHAPTER NINETEEN
ASSASSINATION

Marguerite helped Guy pack his few belongings in a single bag. It wasn't how she wanted to spend their last hours together, but it had to be done. Tears welled up in her eyes, but she was determined not to cry. It would make it harder for him, and he looked miserable enough, despite the unforgettable night they had spent in each other's arms.

It was agony waiting on the porch for Charles to arrive to drive him to the train station. They sat holding hands and not talking, and when she heard the truck engine her chest hurt. *I must be strong. I must show him I am in control of myself.*

An unsmiling Charles heaved the bag into the truck and then stood back while Marguerite and Guy slowly walked over. At the passenger door, Guy turned to her. "As soon as this madness is over, I'll be back."

She clung to him. "Please be careful," she whispered. "Come back to me in one piece."

He kissed her, then kissed her again and climbed into the cab beside Charles. When the engine started Guy reached for her hand through the window, and when it pulled away, their fingers slipped apart. Tears stung her eyes, but she waved and smiled until she could no longer see him. Then she turned away and dropped her face into her hands.

I cannot lose him. Oh, God help me. I cannot.

She spent a listless day and a sleepless night at Charentais while *Maman* hovered and looked worried, and the following morning she dressed for work as usual and waited for Charles to drive her to Caen. On impulse she asked him to stop at Perdu, and he dropped her in the yard just as Bérénice was entering the house.

"Bérénice?" She followed her cousin inside.

No answer. She started up the stairs and Bérénice suddenly stepped out of her bedroom, her cheeks pink.

Marguerite stopped. "What's going on?"

"Nothing," her cousin said quickly. "I thought you were going to Caen today."

"I wanted to thank you for last night. It was it special."

"I wanted to do it, for you." Bérénice looked away. "Don't you have to go to work?"

"Why are you in such a hurry for me to leave?" She glanced over her cousin's shoulder into the bedroom where a pile of dirty laundry, both men's and women's clothes, lay on the floor. Slowly it dawned on her.

"*Mon Dieu*. Bérénice, tell me!"

Her cousin's face flamed. "José was here last night. But it's not what you think."

"Of course it's what I think!"

"José and I are . . . well, we have always been close."

"But he's gone. I thought Red sent him on a mission."

"He comes back. Late at night. I'm-- I'm thinking about leaving Perdu to be with him."

"Not you, too! You can't!"

Bérénice ran her fingers through her hair. "Papa forbids it, of course. José's on the run. But, well, we want to be married anyway."

Marguerite's brain swam. "I need to sit down."

They sat close together on the parlor couch, and Marguerite took Bérénice's hand and held it in her lap. "When did you decide this?"

"A week ago. He took me up to a field when the moon was full, and that's when we talked about it. We purposely did it at night, after curfew, to spit in the eye of the Nazis. Oh, Marguerite, it was beautiful!"

Marguerite felt a knife thrust into her vitals. She was happy for her cousin, but it made Guy's departure leave an even sharper ache in her chest.

* * *

Over the next weeks Marguerite's friendship with Yvonne deepened, and as their reputation as collaborationists became more established, they enjoyed some protection from Gestapo suspicion. But that isolated them from other townspeople. They spent more and more time with each other, especially in Ville de Pommes.

In Caen she kept busy with the accounts and the clinic. Any decline in Auriol Distributors production brought the German military to inspect the producers' farms, so workers at the warehouse labored extra-hard to keep business steady. However, the quality of the liquor they shipped was unpredictable.

Marguerite also joined a small OCM cell that included Peter, Charles, Roland, and Gilbert—a new recruit—as well as Yvonne and Alfred. Gilbert was 23 with longish brown hair and innocent-looking blue eyes, and he was very thin. Everyone was thin these days, even Charles. Three years of Nazi occupation on the heels of the Great Depression was taking its toll on everyone. Gilbert had escaped from a forced labor camp and gone underground. Now he lived in the warehouse basement, but his presence displaced other refugees, and Richard didn't like it.

She admired her fellow OCM members. Roland's experience with the *maquis* in southern France gave him first-hand knowledge of what could go wrong on missions and insight into contingencies. Charles could talk himself out of any tough situation, but when his affable blarney failed, he didn't think twice about pulling out his revolver.

Alfred went along on some missions, but since he was their only doctor, the OCM tried to limit his direct involvement to protect him. Marguerite and Yvonne served as female decoys, lookouts, and backups. As her experience grew, Marguerite found she had a talent for planning, as well.

One late April afternoon Peter called a meeting at the abandoned warehouse where Marguerite had first met the OCM team. He sat at the head of the table, his expression grave. "The *Milice Francais* is sending expert interrogators into northern France to expand their control in the area. Two of them are coming by train from Paris. One is called Arnaud Araignee; the other man is his aide. We don't know their real names."

Marguerite's stomach tightened. Whatever their assignment would be, she knew it was important; even Alfred was at the planning table.

"Araignee is one of their top interrogators," Peter continued. "He has perfected techniques he learned from the Gestapo. If he learns the prisoner has a fear of, say, spiders, he locks them in a windowless room infested with spiders and turns out all the lights. In 20 to 30 minutes the prisoner is screaming to be let out. Araignee questions him again, and if he doesn't get answers, back into the darkness he goes."

Marguerite shuddered. "That's inhuman."

"*Oui*," Peter agreed. "The man was well trained. He's also not afraid to use extremely painful methods. He has the blood of many Frenchmen on his hands."

"Why is he coming to Caen?" she asked.

"To train more interrogators. The *Milice* intends to welcome both men at a lunch the day after tomorrow. The morning trains from Paris arrive at nine and eleven; we're guessing they will be on the eleven o'clock train."

"How do we know that?" Roland wondered out loud.

"We've known for weeks that they were coming; we just didn't know when. One of our informants in the catering business received a lunch order to be delivered to *Milice* headquarters. They actually bragged that the 'real' *Milice* were coming."

"How many at this lunch?" Charles asked.

"Two coming in on the train, plus the welcoming committee. Let's say four altogether. OCM wants the two interrogators assassinated."

Marguerite gasped.

Peter then unfolded a map of Caen and spread it on the table. "This is the route from the train station to *Milice* headquarters. Last week the British parachuted in a .50 caliber machine gun. At close range, say 60 meters, .50 caliber bullets will shred automobile sheet metal like paper. OCM has loaned it to our unit, but they want it back."

"How can we use it?" Marguerite asked.

"If we can get the *Milice* car within range of the gun, we'll get the job done."

She shook her head. "How do we know what car they will drive?"

"They use a black Peugeot, like the Caen police. Araignee and his aide will probably be in civilian clothes, but the welcoming committee will be wearing *Milice* uniforms--blue coat, khaki shirts, black ties, oversized blue berets."

"Will they be armed?"

"We have to assume they will all be armed."

She thought for a moment. "The train station will be crawling with police and military men, and we'll have thc same problem around *Milice* headquarters."

Peter cocked his head. "What problem do you see, Marguerite?"

"Too many chances to be arrested. Too many witnesses."

"We can turn the assignment down," he said quietly. "Command says if we can get them, fine. But if we want to pass, that's up to us."

She sent him a long look. "Give me some paper."

He handed her a blank sheet, and she picked up a pencil and began to draw. "This is a sketch of this point, here." She pointed her pencil at the map. "This is the most likely route. We set a trap here . . ." She tapped a spot. "It's the perfect place for an ambush."

The men gathered around her, studying the drawing. "There's a bombed-out two-story house here," she continued. "It was hit last month and it's still abandoned. You can set up the machine gun on the ground floor, and when the car stops at this stop sign here, you fire the machine gun through the front window of the house."

Peter nodded. "*Bon*. There's a wall across the street, so we won't be firing bullets into anyone's home or business. As long as there are no pedestrians, it should be a clean kill."

Marguerite flinched at the word.

Roland cleared his throat. "How will we know which car to hit? Whoever mans the machine gun needs to know for sure."

She thought for a minute. "Charles and I will take the truck. He will walk into the depot and wait for the *Milice* men to get off the train, follow them, and get a description of the car and the license number. I'll wait in the truck. When Charles comes out, I'll pick him up and we'll leave. He can drop me off at the ambush site and I'll wait at the end of the block. When I recognize the car, I'll signal the machine gunner."

Alfred frowned at her. "How will you get away?"

"Charles can circle the block and wait for me. I'll slip around to the alley and find the truck."

"How do we get the machine gun out?" Roland asked.

"I know the house," Peter said. "It has a back entrance. We'll go in and position the gun on the first floor, then after the hit we can break it down, bring it out the back way, and load it into the truck.

"Be sure to take rags," Roland advised. "The gun barrel will be hot."

Peter nodded. "Roland, you will man the gun. Gilbert will be your backup. I will stay behind the house in the truck, with the engine running."

"What happens if something goes wrong?" Marguerite asked.

"If you and Charles aren't in place by eleven-thirty, we'll abort the mission. If something does go wrong, you can come around to the back and warn Roland and Gilbert to get away. When it's over, we'll meet at Auriol Distributors."

"What if there's pedestrian traffic?" Alfred queried. "We can't risk shooting civilians."

"The area has been completely bombed out, so there shouldn't be any people in that neighborhood," Marguerite answered. "Charles and I can walk the route this afternoon."

"Good idea," Roland agreed. "I'll come with you. I'd like to get inside the house, check the line of fire. We should bring some tools in case the house is boarded up."

"Tomorrow," Marguerite said slowly, "Charles and I will go to the depot at eleven and drive the route to get an idea of the traffic at that time of day."

"What about my gun?" asked Charles. "Should I bring it?"

"Bring it," Marguerite suggested. "But leave it with me. The police make routine stops at the train station, so you don't want to have it on you."

The following morning, Marguerite put the truck in gear and started the trial run with Charles. The intersection was a four-way stop; the abandoned house sat on the left. She parked the car and she and Charles walked the block to the front of the house.

Boards covered the first-floor windows and doors; both floors were intact, but she could see the sky through the second floor window. Rubble from the bombing had been cleared away from the street and piled onto the sidewalk halfway up the first story. No one on that side of the street would be hit by bullets.

A cold wind funneled between the buildings, cutting through her wool coat. The danger of the assignment and the overcast sky made the street feel forbidding. They got back in the truck and drove to the train station and Marguerite braked to a stop. "Charles, look at those men over there." She tipped her head toward two men standing in front of the depot; neither had luggage. The larger one wore a tan trench coat and grey hat. His partner wore no hat but had a similar tan trench coat with the collar pulled up. Both wore dark trousers and black shoes.

Police. . .or Gestapo.

They were watching every passenger that entered or exited the station. After a time one nudged the other and they casually moved toward a solitary man with a single suitcase who was just leaving the station. The larger man pulled out his wallet and opened it; the passenger examined it and then presented his identity papers. When the police were satisfied, the passenger grabbed his suitcase and hurriedly walked away.

She put the truck in gear. "What do you think, Charles?"

"Sure as I'm sitting here, those men are Gestapo. We'll have to be careful."

"Tomorrow, leave your gun with me. I don't want any trouble."

Charles pursed his lips and didn't answer.

"Charles, I insist. I'll return the gun when you get back to the truck."

He gave her a quick, unconvincing nod. She wished she could ignore the chill crawling up her spine.

CHAPTER TWENTY
TRIAL RUN

Charles arrived early the morning of the trial run. It was overcast and cold so Marguerite wore the collar on her gray wool coat turned up; the garment hung below her thighs and had large pockets where she could hide her gun. Her dark blue beret matched a mid-calf wool skirt.

She drove the truck to the depot, where Charles got out and casually strolled onto the platform. Marguerite studied the front of the station, noticing that the police gave special treatment to official vehicles by waving civilians through the drop-off zone while allowing government cars to park.

Charles followed a disembarking couple out of the station as if they were the two *Milice* targets. Marguerite picked him up, memorized the license plate of one of the official cars, then raced to the ambush site, stopped at the beginning of the block, and got out. Charles slid behind the wheel and drove to the stop sign, where he halted, turned right, and disappeared around the corner.

Marguerite chose a car at random and took off her beret to signal Roland, then moved on. She timed her trial walk so she would be two car lengths behind the target vehicle when the machine gun opened up, and then hiked to the corner and circled around behind the house.

The back door was open, but it was so dark inside she had to feel her way along, tiptoeing through the rubble into the front room. The light was dim, barely enough to see. The three men, Roland, Gilbert, and Peter, glanced at her over their shoulders, but when she started to speak Peter raised his hand. "Keep your voice down," he whispered. "We can't let anyone on the street to know we're in here."

Roland had constructed his machine gun platform out of wooden crates with planks laid across the top. "That looks rickety," she whispered. "Will it be dangerous?"

He turned his angular face away from her. "It will be more dangerous for the *Milice*," he said shortly. "We couldn't use nails because we didn't want to make noise."

"When are you moving in the gun?"

"First thing tomorrow morning. This back entrance is a real luxury. There has been no traffic in the alley since we've been here."

"Did you see me signal from the street?"

Gilbert narrowed his blue eyes and shook his head. "I saw you wave your hat, but I wasn't sure which car you were indicating."

"Tomorrow I'll cross half-way into the street, just behind the *Milice* car so there will be no mistake in identifying it."

Roland stood up and stretched his skinny frame. "Don't get too close to it."

When she nodded, he tipped his head toward the door. "After the kill, Gilbert, Peter, and I will drop off the gun and meet you at Auriol Distributors. God willing," he added under his breath. He crossed himself. "Let's get out of here and get some rest."

Back at Auriol Distributors, Alfred waved at her to wait on the warehouse floor while he finished talking to one of the truck drivers. "Well?" he asked when he joined her. "How did the trial run go?"

"There were a few wrinkles, but I think we smoothed them out."

His face looked somber. "In an operation like this, one wrinkle is too many."

She climbed the stairs to the empty office, hid her gun at the back of a desk drawer, and sat down to finish some paperwork. But her mind kept drifting to tomorrow's mission. *Mon Dieu, I have spent the last two days planning a murder.*

She dropped her forehead onto her palms. The war had changed her. Could she really participate in killing four human beings? Then she thought about Araignee and the torture she knew he inflicted on French citizens. *And he is coming here to train more interrogators just like him.* The Résistance had no choice; tomorrow's assassinations were necessary.

She couldn't sit still, so she went downstairs to watch the trucks loading and unloading. One of the drivers, a weathered, grey-bearded man with tired eyes, engaged her in conversation, but she couldn't focus on anything he said. She smiled and nodded with feigned interest, which usually kept the men talking, but after ten minutes she realized she couldn't remember a word he said. She excused herself and went back up to the office.

Tomorrow she must concentrate. She couldn't afford to make a mistake; even a small miscalculation would put the entire team at risk. Her heart began to pound. She wanted it to be over. She closed her eyes and tried to calm her nerves, then heard someone clatter up the stairs. She looked up to find Alfred watching her.

"Something arrived for you today. It's in my office." He gave her an odd smile and pulled a sealed white envelope from his middle desk drawer. Marguerite stared at it. It had been folded and re-folded, but no name appeared on the front and nothing was written on the back. "Where did you get this?"

"A driver from Rennes dropped it off this morning. He said to deliver it to Patrice Cerne."

With a gasp she ripped it open to find a single page in Guy's handwriting.

4 March 1944
My dearest Marguerite,

I hope this letter finds you safe. It has taken me a few weeks to set up an exchange with you. Every week the man who brought you this will arrive with another letter from me. If you can, please have a letter ready to send back with him.

I have made many friends here. The Bretons barely tolerate the mainland French, but they hate the Nazis. The maquis and the Résistance operate much more openly here, making this a very different struggle. One of my new friends suggested that after we drive the Nazis out of Brittany, we should drive the French out next. He said it in jest, but I'm not sure he was really joking.

We are working hard to sabotage the Germans, and every time we strike it brings you and Liberation closer. Our operations take planning and patience. Patience is hard for me because the delays keep us apart. Action is easier because it brings you closer. Once we gain Liberation, you and I will live together, grow apples, and bore our children with stories of the Occupation and the Résistance.

Be safe. Don't take chances. Please write as soon as you can as I long to hear from you.

I love you.
Guy

She finished reading the letter and swiped tears off her cheeks with a trembling hand. Then she re-read it and put it away in her desk drawer to read again later.

The stairs behind her creaked and Roland appeared. "Alfred said you received a letter. Are you all right? You look like you've had bad news."

"*Mais non*. It was a letter from Guy."

He nodded and smiled at her, which touched her heart. Roland never smiled.

The next thing she knew Charles hurried in from the living quarters. "Marguerite, come quickly! Patrice Cerne is dead!"

"What?"

"Come with me." He grabbed her hand and pulled her toward the radio.

The Vichy government has announced that the Milice in Bayeux discovered the whereabouts of the terrorist Patrice Cerne. When the Gestapo attempted to arrest her, the woman resisted and was shot dead. Let this be a warning: Resisters will be hunted down and arrested.

"*Alors*, last time I checked I was still alive," she joked.

Charles stared at her. "Either someone claiming to be Patrice got herself killed or . . ." His usually jolly demeanor evaporated ". . . or they're lying, trying to draw you out."

An icy hand reached into her chest and squeezed. *Draw her out?* Was it a trap? Suddenly she was terrified. Tomorrow Patrice Cerne was going to help ambush and kill four men. She would be seen, maybe remembered. If anything went wrong she could be arrested, and then . . .

She couldn't think about that. Instead she thought of *Maman*, her unexpectedly calm, strong mother. No matter what happened, *Maman* faced it and then quietly went on.

And so would she.

CHAPTER TWENTY-ONE
BEST LAID PLANS

The next morning Marguerite awoke and dressed in a plain brown skirt and white blouse. Sleet pinged against the windows in the living quarters, and she pressed her lips together as she watched it. Visibility would be difficult.

Alfred, Charles, and Roland were seated at the kitchen table, eating breakfast. Alfred looked up from his coffee. "*Bonjour*, Marguerite. Join us."

Her stomach rebelled at the thought of food, but she knew she should eat, even though breakfast was only cheese and wartime bread made with sawdust instead of flour. All of France was eating this now. Even *Maman* baked sawdust bread. It fooled the stomach into believing it was full.

But the cheese was real. "Where did you get this?"

Alfred swallowed a mouthful of bread. "The same place we get everything else, the black market. You can get almost anything you need if you have liquor to trade."

In silence she broke off bits of the cheese and poked them into her mouth, watching the slush slide down the window pane. "Roland, it's sleeting outside."

He squinted at the window. "Not enough to affect our plan. Bullets that can cut through metal will not be bothered by a little sleet."

"How soon will the machine gun be in place?"

"We'll be ready by eleven. I don't want to get there too soon."

The sleet made her uneasy. She ran the operation through her mind, and the more she thought about it, the more nervous she grew. She laid the uneaten cheese on her plate.

"Charles, do you think— ?" *Non*. She couldn't express doubt. They would need all the confidence they could muster.

Charles grinned at her. "I try not to think too much, especially about assassinations."

Alfred wished them luck, and she and Charles walked outside, climbed into the truck, and started off for the train station. Slush coated the streets with a patina of wet snow. The wind picked up.

When they reached the station, she pulled to a stop and Charles opened the passenger door. She reached over and grabbed his coat. "Where is your gun?" She held out her hand. "You're supposed to leave it with me."

"I'm taking it with me."

"*Non*. That wasn't the plan, Charles. We can't change it now."

He looked at her with his twinkling blue eyes and grinned. "Adapt, Marguerite! God is on our side." He touched the brim of his jaunty dark blue beret and ambled off toward the depot.

Marguerite clenched her teeth together. Then, as planned, she parked the truck where she could see the passengers, shut off the engine, and peered through the foggy windshield. She could barely see through the wind-driven sleet. Through a sea of umbrellas that hampered her view she squinted at the departing people and watched Charles amble into the station, stop, and tip his head toward a black Citroen parked in the loading zone. The *Milice* car.

She said a quick prayer. And then she waited.

At eleven o'clock the train from Paris chugged into the station. She waited another 10 minutes, started the engine, and joined the passenger pickup queue. The blinding sleet obscured everything, and she was too far away to see faces under the umbrellas. She edged the truck forward, chafing her hands to keep them warm.

Another five minutes passed. *What had happened to Charles?*

At last he emerged from the depot and Marguerite began to breathe normally, but then two men stopped him and began asking questions. Charles caught her eye and again tipped his head toward the black Citroën just as a group of umbrellas moved toward it. *That was the target car.*

When the umbrellas reached the Citroën, two of the men collapsed them, and now she could just make out two oversized blue berets—uniformed *Milice*—and two men in civilian clothes. The uniformed *Milice* opened the rear passenger doors for the two civilians. *That has to be Araignee and his aide.*

Charles was still being questioned, so she kept her eyes on the Citroën.

Suddenly gunshots erupted and her heart flip-flopped. When she looked back she saw that both the men who had detained Charles now lay crumpled on the pavement, and he was sprinting toward her.

Police whistles screeched. Charles grinned at her, veered away from the truck, and disappeared.

The black Citroën began to move. Her hands shaking, she pulled the truck in behind it and memorized the license number as she pulled past: FR666. *Bon*. Easy to remember, the mark of the devil. She drove as fast as she dared to the ambush site.

The sleet had turned to snow and the streets were slippery. As planned, she pulled into the line at the stop sign in front of the house and glanced over her shoulder for the Citroën.

Once through the stop sign she parked around the corner and raced back to her post. As she passed the house she glanced at the window where the machine gun should be set up, but she could see only darkness. Then a hand appeared, thumb up. She nodded and scanned the street for the *Milice* car.

The black Citroën approached, and she felt a surge of strength and clarity. She let the car roll past her, then stepped out in front of the white car behind it, forcing the driver to slam on the brakes. He laid on the horn, but she ignored it.

The Citroën stopped at the line of cars at the stop sign, and as each car proceeded through, she followed the *Milice* car at a safe distance. At last only two cars were ahead of the Citroën. She could see the muzzle of the machine gun poke out of the front window of the house.

The first car in the line proceeded through the intersection, and then the Citroën pulled up behind the second car. *Now.* She braced for the sound of the gun.

The noise was deafening, and instinctively she clapped her hands over her ears.

On the first pass of the machine gun, the bullets hit the radiator and steam billowed from under the hood. The driver tried to maneuver around the car that was blocking him, but there was no room.

Suddenly the back passenger door of the Citroën swung open, and one of the civilian *Milicien* tumbled out, took cover behind the rear wheel, and drew his sidearm. The machine gun raked the car, but the man kept his head down. Chips from the stone wall behind him filled the air and smoke and steam enveloped the street.

Finally the machine gun went silent. The *Milicien* emptied his revolver at the house window.

In the sudden silence, the drivers who had cowered inside their cars slowly opened their doors and approached the bullet-riddled vehicle. The *Milicien* was leaning into the Citroën, checking on his companions, and Marguerite moved toward him. Just as he looked back at her, she slipped her pistol out of her coat pocket.

He thrust out his hand to keep her away. "Please stand back, *Mademoiselle*. You shouldn't see this."

"*Monsieur* Araignee," she said softly.

He spun toward her, his eyes wide, and she raised the pistol and fired a single shot into his forehead. Blood sprayed over her face and blouse. She noticed the body in the back seat twitch, and she leaned into the car and fired two shots into his temple, then moved to the driver's compartment and fired a bullet into each of the *Milice* officers slumped inside.

Calmly she returned her gun to her coat pocket, walked around the corner, and climbed into the truck. It all seemed unreal, that she could kill people and then simply start the engine and pull away from the curb. Behind her the faint wail of approaching sirens rose in the cold air. The sound grew louder and louder, and then the emergency vehicles passed her going in the opposite direction.

She drove toward Auriol Distributors, checking her rear view mirror again and again. No one followed her.

CHAPTER TWENTY-TWO
CONSEQUENCES

Marguerite stopped in a narrow alleyway and used wet snow to wash the blood off her face and hands. She tried to clean the blood off her blouse but only smeared it, so she buttoned her coat to cover the stains. She couldn't stop worrying about Charles, kept hoping he would appear, even though she knew he wouldn't be able to find her. *Damn him. Why hadn't he left his gun with her?*

Instead of returning to Auriol Distributors she drove back to the train station and spent half an hour searching the surrounding neighborhoods on foot. There was no sign of him. Finally she gave up and drove back to the distribution center. *He will be all right,* she repeated to herself over and over. He *must* be all right.

She arrived shaken and out of breath and dragged herself up the stairs to find Alfred. "Have you seen Charles?" she panted.

He looked up from his desk in surprise. "*Non*. Isn't he with you?"

She shook her head. "He took his gun with him, and two policemen stopped him at the train station. He shot them both and then ran. I couldn't believe my eyes."

"But why? The plan was— "

"I know," she said dully. "After the ambush I went back to the station to look for him, but there was no trace." She flopped down at her desk and dropped her head in her hands. "I'm really worried. What happens if they catch him?"

"Was the ambush successful?"

She looked up at him. "*Oui*," she said in a dull voice. We got them all."

Alfred's graying eyebrows went up. "All of them? Well done, Marguerite! That is the important thing. The OCM will be pleased."

"*Oui*, but… Oh, I could just kill him!" She stood and unbuttoned her coat. Alfred stared at her blood-stained blouse. "You are hurt!"

"*Non*, I am fine. I had to shoot one of them up close."

"*You* shot one?"

"During the shooting, one of the *Milicien* escaped and returned fire. I had to do something."

"And you killed him?"

"*Oui*," she said, distracted. It all felt unreal, like a terrible dream. She could scarcely believe she had shot that man . . . and the others, as well. She had to get her mind off it. "I'm going back to the depot. I *must* find Charles."

"*Non*. Wait here for Roland and Peter. If Charles doesn't turn up when they arrive, you can all search for him."

She paced back and forth in front of her desk. *I shouldn't have given him his gun.* "Alfred, my nerves are stretched thin; I have to go look for him."

The physician rose and laid his hand on her shoulder. "Go and change your blouse, Marguerite. Then . . . " His voice trailed off. "Then we shall see."

She pulled her bloody top away from her chest, looked down, and released a long sigh. She marched into the spare bedroom to wash and change her clothes, and before she finished dressing she heard someone clatter up the stairs.

Roland met her with a questioning look. "You showed up at the ambush alone. What happened to Charles?"

She drew in a shaky breath. "Charles took his gun with him, and he shot two policemen at the station. The other police were chasing him away from me, so I had to proceed as planned alone."

Roland clenched his fist. "They may have caught him. If he was arrested, they might be coming after us this very minute."

Peter hadn't stopped staring at her since they arrived. "I cannot believe what you did, Marguerite."

Alfred sent him a questioning look. "What was it she did?"

"She shot one of them," Peter said. "Then she crawled into the car to kill the other three."

Now Alfred was staring at her, too. "Truly, Marguerite? You did that?"

"That's what we were supposed to do, wasn't it?" she said quietly. "Kill them?"

Peter looked away. "We have to telephone the OCM. Let them know Charles is missing. They have contacts at the police station, but in the meantime, we should look for him."

Getting into the truck with Peter was a relief; at least she was doing something. They drove for hours, searching alleys and abandoned buildings, even *tabacs* and cafés. Nothing. Finally they returned to the warehouse to wait for some word.

Marguerite dragged herself off to bed but found she couldn't sleep. Every time she closed her eyes she saw Charles racing toward the truck and then veering away at the last minute.

Around two in the morning she heard a noise in the warehouse below. She sat upright, then hugged her nightrobe around her and peeked into the office. Roland and Peter grabbed their revolvers and crept to the top of the stairs.

For a long while no more sounds came from below, and then suddenly there was Charles, climbing up the stairs with a broad smile on his face.

Marguerite flew at him. "When I say leave your gun, you're going to leave your gun! Do you understand?" She waited until he reached the top of the stairs, slapped him hard across the face, grabbed his lapels, and kissed him.

"What's all this?"

"You idiot! We thought you'd been killed or arrested."

"Arrested? Me? You should have more faith in my creativity. We were successful beyond our dreams today. We got six, not just the four we planned to kill. A spectacular success!"

Marguerite seethed. "From now on," she snapped, "you stick with the plan."

Charles simply smiled.

* * *

By the end of March 1944, Radio London began broadcasting news of the build-up of Allied forces in Great Britain. "That can mean only one thing," Peter said. "The Allies plan to invade northern France from England. The only unknown is when and exactly where."

"Liberation may be closer," Marguerite said, "but the day-to-day lives of the people of Normandy are worse." She couldn't stand seeing the long lines at the bakeries, women in threadbare dresses with ragged, emaciated children. It made her want to throw up.

In early April, Marguerite went to meet Yvonne for lunch in Caen. Peter dropped her off, but just as she exited the car, a trio of uniformed Nazis strolled into the café. A shadow fell across her heart. Steeling her nerves, she walked in to join Yvonne at a small table.

"*Guten Tag*, Babette." She nodded toward the German soldiers taking seats near them. "We cannot talk here," she murmured.

Yvonne pursed her lips. "You're right. Have lunch with me and Yvette and Simone in Ville de Pommes on Saturday," she whispered.

"Are you sure that's safe? The closer we get to Liberation, the more brazen and careless the Résistance getting. Places like cafés are dangerous."

"It should be all right. It's safer in Ville de Pommes than here."

Marguerite nodded. "Go ahead and set it up." She tried to keep her gaze off the soldiers at the next table.

"*Ja*, I'll call them. Do you have any news?"

Marguerite smiled at her friend. "The truck driver from Rennes is due tomorrow. I expect another letter from Guy. I worry about him now that— "

Yvonne cut her off. "I envy you. I'm still not over Etienne."

Marguerite leaned toward her. "The waiting is hard," she murmured. "Too hard. I am desperate to be with Guy."

Yvonne blinked.

"He's in a *maquis* unit," Marguerite intoned. "I've made up my mind. I'm going to join him."

"You could get yourself killed!"

"Ah, *non*, I won't."

"Marguerite, keep your voice down." Yvonne cut her eyes toward the table of Nazis, and Marguerite realized they had stopped talking. *Had they heard them?* She waited for them to resume their conversation. Yvonne picked up her cue and stirred her coffee without speaking. Finally the Nazis began to chat.

They finished their lunch in silence and left the café. When she returned to the Auriol distribution center, she found Richard leaning against a desk in heated conversation with Alfred. The doctor motioned to her, pulled a plain white envelope out of his middle desk drawer, and handed it to her without a word. She snatched it and tore it open.

Richard shot her a quizzical look. "Anything you want to share?"

"*Non.*"

He grinned at her. "Would you like to go to Rennes and see Guy?"

Marguerite gasped. "Are you teasing me?"

"*Non*. Would you like to go?"

"*Oui*." she said breathlessly. "When?"

"In two weeks. Robert will drive you."

Two weeks! How can I wait that long?

"Oh, Richard, *merci*. I was afraid I would never see Guy again. *Merci!*" Her mind raced and she had to force herself to be calm.

When Richard left, she tried to plan what she would take, what she would say to Guy, what she would wear. But she found it difficult to think clearly when it involved seeing Guy. All at once nothing seemed important, not what she should take or what she should wear or anything else. It was only important that she see him.

She told *Maman* when she went home to Ville de Pommes for the weekend. The words were scarcely out of her mouth when she realized she had made a mistake.

"*Non*," her mother said flatly. "You are not going to Rennes."

"What do you mean? Why not?"

"It's dangerous in Brittany. Haven't you been listening to Radio London? There is fighting between the Résistance and the *Milice* and the Nazis, and the police. Everywhere there is fighting."

"I need to go, *Maman*. I must see Guy, even for an hour."

"*Non!* I forbid it. There is nothing more to say." She turned on her heel and stalked into the kitchen.

Marguerite stood in the middle of the living room staring at the empty doorway. *I am going to Rennes, and that's all there is to it.* "I'm going over to see Bérénice," she called into the kitchen. "Don't wait up for me. I'll stay overnight."

She took the stairs up to her bedroom two at a time, threw a change of clothes in her bag, and grabbed her linen jacket. She climbed the hill to Perdu, trying to slow her heartbeat and think rationally.

"Bérénice?" she called through the kitchen door. "Bérénice, are you here?"

"I'm up here. I didn't expect you."

"I had an argument with *Maman*. I have arranged to go to Rennes to see Guy, but *Maman* forbids it."

Her cousin rattled down the stairs. "She's right. Brittany is the only place in France where the Résistance controls the interior. José says it's because the Nazis aren't interested in taking the interior yet. They only have enough troops to guard the U-boat ports in Brittany, but in the interior, the Résistance outnumbers them. Anyway, the fighting there is open, not secret. If you go to Rennes, you could get caught up in it."

"I still want to go."

Bérénice shrugged. "Consider yourself warned. Did I tell you that José is in Brittany, too?"

"*Non*, you didn't. Do you think he's with Guy?"

"Has Guy written anything to you lately?"

"*Non.* Has José?"

Bérénice shook her head. Marguerite took her hand. "Do you think anything is wrong?"

"Maybe," her cousin said shortly. "Maybe not. It's awful not knowing."

Marguerite couldn't sleep that night. She tossed and turned in the spare room at Perdu and finally crawled out of bed, pulled on her socks to keep her feet warm, and padded downstairs. The coals in the fireplace were almost cold, so she laid a small log on the embers and curled up in a big chair where she could see outside into the farmyard.

It was snowing. The late spring snowfall was beautiful, the big wet snowflakes quiet as they floated to the ground. There was no wind. How serene it looked, the farmyard asleep and peaceful. She sat down cross-legged on the floor in front of the window and watched the snow drift onto the bunkhouse, the barn, and the cellars. The yard looked virginal, no footprints, no tire tracks, no animal tracks. *Someday all of France will know such peace.*

Bérénice touched her arm and Marguerite jumped. "You startled me!"

Her cousin joined her on the floor, draping her arm around her shoulders. Together they watched the snow sift down.

"Marguerite, what are you thinking?"

"I'm thinking how ironic it is that I am here enjoying the snowfall in this warm house with you while our men may be watching the same snow storm, cursing the cold and the wet, and struggling every day to bring Liberation."

Bérénice said nothing and Marguerite let the silence wash over her. "I'm worried," her cousin said at last. "José says the *Milice* and the Nazis are more aggressive than ever and they've had some narrow escapes. The last time he came to Perdu he was almost captured. Richard thinks the *Milice* is watching us." She squared her shoulders. "When I think about José, it makes me frightened."

"But there have been no arrests, have there?"

"*Non.* You know, I never worried about survival before; now I worry all the time. The Gestapo is getting closer and it's getting harder and harder to not think about what will happen to us."

Marguerite rested her head on her cousin's shoulder and then sat upright when a light went on in the bunkhouse. The door opened and she saw a black form move into the yard.

"Who is that?" asked Marguerite quietly.

"Our lookout. Richard sends him out twice each night to keep an eye on things. He says we must stay vigilant." She gave a little shuddery sigh. "I want to survive this war. I don't want to be the last one killed before we are finally free."

They watched the lookout quietly make his way across the yard, leaving a single set of footprints in the snow. He disappeared behind the barn, then reemerged and circled the entire farmyard before returning to the bunkhouse. The light winked off.

Marguerite got to her feet, pulled Bérénice up, and kissed her cheek. "I hope you and José will find happiness when we're free," she whispered.

Bérénice swiped uncharacteristic tears off her cheek and hugged her. "I don't ask God for much, not since my mother died in Spain. But I pray that someday all of us, you and Guy and José and myself, will be together on our quiet little farms watching the snow fall like this."

Marguerite squeezed her cousin's hand. *I am going to live through this awful war, and I will know peace again one day. The Nazis will never deny me that.* Tomorrow she would meet with Yvonne and their friends at the café in Ville de Pommes and hear all the news.

She wondered why she suddenly felt uneasy.

CHAPTER TWENTY-THREE
RESCUE

Marguerite slept late the next morning, and when she rose, Bérénice was gone. She'd left no note, so she assumed her cousin had gone to be with José. She hiked back to Charentais and dressed in a green linen frock with lace trim for lunch with her friends at *Café Angéle. Maman* frowned when she admitted she was going into town, but when Charles arrived to drive her into Ville de Pommes, her mother softened under the Irishman's charm. "Escort a beautiful young woman on a fine spring day? I live for this."

Both Marguerite and her mother rolled their eyes. "*Merci,* Charles. But skip the poetry, all right?"

Charles tramped toward the barn for the truck, leaving Marguerite shivering in the crisp morning air. When he returned, she climbed in, rubbing her hands for warmth.

"Where shall I take you, *Mademoiselle*?"

"*Café Angéle.*"

He shot her a look. "That café is not safe, Marguerite. Too many people hate those collaborators and their friends."

She sighed. "You and my mother both worry too much."

The café was almost empty, and Marguerite wondered why. Usually it was crowded on Saturdays. She sat down at a table near the back. Five minutes later Yvonne entered, and then came Simone and Yvette. All three wore spring dresses, complete with hats and gloves. Marguerite hadn't worn gloves since

. . . she found she couldn't remember.

The waiter took their order and disappeared into the kitchen. No one was behind the counter and the waiters were gone; all at once she felt uneasy. Suddenly she heard a shout from the street. "Traitors!"

Instinctively she started to rise, and then there was a flash of light.

She remembered a shout from inside the café. "Bomb!" But she didn't remember the explosion. She remembered darkness and a muffled voice. "Here's another one." Though her eyelids were closed she could still see light through them.

She willed her body to move, but nothing happened. She felt nothing. *Am I dead*? Someone picked up her wrist. "She's got a pulse," the voice said. She remembered thinking, *that's good.*

Her next memory was of lying in some sort of vehicle, and pain. Terrible pain.

* * *

Her eyelids fluttered open. *Where am I?* She tried to orient herself, but something covered her left eye. When she tried to move her legs her body screamed with pain. Her temples throbbed. She turned her head and saw Bérénice in a chair next to her bed.

"Where am I?"

Bérénice lurched. "Marguerite? Marguerite, can you hear me?"

"Where am I?"

"You're in the hospital. In Caen."

"What happened to me?"

Her cousin snapped her book closed and leaned toward her. "Someone threw a bomb into *Café Angéle*."

"Where are my friends?"

"Yvonne and Simone are at home, recuperating."

"What about Yvette?"

Bérénice paused. "You need to rest. I need to tell the nurse you're conscious."

"Wait! How long have I been here?"

"Three days. We— We weren't sure you were going to make it."

Marguerite tried to sit up but could not get her arms to work. "Am I all right?"

"Well, *non*, you're not. You have stitches in your left leg, your left arm, and your face, and you had a concussion. Your left eye is all right, just scratched, but you have a gash on your face. That's why you're bandaged."

Marguerite closed her eyes. "Who did it? Who threw the bomb?"

Bérénice carefully closed the hospital room door. "We don't know yet," she whispered. "Someone said whoever threw the bomb yelled 'traitors,' so we know they weren't trying to kill Nazis. But so many renegade Résistance groups are springing up everywhere we may never know who did it. The closer we get to Liberation, the more reckless everyone is getting."

Marguerite groaned. "Everything hurts, especially my head. What happened to the other people at the café?"

"Three were killed. Yvonne was hurt, but not as seriously as you. Simone was unhurt because she was protected by the table and Yvette."

"What happened to Yvette."

Her cousin bit her lip.

"Bérénice, what happened to Yvette?"

"She was . . . she was killed."

"*Non! Mon Dieu, non*." Tears welled in her eyes and she lifted her good hand to wipe them away.

"Dr. Morel saved your life," Bérénice said, her voice quiet.

"Dr. Morel?"

"*Oui*. He heard the blast and ran from the *tabac*. They had to dig you out of the rubble, and a piece of steel had pierced your leg. He removed it and stopped the bleeding."

Talking was exhausting, and the relentless pain in her head made it hard to concentrate. She had to stop. She reached out to Bérénice, clutched her arm, and drifted off.

* * *

"Marguerite, how are you doing?"

She opened her eyes and saw a blurry Richard and Alfred standing beside her bed. Bérénice closed the hospital room door and stood with her back against it.

"I am fine," she managed.

"You are not fine," Alfred said. The physician lifted the bandage on her face and inspected the wound, then signaled Richard to come closer. Marguerite let her lids drift shut but she could hear them talking.

"Do you know anything about sutures?"

"*Non*."

"See these? They put in only seven stitches. They should have used four times that many to minimize scarring. Whoever did this is either incompetent or they intended to leave a scar on her face."

"If we get her out of here, can you repair it?"

"*Non*, not until the skin is completely healed. It should have been done immediately. And look at this; these bandages haven't been changed since I was here yesterday, and there may be an infection in her leg. The care here is abominable. We need to get her out of here."

Richard frowned. "I was afraid of that. The staff knows she was hurt by a bomb thrown into a collaborationist café. They hate collaborators. The other patients don't want to be in the same room with her. How long before we can move her?"

"At least another night, and then we'll have to be careful. We'll need to keep her in Caen. A trip to Ville de Pommes would be too much. They almost lost her in the ambulance."

"Alfred, can you stay overnight here with her?"

"I can. I need to change her bandages now and again in the morning."

When she awoke the next morning, *Maman*, Alfred, and Bérénice were there. Her head still ached, but not as much as the day before.

Maman touched her hand. "We've made arrangements to have you discharged, *chou-chou*. The staff wants you out of here, so it was easy." She sounded so calm and matter-of-fact Marguerite wanted to laugh.

Richard strode into the room. "They're going to discharge her in an hour. Let's get her ready."

Alfred bent over her and inspected the dressings. "Marguerite, I'm going to change your bandages again."

He carefully cleaned and rewrapped each site. "*Alors*, she's ready to go."

Her mother shooed the men out. "Wait outside while we get her dressed."

Marguerite tried to sit up, but the effort was too much. *Maman* gently lifted her legs to the edge of the bed, then helped her to sit up while Marguerite braced herself against the pain. Bérénice gingerly untied her hospital gown, and they pulled her to a standing position and slipped a dress over her head. *Maman* knelt to help her with her shoes while Marguerite panted with fatigue.

Alfred and Richard returned with the discharge nurse, an officious woman who went directly to Marguerite. "An orderly will come to get you," she snapped. She left the room without another word.

After ten minutes of waiting, Marguerite grew dizzy. "I feel faint," she murmured. Instantly, *Maman* was beside her, and she and Bérénice helped her lie back down.

For the next half hour Richard paced and finally he left the room, returning at once with a young orderly pushing a wheelchair. With no introduction the man reached under her armpits and tried to pull her upright. She cried out.

Richard leaned across her bed, grabbed the man's white hospital jacket in his big fists, and yanked him forward. "The next time she says ouch, you'll be the one feeling pain. *Compris*?"

The man glanced aside. Richard tightened his grip and shook the man, hard. "Do you understand me?"

The orderly's eyes went wide. "*Oui*," he said in an uneven voice.

Richard released him with a shove, and the man stole glances at him as he and Bérénice settled Marguerite into the wheelchair. The orderly stepped behind her, turned the wheelchair sharply, and bumped it into the door jam. Marguerite screamed.

Richard grabbed the man with both hands and threw him against the wall. Then he took his place pushing the wheelchair. Marguerite's head began to pound. "Where are we going?"

Richard laid his hand on her shoulder. "To Auriol Distributors. We have your room ready upstairs, and your mother will stay with you until you are able to travel to Ville de Pommes."

Maman would stay with her? She began to cry.

Richard loaded her in the back seat of the Peugeot with *Maman*. Bérénice and Alfred climbed in next to him. He drove very slowly to the distribution building, but when he turned the last corner, he pulled over and stopped. Four police cars were parked in front. "I don't like the looks of this," he muttered.

The front door of the warehouse opened and four workers were marched out in handcuffs. Richard twisted to look back at Marguerite. "How are you doing?" he asked in a low, calm voice.

"I am well," Marguerite said. Her voice shook. "Get us out of here."

"I'll have to take you to Ville de Pommes. Are you up to it?"

She tried to laugh. "Do I have a choice?"

"Probably not. One hell of a time for this."

Richard took over an hour to slowly drive the 25 kilometers to Ville de Pommes, and when they arrived he headed straight for the hidden entrance to the Cave.

"I thought we were taking her home," *Maman* said. "What are we doing here?"

“She’s safer here,” Richard replied. “I need to go back and see what’s happening in Caen. If there’s trouble, I want Marguerite down here.”

He helped *Maman* out, then very gently maneuvered Marguerite across the back seat and lifted her into his arms. He carried her into the empty Cave and laid her on a cot where Bérénice covered her with a blanket. “How does she look, Alfred?”

The physician checked her wounds. “Not too bad. There’s still some seepage, and she’ll need a few weeks to heal.”

“Stay here and look after her,” Richard directed. “We’ll send some food down later. *Madame* Auriol, do you want to stay with your daughter, or can I drive you back to Charentais?”

“I will stay,” her mother announced, her tone resolute.

“*Bon*. I’ll go back to Caen and find out what’s going on.”

Marguerite stretched her hand out to him. “Richard, please be careful. I have a bad feeling about what’s going on back there.”

CHAPTER TWENTY-FOUR
REPRISAL

Marguerite opened her eyes, rolled onto her right side, and pushed herself up into a sitting position. After two days of rest in the upper level of the Cave, her headache was almost gone and she could walk with minimal pain. Alfred was coming today to remove her last sutures, for which she was grateful because they had begun to itch.

She moved slowly to the stairs. “Is anybody down there?”

“Marguerite?” Bérénice appeared at the bottom of the stairs. “You’re up?”

“I’m coming down.”

“Are you sure? Put some clothes on if you are. Alfred will be here any minute.”

She changed into a blue flowered dress *Maman* had sent over with Bérénice and unwound the annoying bandage from the left side of her face because it was driving her crazy.

Bérénice’s eyebrows shot up when she saw her.

Marguerite touched her face. “It’s bad, isn’t it?”

Her cousin stared at her. “What?”

“My stitches. They look bad, don’t they?”

“*Non. Non.*”

“Give me a mirror.”

“I… I don’t have one with me.”

She snatched up Bérénice’s purse and searched it, holding her left hand close to her body. When she found her cousin's compact she pulled it out.

"Oh, there it is," Bérénice faltered. "I thought..."

"Don't lie to me, Bérénice. Ever." She examined the wound on her face, touching it gingerly with one finger. "I look terrible, don't I?"

"You can use makeup to hide the scar."

Marguerite continued to peer into the small mirror. "Perhaps it will look better after the stitches are out."

"It isn't fair," Bérénice blurted. Men get scarred and it's a mark of courage. For a woman, it's disfiguring!"

"*Non.*" She snapped the compact shut and leveled her gaze at her cousin. "It *is* a mark of courage. I will be proud of it. It is my Résistance badge. Did you find out who was responsible?"

"*Non.* The police think it was the OCM, but no one in the OCM knows anything about it."

At that moment Richard and Alfred walked in. The physician sat Marguerite down, unrolled a package of scissors and some tweezers, then pulled a small bottle of alcohol and some cotton from his pocket. "I'm going to take out your stitches. Are you ready?"

She nodded. "*Oui.*"

He snipped sutures and removed them with the tweezers. As he worked, Richard prowled the Cave like a caged animal. "The workers arrested in the Gestapo raid on the warehouse are being interrogated," he said heavily. "They're holding them in Caen Prison, and we have to assume their techniques are yielding results."

Marguerite flinched.

"There's more bad news," Richard continued. "Peter was arrested with them."

Her breath hissed in. *Oh, non. Peter knows everything about the assassinations, Réfugié, everything.*

"The SS is burning the homes of suspected Résistance sympathizers. I don't want you caught in the middle of a raid, so I want you and Bérénice to stay down here in the Cave. I've arranged for your mother to stay with Germaine in Paris until we understand what the Gestapo knows. Someone will drive her to the train station."

Alfred tweezed away the last stitch on her face and started on her arm. "Are you feeling all right, Marguerite?"

"*Oui*, fine. Just keep going."

Just as he bent over her arm an explosion shook the Cave. Dust and dirt sifted down from the ceiling.

Bérénice turned pale. "*Mon Dieu,* what was that?"

Suddenly a loudspeaker blared. "*Achtung! Achtung!* You will surrender Marguerite Auriol immediately."

Marguerite's heart stopped. "How could they know I'm here?"

Richard flipped off the light switch and cracked open the inner door. "Bérénice, follow me with the flashlight." He eased open the outside door and Marguerite heard a series of pops. "Gunfire," the big Irishman muttered.

He closed the door, took the flashlight from Bérénice, and scrambled up the stairs. Within seconds he returned and tossed Alfred an American .45 caliber Colt while Bérénice fished her revolver out of her purse.

"Where's mine?" asked Marguerite.

"You don't need one," Richard answered. "You wait here. You'd be a liability limping around out there." He glanced at Bérénice, then Alfred. "Are you ready?"

Marguerite watched them squeeze one by one through the crack in the door. She was pushing it closed after them when she heard the gunshots. Shaking, she bit the inside of her cheek and retreated into the Cave, closed the inner door, and flipped on the light switch. Nothing happened. She flipped it up and down several times. Still nothing. *Why are there no lights?*

Using the flashlight she climbed the stairs to the second floor where she found a revolver and some ammunition, then returned to the tunnel, eased open the outside door, and peered into the darkness. Another faint burst of gunfire forced her to duck back inside, and she waited in the dark for what seemed like an eternity.

Three tremendous explosions shook the Cave. Unable to stop herself, she opened the outside door.

A flash of light followed by a deafening crack startled her and she stumbled backwards, her heart pounding. It was raining! Lightning flashed, followed by claps of thunder. She stepped outside and worked her way around the hedgerow and up the hill, slipping in the mud. Near the top she slipped again and felt the stitches in her leg tear open, but she kept going. Water streamed down and the mud was thick and slippery.

When she reached the hilltop she gasped at the carnage. The house, the barn, the bunkhouse were piles of rubble, and flames licked at the remaining timbers. Another lightning flash illuminated an SS helmet on a figure moving around the yard. Soldiers! She stifled a cry and carefully retreated back down the hill.

Hours passed in the dark and at last it grew quiet. She waited another hour and slowly stood up. She couldn't stand not knowing, so again she climbed the hill. At the top she stopped dead. A man lay face down with a .45 in one hand. She approached cautiously and when he didn't move, she rolled him over.

Alfred! Automatically she checked for a pulse. Nothing. Then she turned away and vomited.

Farther on in the farmyard she saw hand sticking out of what was left of the bunkhouse. An SS helmet lay in a pool of blood in the yard. She knew the Nazis retrieved their dead and wounded; only Résistance bodies would be left out in the rain. She waited, hidden in the burned-out barn, but no one came.

In the bunkhouse blood was everywhere. She found Roland propped against the door frame, his eyes open and a handgun in his lap. Next to him was another body. *Oh, dear God, it was Charles! Brave, foolish Charles.* She checked his gun, found it empty, and slipped it into her pocket.

Blood was running down her left leg, but she ignored it, limping from building to building looking for more bodies. She discovered another German helmet. But when she saw what was lying beside it, she froze. She bent to pick up the small revolver. Its grip was taped, and when she peeled back the tape she saw it was broken.

Mon Dieu! It was Bérénice's revolver. She clicked open the cylinder and counted six spent cartridges. Sobs racked her body.

All at once she thought of *Maman. You cannot cry, now. Control yourself!*

In the lightning, she could see black smoke floating into the sky from the direction of Charentais. *Non. Oh, non! They had burned her home?*

Weak and dizzy, she sank to the ground and waited until she could stand, then found her way back to the Cave, reloaded Charles's gun, and sat alone in the darkness, trying to think what to do. Richard and Bérénice were either dead or under arrest and being interrogated. She clenched her jaw, imagining her cousin dangling naked over a bathtub of ice water. She hoped she was dead and not suffering.

She prayed that *Maman* was in Paris with Aunt Germaine. And then she remembered her instructions: *If someone is arrested, go underground. Assume the Nazis know all.* She realized suddenly that under torture someone might disclose the location of the Cave. *I have to get away from here. I am completely on my own.*

Using the flashlight, she inventoried the upper floor and found a lantern and matches. She lit the lantern, turned off the flashlight, and changed into dry clothes from the valise *Maman* had brought her. She plucked out the rest of her stitches in her arm and leg and bandaged the area where the stitches had burst as best she could using strips of torn-up sheets. Then she picked up the small valise and ventured outside into the morning light.

Miraculously, the Perdu farm truck sat behind the smoldering barn. Bullet holes riddled the cab. She found the hidden set of keys, blackened but still usable, in the smoking ruins of the Perdu kitchen.

The engine roared to life. She drove to the outskirts of Ville de Pommes, hid the vehicle behind the bakery, and started to walk. She needed help.

The back entrance to Dr. Morel's clinic stood open, and she slipped into his office, quietly closed the door behind her, and waited behind his desk with her gun in her lap.

An hour passed. The clinic was busy at this hour, and the veterinarian did not enter his office until late morning. She fought to stay alert and finally the door opened and Dr. Morel stepped in. He stopped short. "Marguerite! What are you doing here?" Quickly he shut the office door. "My dear, why the gun?"

She pushed the pistol into her pocket and explained all that had happened. When she finished, his face looked drawn. "The police were here looking for you."

"When?"

"Yesterday. They suspect you work with the Résistance."

"Have you heard anything about Bérénice or Richard? Or my mother?"

Dr. Morel shook his head. "*Non*. The rumors are that the Nazis arrested or killed everyone at Charentais and Perdu and destroyed all the buildings. They say no one escaped."

She began to sob. "I hope everyone was killed. If they were caught I can't bear to think what the Nazis are doing to them."

He pressed his handkerchief into her hand. "Don't assume the worst, Marguerite. How did you escape?"

"I hid in the Cave at Perdu."

"Let me look at your face. Come closer to the light."

"Could you put a clean bandage on my leg? I tore out some stitches and I couldn't bandage it very well." She raised the hem of her skirt to reveal the blood-stained strips of sheeting.

The doctor stepped out and returned with clean bandages, alcohol, and cotton. He started with her leg, then worked his way up to her face, carefully examining and cleaning each wound.

"What do you want to do?" he asked when he finished.

"I'm going to Rennes and find Guy. I have the train tickets Richard gave me, but now they're outdated."

"*Alors*, we need to get you on the train to Rennes. But they'll be looking for you in Caen, so I'll take you to Bayeux. You can catch the train there."

"You?"

He ignored her question. "I'll have to hide you in case the police come back." He turned toward the office door. "Jenna," he called. "Will you come in here, please?"

Marguerite tensed, slipped her hand into her pocket, and gripped her pistol.

"It's all right," Dr. Morel said. "She can be trusted." She nodded but kept her finger on the trigger.

The door opened and Jenna Benault walked in. She stiffened at the sight of Marguerite but said nothing.

"Jenna, do you have any makeup in your purse? I need to hide Marguerite's wound."

Jenna bent to examine her face, left the office, and returned with a large broad-brimmed sun hat. "I don't use makeup because it's too hard to get. Besides, your problem isn't just the makeup. Do you have any money?"

"*Non*. I don't."

"Here, take this." She pressed some francs into Marguerite's hand. "It's not much, but you might need it."

"*Merci*, Jenna."

The receptionist opened her mouth to reply when a voice boomed at the front entrance. "*Guten Tag, guten Tag*. Who is here?" Marguerite's breath stopped.

"Jenna, delay whoever that is." When the receptionist left, Dr. Morel took Marguerite's hand. "Go out the back way, Marguerite. Find someplace safe and wait. Come back in an hour, and I will drive you to Bayeux."

She grabbed Jenna's hat and slipped out the back entrance. Casually she tilted the hat at an angle to hide her face and strolled to the town park where she knew she could hide. An hour later, she re-entered Dr. Morel's office and left a note on his desk. 'In the car.' She positioned Jenna's hat next to it.

She made her way out to his Citroen, fished his extra pair of coveralls out of the trunk, and tossed them into the back seat. Then she crawled in and pulled them over her head. She thought about *Maman* and prayed she was safe. Just when she thought she might survive this ordeal, she heard men's voices coming from the clinic.

"Lastrange, you've searched the clinic. She is not here."

"Dr. Morel, I am not stupid. She is a friend of yours, so naturally she would come to you. Do you mind if I search your car?"

"*Nein*. But you are wasting your time."

She heard the trunk open and felt the car rock as the officer shifted the contents. Then the rear door at her feet opened and he began rummaging around. In the next instant he tugged the coveralls exposing her head. Startled, he jerked up, staring at her, and reached for his gun.

She fired her pistol first.

Lastrange's heavy body collapsed on top of her. Dr. Morel pushed his legs into the back seat and slammed the rear door. She lay still, and in a few seconds Dr. Morel climbed into the driver's seat and started the engine.

"Where are we going?" she called.

"Away from here. Sergeant Boulot was in the clinic with Lastrange. I told him that Lastrange saw something and had run off to the north, and Boulot swallowed the bait. We're going the opposite way. Just stay where you are."

After some minutes, the car stopped, the back door opened, and the dead weight was lifted off her. She recognized the rear yard of the church near the trashcans. Morel dragged the body off of her. She helped him drag it behind the trash cans and cover it with garbage. "A fitting end for a traitor, don't you think?"

"*Oui*, I do, Doctor." The vet hadn't seemed surprised that she had killed Lastrange. Perhaps he knew her better than she thought.

He yanked open the trunk. "Take anything with blood on it and put it in the trashcans. Then wipe up as much blood as you can with those overalls."

She limped to a faucet, wet the coveralls, and cleaned the blood from the inside of the windows and the ceiling. The vet tossed them over Lastrange's body. "Now," he barked, "let's go."

"I must change my dress—it's bloody."

"We don't have time." He reached deep into the trunk and pulled down the back wall, revealing a small space. "Climb in there."

She scrambled over the medical supplies, her valise clutched in her hand, and curled up sideways in the hidden space. Morel replaced the false back, reloaded the supplies, and slammed the trunk closed. She listened to the sound of the engine and the tires on the road, and when the noise roughened she guessed they had left town and were in the country. Finally the car bumped to a stop and the engine went silent.

Dr. Morel pulled away the false back, and Marguerite crawled out, stretched, and smoothed out her blood-stained dress.

"Are you all right?"

"*Oui*. But why is there a hiding place in the trunk of your car?"

"None of your business," he said curtly. "What we need to think about is what to do next."

"Oh, please, take me to Charentais. I must know if *Maman* is all right. She was supposed to go to Paris, but…"

"*Bon*. To Charentais then."

He tossed her valise in the back, hurried her into the passenger seat, and started the engine.

CHAPTER TWENTY-FIVE
LEAVING HOME

The farmyard at Charentais was full of debris from the explosions which had destroyed the house and damaged the cellar building, the bunkhouse, and the barn. Marguerite climbed out of Dr. Morel's Citroën and walked through the destruction, clenching her hands into fists. *Is it good or bad that there are no bodies?*

She dragged herself back to the car and slumped in the front seat. "I've seen enough. Please take me to Bayeux."

The doctor backed down the drive, turned west, and drove in silence for a few kilometers. "Marguerite, have you heard of the *Maquis de Pommes*?"

She looked at him sideways. "*Non*."

"No one else has heard of them, either. They're Résistance fighters who haven't done much fighting, just sit and talk about it a lot. They asked me to join them, but I was undecided until a few days ago."

"What happened a few days ago?" she asked without enthusiasm.

"They decided to bomb a collaborationist meeting place."

She jerked upright. "*Café Angéle*? You bombed *Café Angéle*?"

"I tried to stay out of it. They didn't tell me they intended to bomb the café. Had I known, I would have talked them out of it." He swallowed. "I think they were trying to kill Yvonne Callion."

"But why? Yvonne is— " She snapped her mouth closed. Could she tell him that Yvonne worked with the Résistance?

Morel sighed. "Why? Because two of the men had lost sons to the forced labor Callion Construction uses on the beach defenses."

"The fools! They injured two Résistance agents, me and Yvonne Callion. She's an OCM agent."

He groaned. "I was afraid of something like that. You can't just toss a bomb into a crowded place; you never know who will be hurt. What a tragedy. That's what guerrilla war is, amateurs with explosives."

Marguerite said nothing. She could not believe Dr. Morel would ever condone bombing a café full of people.

At the Bayeux train station Dr. Morel exchanged her outdated ticket, and the clerk came out from behind her post and spoke quietly to her. "Find a seat in the back of the train, *Mademoiselle*. The Allies are shooting at the trains along the coast, and when they see one, they go after the locomotive. Sometimes they're not very good shots and they hit the first coach car."

All of a sudden she felt unsure. She would be riding in a train the Allies would try to destroy? "*Merci*, *Madame*. I will remember that."

"And the train will probably be late because of Résistance activities along the line." The clerk glanced furtively around and spoke from behind her hand. "If the Résistance has done nothing else, they've made the trains late."

Dr. Morel escorted her to the platform and waited on the bench with her. "I feel responsible for you, Marguerite. Responsible for your injuries."

She turned to him and grasped his hand. "You shouldn't. Chances are you could not have stopped it."

"Perhaps. Perhaps not. It haunts me."

"I will miss you, Dr. Morel. You have done so much for me." She leaned over and kissed his cheek.

He pulled away awkwardly and she saw him blush. "God keep you safe, my dear."

Her eyes stung.

"Here," he whispered. "Take this money." He pressed some bills into her hand. "That should help until you find Guy."

"But that's all you have!"

"Don't worry, I have other resources." He stood up. "I will leave you here. I need to find someplace to sleep tonight."

She rose, dropped her valise onto the platform, and hugged him hard. "You've been like a father to me, Dr. Morel. You help me see things clearly, and lately I've been confused about a lot."

"You have grown these last few years. You have seen and done more than most people will do in their entire lifetime, and you're what, twenty?"

"I turned twenty-one last week. No one remembered."

He reached into his jacket pocket and pulled out a small metal object. "This is my Saint Anthony medal. I wear it always, and now I want you to have it. Happy Birthday, Marguerite."

"*Merci*," she said, her voice breaking.

"You know, I admire this Patrice person you've invented. You have her strength and courage and also Marguerite's kindness. Stay safe."

His last words were almost drowned out by the approaching locomotive. "Here's your train," he shouted.

The huge steam engine rumbled past and slowed to a stop. She threw her arms around him one last time as the coach doors opened and a team of conductors stepped out to put down small iron steps. The stream of debarking passengers slowed and the crowd waiting on the platform began to step into the coaches. Marguerite kissed Dr. Morel's cheek, turned away, and boarded the last car.

There were no empty seats, so she walked forward to the next car, but it was full as well. The closer she got to the front of the train the more empty seats she found. Advice about where to sit was no secret. She sat down in the second car from the locomotive and decided that at each stop, she would move farther back.

The train lurched forward, and through the window she saw Dr. Morel waving at her. The train moved away, and he grew smaller and smaller until she could no longer see him.

She stared out the window at the scenery without really seeing it. Her head throbbed and both her arm and her leg ached. *Where was Maman? And Bérénice and Richard. Were they dead? Under arrest? Being tortured?* She shook the questions out of her head.

All the way to Rennes she was appalled at the destruction visible from the train window, shells of burned-out buildings, torn-up streets, even the remains of a wrecked locomotive tipped on its side.

At the station in Rennes, she stepped off the train and gazed about her. The sky was slate grey, and it was wet and miserably cold. Shivering, she decided to start her search for Guy at a wine shop across the street. Inside, she asked the proprietor where the liquor warehouse was located. He wrote an address on a slip of paper and handed it to her.

Next door was a dusty-looking jewelry shop. She went in and bought a chain for her St. Anthony medal. Then she hailed a taxi, which delivered her to a warehouse about the same size and layout as Auriol Distributors except that the offices were on the ground floor and there were no living quarters. Three clerks were bent over their desks.

"*Guten Tag*. I am looking for the driver who delivers to Caen. I think his name is Robert."

One man looked up, studied her for a long moment, and shrugged. "He's in Bay Three, loading up."

At Bay Three she found a heavy-set man in a workingman's jacket and a black beret lounging against the wall.

"Robert?"

He straightened. "That would be me."

"May we speak privately?"

He eyed her with suspicion. "Who are you?"

She took a deep breath. "I am sometimes known as Patrice Cerne," she whispered.

He took a step back and stared at her, the color draining from his face. "Did you say Patrice Cerne?"

"*Oui*," she murmured.

Robert motioned her to follow him to a secluded corner of the building. "What can I do for you?"

"You delivered some letters to Auriol Distributors in Caen. Do you remember?"

"I remember. What do you want?"

"Those letters were meant for me. Could you take me to the man who sent those letters?"

He looked off to one side without answering. Then, after a long pause, he nodded. "I need to make some telephone calls." He pointed outside across the street. "Go to that corner and wait. No one should see us leave together."

She nodded, walked outside to reclaim her valise, and waited on the back corner. Her hair was wet and her teeth chattered with the cold. Bless *Maman* for sending a warm jacket along with her other clothes!

A truck rumbled up and braked, and without a word she opened the passenger door, threw her bag onto the seat, and jumped in. The warmth from the truck's heater washed over her chilled body, and she reached her hands toward the vent.

"*Bonjour*, Patrice Cerne," Robert said.

"*Bonjour*, Robert. Is it always this cold and wet in Brittany?"

"It is always cold and wet in Brittany except during the winter, and then it's cold and snowy. May I see your identification?"

She dug her identity papers out of her purse and handed them over. He glanced at them and passed them back without looking at her. Immediately her instincts told her something was wrong.

"We were surprised when you showed up," he said.

"Who is 'we'?" she asked cautiously.

"You know better than to ask a question like that, *Mademoiselle*. Two days ago I made my regular run to Auriol Distributors and found the building closed up. I dropped my load at another warehouse and asked what happened at Auriol. They said the Gestapo suspected the Auriol family of supporting the Résistance, so they arrested or shot everyone. That's why I was surprised when you showed up."

"I hid, then escaped when the Nazis came. Where are you taking me?"

"Where I pick up and drop off the Patrice Cerne letters. It's about sixty kilometers from here."

"Your foreman lets you take the truck wherever you wish?"

"This is my regular route. I deliver to Brest."

On the way out of Rennes, Marguerite noticed posters warning against aiding paratroopers. "Paratroopers? Are there paratroopers here?"

"*Oui*. Free French paratroopers."

"Free French! What are they doing here?"

"They're French Special Air Services trained by the British as commandos. They're training *maquisards* to support the Liberation by attacking roads, railroads, communications, and command posts. We've been practicing with small missions against the Germans."

"I cannot believe it, a Free French Army operating in Brittany!"

"Not a uniformed army, *non*. But there's thousands of us. When the Germans set up the Unoccupied Zone, they let Pétain keep an army of a hundred thousand men. It is full of Résistance sympathizers."

"But Brittany was a part of the Occupied Zone."

"*Oui*, it was. But the Bretons are stubborn. We formed an interior army anyway. They operate mostly around the Nazi submarine pens in Brest, Lorient, and Saint Nazaire, and they control the Breton interior."

This was the first Marguerite had heard about the Liberation from someone directly involved. She had no idea there was such open resistance to the Occupation anywhere in France.

The road turned into an isolated two-lane affair with little traffic. The area was heavily wooded, the forests broken up by isolated farms with cleared fields planted in potatoes or wheat and an occasional apple orchard or herd of cattle. It looked so normal she wanted to cry.

The mist gave way to rain, and as they drove deeper into the countryside, Robert turned on the windshield wipers, which slapped away the moisture.

"If we are stopped, what do I tell them?" Marguerite asked.

"Stopped? Stopped by who?"

"The Germans. What if we run into a roadblock?"

He gave a short bark of laughter. "If we run into a roadblock, it won't be Germans. A lot of young men fled into the countryside to escape forced labor. I've been robbed a couple of times by thieves who have nothing to do with the Résistance; they're simply criminals on the run. You won't see German roadblocks in this countryside. If we do, I have travel permits."

"Which identity papers should I use?"

"Thieves won't ask for identification, *Mademoiselle*. Only the Germans. Use your Auriol papers. Patrice Cerne is a name known in these parts."

She made the adjustment in her purse and checked the pistol in her jacket pocket. Robert glanced at her, a question is his eyes. "Are you armed?"

"*Oui*."

"When we meet your escort, keep your hand away from the gun. They will be on guard and I don't want you shot."

"I understand."

He drove on through a thickly wooded area with no traffic other than horse-drawn carts. "We're getting close. See that tall juniper at the top of the hill?"

"I see it."

"We'll stop there and check with their lookouts. They watch the road for strangers." He slowed the truck and pulled to the side of the road. A pair of unshaven men armed with rifles stepped out of the underbrush and gestured. Robert rolled down his window and leaned out.

"Is she with you?" one of the men yelled.

"*Oui*, she's with me."

The sentry nodded and waved them through. They drove another ten minutes and again stopped in a wide spot on the side of the road. "We wait here until your escort comes," Robert announced. Suddenly, he looked at her. "How did you escape the Nazis?"

Marguerite opened her mouth to respond when an ancient Peugeot pulled up in front of them. "Here's your escort," said Robert. "Let's go."

They stepped out onto the ground and four men wearing dark clothes and berets surrounded them, their rifles pointed at Marguerite. The leader spoke quietly to Robert, "Is this Patrice Cerne?"

Robert gave her a long look. "*Oui*, but be careful. She's armed." Then he reached out and fastened his meaty fingers around both her wrists.

CHAPTER TWENTY-SIX
PATRICE CERNE

Marguerite struggled to pull her wrists free from Robert's grip. "What are you doing?"

"Her gun is in her right pocket," he growled.

One of the guards lowered his rifle, reached into her jacket pocket, and confiscated her pistol. She pulled free from Robert. "What is this all about?"

"Yesterday I brought someone else here calling herself Patrice Cerne," he explained. "Just before we left Rennes today I called ahead to tell them I was bringing *another* Patrice Cerne. Fortunately we have someone from *Réfugié* here; he knew yesterday's Patrice Cerne and has vouched for her."

A sentry added, "That makes you a *Milice* infiltrator. We know how to deal with the *Milice*."

"But, I *am* Patrice Cerne! There's some mistake."

"*Oui*, *Mademoiselle Milice*, and you have made it."

Robert jerked a thumb in her direction. "This one knows too much. You should shoot her now and bury her in the woods."

Marguerite gasped. "*Non!* Take me to the *Réfugié* agent. If he is truly from *Réfugié*, he will identify me."

"We will take you to him for 'aggressive' questioning," the sentry snapped. "Before we execute you, maybe we will learn something."

She was so tired and cold she couldn't think. The guard produced handcuffs and locked her hands together in front of her; then they manhandled her into the back seat of the car. One of the men spoke into a walkie-talkie. "We have her."

"*Bon*," a scratchy voice responded.

Robert reached into his cab, grabbed her valise, and tossed it to the one of the guards. The driver twisted to face her. "You didn't count on the real Patrice Cerne being here, did you, *Mademoiselle Milice*? We've had enough of you traitors. In an hour you'll be in front of a firing squad."

Marguerite worked hard to appear calm, but inside she wanted to explode. *This cannot be happening!*

The car pulled onto the road. After five minutes it slowed and turned down a muddy, unpaved lane into the forest. A few kilometers into the woods, it stopped suddenly and two sentries in dark clothes and berets appeared with machine guns slung under their shoulders.

"Get out, *Mademoiselle Milice*," the driver ordered.

She scrambled out of the back seat. "Take me to this Patrice Cerne imposter!" she demanded.

"Soon enough," he muttered. He got out, handed her valise and pistol to one of her guards, and pointed to a muddy trail. "Up there."

She labored up the trail, rain blowing into her face, and emerged in a large field where she stopped dead. The scene in front of her was incomprehensible. A sea of tents dotted the area and thousands of men were roaming about. A farmhouse and a large barn stood in the center.

Marguerite turned to her escort. "What is all this?"

"Quiet!" he barked. He prodded her forward with his rifle barrel and shoved her through the opening of a large tent guarded by two armed sentries.

Inside, three men slouched behind a table and armed guards stood around the gloomy interior. Her guard unlocked her handcuffs, took her gun from his pocket, and slapped it onto the table. "We found this on her."

The bearded, disheveled man seated in the center briefly inspected her pistol and put it back down while she rubbed her wrists. "Good afternoon, *Mademoiselle Milice*. Welcome to *Château Marneé*. Your stay with us will be uncomfortable. And short."

"They told me someone claiming to be Patrice Cerne is here. I demand to see this imposter."

"You are in no position to make demands, *Mademoiselle*. Nevertheless, since you wish to meet her…" He turned to an aide. "Get Patrice Cerne."

Marguerite balled her fists and paced back and forth, thinking of Papa's execution and the assassination of the *Milice* interrogators. Fury overwhelmed her. *Who would dare to impersonate me?*

The man pointed at her face. “That scar says you’ve had a session with the Gestapo. Did you agree to find us for them?”

Marguerite glared at him. “I have never been arrested by the Gestapo or anyone else! When that imposter gets here, I’ll strangle her. No one, *no one,* lies about me.”

The aide returned and pulled the tent flap aside for an unshaven, swarthy man with a rain-spattered, wide-brimmed hat and a black walrus mustache. He shambled in followed by a small woman with wet black hair obscuring her face. Both were rain-soaked.

Marguerite stepped forward to confront her, but at that moment the man removed his hat and Marguerite stopped and stared at him. There was something familiar about his eyes. And then white teeth appeared under the big mustache and his face broke into a grin.

“José!” She bolted toward him and threw her arms around his neck. Weeping, she kissed both his scratchy cheeks. “What are you doing here?”

“They asked me to bring Patrice Cerne.” He stepped aside and turned to the small woman standing behind him.

“Welcome to *Château Marnee,*” the woman said. A beaming smile spread across her face and she opened her arms wide.

“Bérénice!” sobbed Marguerite. She threw her arms around her cousin. “*Mon Dieu*, Bérénice! I thought the Nazis had arrested you.”

Bérénice swiped tears off her cheeks with her fingers. “We got away. Red and me.”

“Oh, thank God,” Marguerite said, her voice unsteady. “How did you escape?”

“When we left the Cave, we stumbled into a gun battle at the bunkhouse. Red and I worked around behind the storage building until we ran out of ammunition. Then we escaped into the hedgerows.”

“But I found your gun. I thought you were … ”

“I dropped it when it was empty. We walked to the Villeneuve farm, and they hid us until Red could send me here. He had plans in place for you to see Guy, so all I had to do was get to Rennes and pose as Patrice. It was easy.”

Marguerite held up her hand. “They thought I was the *Milice* because someone claiming to be Patrice Cerne was already here.”

“I was afraid of that,” her cousin said quietly. “They find infiltrators all the time.”

“What happens when they find one?”

Bérénice shrugged. "They shoot them. They have no jails, and they can't afford to send them back to the Nazis."

"Is Richard here, too?"

"*Non*. He stayed behind to find you." She reached to touch Marguerite's scar. "That still looks pretty bad. Does it hurt?"

Marguerite ignored the question. "What is this place?"

"This is the headquarters for the *Saint Marcel Maquis*. When the invasion comes, the partisans here will be absorbed into the Free French Army. There's easily fifteen hundred of us here all the time. Free French commandos are training the partisans. José and I just received instruction on demolition."

"How can so many partisans be in one place inside occupied France?"

"It's a different war here. The Bretons are . . . different. Before the Occupation, they barely tolerated the French and they don't tolerate the Nazis at all. The Germans leave central Brittany alone, so we can operate more openly than we could in Normandy."

"Bérénice, tell me where Guy is."

"He's out on a mission. When I arrived yesterday, the news went around the camp that Patrice Cerne was here. Guy found me, but he was disappointed I wasn't you. It was all we could do to keep him here, so they sent him out on a mission. He should be back tonight."

"Could I get something to eat while I wait for him? I haven't eaten since yesterday."

"Come with me." José led them across the muddy field and through rows of tents to the main house, a two-story stone building with a grey slate roof and a long attached barn. The rain had stopped and the air smelled of pine and woodsmoke.

A tall man stepped out of the barn. "*Bonjour*, Guin," José called. "This is Marguerite Auriol. She's looking for Guy Massu. Marguerite, this is Guin Gwyer. He's in charge until more French commandos get here."

"Welcome to *Château Marneé*, Marguerite."

"*Merci*, Guin." He was young and handsome and he was holding a Sten submachine gun under his arm. Unruly brown hair peeked out from under his beret.

"Come into the barn," Guin said. "It's warm and dry in there."

Inside, she scanned the room where 20 or 30 long wooden tables were set up and a few hundred men and some women were eating. An open kitchen at the far end housed bubbling pots. To the left, 20 cots were arranged in four rows. A woman wandered among bandaged men, checking wounds.

Bérénice and Marguerite found an empty table and sat down. She gestured at the injured men on the cots. "Who are they?"

"Wounded *maquisards* from their raids on the Germans," her cousin explained.

José brought three bowls of stew and Marguerite began to eat with relish, then noticed a group of men gathered around the end of a table, listening to a radio. "José, what's that all about?"

"They're listening for the first alert."

"The first alert?"

"London will broadcast two alerts before the Allies invade France. The first alert is a general notice to Résistance organizations to get ready for whatever job London has assigned them. Then they will broadcast a series of second alerts, which cue specific groups to perform their pre-assigned jobs."

"Does *everyone* here have jobs to support the invasion?"

José laughed. "This is not the largest camp in Brittany. There are thirty to forty thousand armed partisans throughout Brittany."

"What are you assigned to do?"

"We're supposed to return to Normandy and work with the Résistance."

"We?"

"Guy has arranged for Bérénice and me to be smuggled back to Normandy by the same driver who brought you. Don't worry. There is plenty of room for you. We are to disrupt communications; our specific job will be assigned when we get there."

A bubble of joy welled up in her chest. She set down her fork because her hand was trembling. *Liberation is really coming, and I'm going to be part of it.* "José, how do we know when to listen for the alerts?"

"They come at the end of the six o'clock BBC French language broadcast. It's a five-minute segment with a stream of nonsense sentences like 'The tree is blown by the storm. The stew is ready. Three cows walk where horses ran.' Mixed in are prearranged signals to various Résistance organizations."

"Tell her about tonight," Bérénice prompted.

The dark Spaniard grinned. "Ah, of course. If the weather clears, we are to light a fire in a large field near here to signal a parachute drop from the British. We can always use another set of hands."

"Aren't there any Germans in the area?"

"*Non*. They leave us alone."

Marguerite finished her stew, and they left the barn to find that the shadows had deepened. They fell in with a stream of men and women headed down a trail to a clearing with a huge woodpile in the center. She blinked. "Are they going to burn that mountain of wood?"

"After it gets a little darker, they'll light three of them," José replied. "They form a triangle, so the planes can see the drop zone."

"But, *mon Dieu*, every German soldier for a hundred kilometers will see them!"

He shook his head. "Let's just say the Nazis in Brittany are more casual about security."

When the signal fires were lit, Marguerite drew close to the flames to absorb the heat and suddenly a cheer went up from the crowd. Allied planes roared overhead. People scattered to collect the parachutes as they drifted to the ground. Marguerite and Bérénice helped carry the metal canisters back to *Château Marneé*.

Back in camp, there was more excitement. Guy's group of partisans was returning.

CHAPTER TWENTY-SEVEN
THE SONG OF THE BANSHEE

Marguerite brushed the hay off her dress, slipped her gun in her pocket, and woke Bérénice to join José at breakfast. She sat down beside him and buttered a slice of coarse bread. "Is Guy back yet?"

"Not yet. He should be back this morning." He nodded to a woman collecting breakfast bowls from the injured men. "Marguerite, after breakfast I want to introduce you to Collette. She's in charge of our field hospital."

When they finished eating he guided her over to the woman. "Collette, this is Marguerite Auriol, the real Patrice Cerne."

"Oh!" The woman extended her hand. She was tall, in her twenties, and very striking, with red hair pulled back into a bun at her neck. The sleeves of her blue-flowered dress were rolled up above her elbows, and she wore an embroidered apron and heavy black shoes.

"I heard you were in camp," she said, her Breton accent apparent. "I have always wanted to meet you."

"Collette is the angel of *Château Marneé,*" Bérénice explained. "She tends the wounded."

"Can I help?" Marguerite asked.

"*Oui*, of course." She turned to José. "Could you leave Marguerite with me?"

He nodded, and Collette introduced her to each injured man and described his wounds. Marguerite explained that she had hospital emergency room experience, and for the rest of the morning she and Collette changed dressings and dispensed what medicine they had.

At noon a man in filthy trousers and a torn shirt rushed up to them. "Another injury is coming!" Marguerite's heart leaped into her throat. *It was Guy, she just knew it.*

Collette closed off a wooden table behind some burlap curtains, and a group of men carried in a tall man and laid him down. Marguerite peered down at the blackened face. *Not Guy, thank God.* All at once one of the bearers grabbed her shoulder and spun her around.

"Marguerite! Marguerite, what are you doing here?"

The injured man groaned.

"Guy! I have much to tell you, but it must wait."

He squeezed her hand and nodded. "I understand. Later, then."

Another hour passed, then two, as she and Collette labored over the wounded man. He had been shot in the fleshy part of his shoulder and something, or someone, had broken four of his ribs. They removed the bullet and bound his chest, and when he was finally stable, Marguerite stepped outside to find Guy.

She walked toward the barn, but before she had taken 20 steps, someone behind her shouted. "Marguerite!" Guy gathered her in his arms. "When Bérénice arrived, I wondered where you were. She said she left you in the Cave, but— "

"Richard had given me train tickets to Rennes, but getting here is a very long story."

"I have lots of time for a very long story, so tell me. Oh, Marguerite, I've been worried about you!" He pulled her close and kissed her. "Let's get some privacy."

He walked her to a secluded place in the woods, sat down on the ground, and pulled her onto his lap. Then he pressed his lips against her neck, her eyelids, behind her ear until she drew away. "Guy, stop. I need to talk."

She laid her head on his chest and told him everything, about the bomb at *Café Angéle*, killing Lastrange, her escape with Dr. Morel, everything. He listened in stunned silence. Finally he laid two fingers over her mouth.

"You seem very calm about all of this. Are you all right?"

She looked up at him. "I'm confused, Guy. So much has happened it's difficult to know who I am anymore."

"It's true. I see the difference in you."

"The worst part is I'm not sure I like what I am becoming."

"I think you have no choice, Marguerite. We are all changing. Bérénice told me how your face was scarred." He gently traced it with his fingertips.

"Do— do you think it is ugly?"

He tightened his arms around her. "*Non.* Nothing about you is ugly. Nothing at all. I wouldn't change anything about you." He kissed the top of her head. "Now, we need to talk about what's happening here."

She tilted her head back. "I had no idea about all these partisans here."

"I wrote you that Brittany is unusual, remember?"

"Guy, when do you think the Allies will invade? I'm anxious for it to start and afraid at the same time. Does that make sense?"

"It does. We've worked hard and waited so long, and now it's almost here. Do you know about the alert broadcast from London?"

"*Oui.* José told me."

"Last night I learned the first alert will be 'It is hot in the Suez'. When we hear that, the invasion will have begun. Our specific signal will be 'The arrow will not pierce'."

"What is our assignment?"

"I'm going back to Normandy with José to cut telephone lines. He's being trained in demolition."

"He and Bérénice were trained yesterday."

"Bérénice, too?"

She nodded. "*Oui.*"

"I asked to fight in Normandy because I thought you were there. If I don't survive, that's where— "

"Don't say such things. It's bad luck. Besides, I'm coming with you."

"*Non*, Marguerite. This isn't *Réfugié* work, this is combat. You and Bérénice should stay here where it's safe."

"We're no safer here than we would be in Normandy. Think, Guy! I've been in gun fights and I've assassinated Nazis and a police officer. You're being kind and wonderful but quite stupid." She brought his hand to her lips and kissed the knuckles. "You are not leaving here without me. Whatever happens, I want to be with you."

"*Non,* Marguerite."

"*Oui*, Guy. *Oui!* Now, do you know how we are getting back to Normandy?"

He sighed, "After the first alert, Robert will pick up José and me— "

"And Bérénice and me," she interrupted, her voice calm.

"He will drive us to an abandoned farm near Ville de Pommes to meet other partisans and get our instructions."

"With me and Bérénice," she said. She thought for a long minute. "Guy, what will we do if the invasion fails?"

"We will make sure it doesn't fail. We take one step at a time, as we have for the last four years. And Marguerite, when we hear the first alert, there will be a celebration here."

"A celebration? What kind of celebration?"

"When there's a parachute drop, they light these enormous signal fires. I swear to God, Hitler could see the glow from Berlin. When we get the first alert, there'll be a huge bonfire. It's a Breton thing, to take our mind off what's coming."

She moved closer to him. "It's time to take our minds off it, now." She reached to kiss him and began to unbutton his shirt.

* * *

Later, they walked to the barn for supper and found a place near the radio to hear the six o'clock broadcast from London. When the program ended, the litany of nonsense sentences began. Two minutes later came words that sent a chill up her spine.

"It is hot in the Suez."

A shout went up from the crowd and people started jabbering in Breton. Guy swung her off her feet and kissed her. "It's started. *Mon Dieu*, it's finally started!"

Men and women rushed everywhere, telling their teams to prepare. Collette found Marguerite and gave her a hug. "Can you believe it? The invasion has finally started. It's the end of this awful nightmare!"

A huge bonfire was laid in the clearing. Men threw planks, branches, logs, even old furniture onto the pile. Four men dragged a wooden platform forward, which Marguerite thought they would throw on top of the bonfire until she realized it was a makeshift stage.

Trucks and horse-drawn carts began to arrive, and as the sun slipped below the horizon the crowd swelled. When it grew dark, she and Guy found a spot near the tower of firewood and watched four men toss burning torches onto it. The flames sent sparks into the sky, and a piper inflated his bagpipe and began walking through the crowd, playing and replaying a haunting tune.

"What's he doing?" Marguerite asked.

"All Bretons within earshot are supposed to answer the pipes."

When the bagpipe quieted, a fiddle started, and the crowd began clapping in time. Suddenly the fiddle stopped and the audience grew quiet. Guin stepped onto the stage and began to speak in Breton.

"Guy, do you understand what he's saying?"

"Some. Let's see . . . we all have to do our job, then something about fighting for our mothers, wives, and daughters."

"What about fighting for our fathers, husbands, and brothers?"

Guy grinned at her. "Then there's a part I don't understand."

The crowd let out a cheer. "Now he wants us to make, uh, sacrifices, I guess, and something about the holy…" Guy shook his head. "…maybe sacred soil of Brittany and France."

Guin finished, threw his hands in the air, and the crowd roared. He stepped off the platform and the fiddle started again, accompanied by drums. All at once Marguerite heard a bone-chilling sound from deep in the woods. "What was that?"

"Unless I'm mistaken, it's the cry of the banshee. It's more an Irish tradition than Breton. The banshee is a ghost with a loving relationship with a family; it comes to reassure them or to announce the imminent death of someone."

A shiver went up her spine. She didn't want to think about death.

A tall, elegant woman in a flowing white dress and long blonde hair rippling down past her shoulders floated onto the stage. She carried herself so her body didn't appear to move, so she looked like an apparition gliding over the earth. When she reached the stage she began to sing, and Guy translated for Marguerite.

"Death comes to you . . . receive the gift . . . and finally rest."

The strange song filled Marguerite with a chilling sense of foreboding. She watched the woman glide off the stage and melt into the woods; the fiddler followed until the music faded into silence.

Marguerite clutched Guy's hand and began to cry.

"Marguerite? What's wrong?" He touched her shoulder.

She pushed his hand away. "I'm afraid. I wonder if the banshee came to tell me someone I love will die."

"*Non*, Marguerite. It's only a folk tale. Come on. Let's go have some Breton calvados. That's different here, too." They followed the crowd to the barn and lined up at a table with various size jars of clear liquid. She held out her glass, received three fingers of liquor, and took it outside. José, Bérénice, and Guy got their rations and followed her into the darkness.

Guy offered a toast. "To friends, family, and France. May God protect us."

"*Vive la France!*"

"*Vive la France!*"

Marguerite took a swallow and the liquid burned her throat all the way to her stomach. She sputtered and coughed, then straightened up and tried to pull air into her lungs. *"Merde!"*

"They like it stronger than we do," Guy explained. "They age it in fruit jars instead of oak barrels, and not for very long."

"Has this stuff ever seen an apple? It could have been made from potatoes."

"It is made from apples."

"Why is it so strong?"

"They distill it until it's eighty to ninety percent pure alcohol."

"Mon Dieu!"

"Have another sip."

She had to admit it warmed her, but after only half of her ration, the woods began to spin. "I'm getting dizzy. I need to be clear-headed for tomorrow, so I'm going to bed."

She shook the cobwebs out of her brain and found her place in the loft. As she waited for sleep she thought about what was about to come and how frightened she was underneath. The banshee had predicted a death; could it be her own? Even if it was, she could not let fear rule her actions. She fingered Dr. Morel's St. Anthony medal around her neck and made a vow.

I will do whatever it takes, give whatever it costs, to bring liberation to France.

CHAPTER TWENTY-EIGHT
THE FIRST STRIKE FOR LIBERATION

Marguerite felt someone prod her awake. "Wake up," Bérénice whispered. "It's morning. We have work to do."

Marguerite shook the fuzziness out of her brain, pulled on her worn blue dress, and searched for her pistol. Her body felt sluggish and her head ached, but she ignored it. Today she was going to be part of the first strike for Liberation, and a wave of exhilaration swept through her. Soon France would be free and life would be the way it was before the Occupation.

She stopped short and sucked in her breath. *Ah, non, it would never be the way it was before. Everything was different. She was different.* Something inside her had changed.

Guy was waiting for her in the barn. "Are you ready for today?"

She kissed him and sat down next to him at the table. "I am, *oui*. I am more than ready."

Outside they met José and Bérénice, who sported new black berets and carried Sten submachine guns. Bérénice presented Marguerite with a beret and José offered Stens to both Guy and herself. She noticed that her cousin wore a ragged pair of dark trousers and a man's shirt. "This is my uniform now," she announced.

"But I have only my dress. Should I-- ?"

"*Non*. After our missions we are supposed to blend in with the civilians in Normandy. Keep your dress."

Marguerite smiled and pulled on her beret. "Where are the cable cutters?

And aren't we supposed to have explosives?"

"They were parachuted into Normandy months ago and hidden," José explained. "We'll retrieve them when we get our assignments."

Guy showed Marguerite how to aim and fire her Sten while it was slung under her arm. Just as she mastered the technique, their driver, Robert, arrived. He shook Guy's hand. "What happened to the imposter I delivered claiming to be Patrice Cerne?"

Guy jerked his thumb over his shoulder where Marguerite and Bérénice stood side by side, their Stens dangling under their shoulders.

Robert's bushy eyebrows went up. "There are two of you?"

"I am the real Patrice Cerne," Marguerite said. "This is my cousin, Bérénice Auriol. She used Patrice's name to reach *Château Marneé.*"

Robert started to smile, but it faded as a series faint of booms echoed from the north.

"We must go," Guy exclaimed. "Marguerite and Bérénice are coming with us, Robert. We need to find room."

"For two Patrice Cernes? It is an honor!"

"What shall we do with the Stens?" asked Marguerite.

"Remove the ammunition clip and the stock and store them under the seat," Guy said. "Now, let's go."

Robert opened the back of the truck and José and Bérénice climbed in, then he closed the cargo door while Marguerite and Guy got into the cab next to him. They broke down and stored the guns. Robert started the truck and rumbled down the road. The way was clogged with automobiles, trucks, horse-drawn carts, and heavy foot traffic moving in both directions, so he had to drive very slowly. Marguerite grew increasingly anxious that they would miss their rendezvous.

The truck crawled forward for the next two hours, and then they heard a series of distant explosions. "What is that?" Marguerite asked.

"The Allies," Robert answered. "They've been bombing along the French seacoast for weeks. I will stay away from the coast for as long as I can, but once I turn north, we'll have to be careful . . . and lucky."

Marguerite shuddered. *We should have planned this better.*

They drove past the outskirts of Le Mans and turned north toward Normandy. The explosions grew louder and more frequent, and now the traffic included German convoys using their horns to demand that civilian traffic get out of their way. Columns of troop transports and an occasional line of tanks plowed through the crooked lane jammed with civilian vehicles.

Suddenly Marguerite spotted four small Allied planes overhead. They banked, leveled off, and dove directly at the military caravan in front of them.

"Get out!" Marguerite screamed. "Get out!"

They scrambled out just as a carpet of bombs exploded half a kilometer ahead. She flattened herself in a field beside the road and then realized that her cousin and José were still in the back of the truck. "Bérénice," she shouted.

She started to get up, but Guy yanked her down and covered her with his body. Allied fighters screamed overhead and their bombs shook the earth beneath her. The pilots found their marks and secondary explosions came from the Nazi trucks on the road ahead.

She struggled out from under Guy. "Bérénice and José are still in the truck!"

"We can't reach them now," he yelled. "Too many Germans."

"We must! They'll be killed."

Miraculously the planes roared away and the German soldiers emerged from the trucks to inspect the damage caused by the planes. Robert started the truck, drove into a small farmyard partially hidden from the crowded road, and parked behind a barn. Guy got out and rolled up the cargo door. A shaken Bérénice and José scrambled out.

He and Robert then jogged back out to the roadway to survey the damage. "There is no way around all those bombed vehicles," Guy said. "We've got to go back."

Robert agreed.

"We'll all have to ride in the cab together," Guy instructed. They crowded in, Marguerite on Guy's lap and Bérénice perched on José's. Once more Robert climbed in behind the steering wheel, drove south to avoid the damaged convoy, and again turned toward Normandy. Bombs exploded around them. Then they entered a fog bank and slowed some more.

Late in the morning Robert growled, "We're getting close to Ville de Pommes. Where's your meeting place?"

"The abandoned Asselin farm. Drop us here. We'll circle around and walk in from the back, just in case there's any trouble." They climbed out, reassembled the Stens, and watched Robert drive away.

"We're late," Guy said. "We should have been at the meeting place hours ago."

They trekked through the thickening fog, Guy leading them from field to field and staying out of sight of the road. The air smelled of smoke with an underpinning of cordite from the bombs the Allies dropped all over the area. Guy peeked over the top of a berm, then signaled them to get down and keep quiet. The fog gradually turned to rain.

Marguerite peered over the hedge and saw a stone shed, too small to be called a barn, but big enough for nine or ten people to meet. The structure stood in one corner of a slightly sunken field. Hedgerows surrounded it. Cars, trucks, and horse-drawn carts were parked at random around the building, but it was unnaturally still. She could see no people.

"Something's wrong," Guy whispered. "It's too quiet. We're supposed to meet in that old shed, but I don't see any lookouts. There should be a guard posted at each hedge opening on this side of the field."

"If anyone is in the shed, they're being held hostage," José said in a low voice. "I smell a trap. There may be German guards on the other side."

Guy nodded. "Let's split up and scout the perimeter. You and Bérénice go along the left side of the field to the far edge. Marguerite, come with me. We'll go up the right side. Meet back here in fifteen minutes."

They crept in opposite directions, moving slowly and screened by hedges. Suddenly Marguerite clutched Guy's arm and they froze. Two German soldiers were hidden, facing away from them, watching the gap in the hedges on the far side of the field. Guy signaled Marguerite, and they retreated to the meeting place. After some minutes, José and Bérénice returned.

"German troops are lying in ambush on the left, watching the hedge opening on the far side," José reported

"How many?"

"Six, I think."

"Two more on the right. We have to assume our friends are in the shed, probably guarded by at least six more soldiers."

"What should we do?"

Guy paused and set his jaw. "We're over an hour late for the meeting, and the Nazis won't be expecting anyone walking in from this direction. Our job is to cause as much trouble for them as we can."

Marguerite pressed her lips together. "What do you suggest?"

"At some point, they're going to move their prisoners out of that building. A couple of guards will probably come out first, then the prisoners, then the rest of the guards. Two of us should circle around to the other side, and when they move the prisoners out and the last guard exits, we start shooting."

"What about the other soldiers?" José asked. "The ones guarding the hedge openings? When they hear gunfire, they'll come running."

"Exactly. You two go to the other side of the shed and fire a few short bursts at the Germans guarding the prisoners as they come out. Try not to hit any of the partisans. As soon as the other soldiers hear the shooting, they'll head for the shed and we'll open up from both sides."

"What about the partisans?" asked Bérénice.

"They'll be out in the open and they'll know what to do. Fire one clip each, then get away from the field as fast as you can. From there, everyone's on their own. Let's go!"

Marguerite went up one side of the field, found a hole in the hedge, and motioned for Guy to join her. He nodded, and she unslung her Sten. Then they waited. She wondered why she wasn't more frightened.

At last the shed door creaked open and an armed guard emerged. After him filed a single line of bereted civilians, their hands in the air. Marguerite chose her target, the first guard. Her heart pounded and she fought the impulse to fire too soon. Finally the last uniformed soldier emerged and closed the shed door.

She squeezed off a short burst. The lead guard crumpled to the ground and she turned her gun on the soldiers running toward them from the far side of the field. Guy's Sten opened up on her left.

Another guard went down, along with two of the partisans. One wounded soldier managed to get up and limp toward the hedges; a partisan pulled the revolver away from a downed guard, put another round into him, and then killed the escaping soldier.

Muzzle flashes sparked on the opposite side of the field and Marguerite heard return fire coming from the Germans. She reloaded her Sten, emptied it, and then drew her pistol.

The partisans scattered in every direction, some to their vehicles. Engines roared to life and cars and trucks headed for the opening in the hedgerow, with German soldiers firing at their backs. Marguerite touched Guy's shoulder. "Let's get out of here."

They dashed away from the shed and raced across a second field, through a hedge opening, and then across another field. As they got farther away, the sound of gunfire faded. They ran until she heard no more gunfire, crossed another field, and found a footpath between two hedgerows. The rain poured down. The trail was too narrow for a cart, much less a car or truck. Panting, they followed it into yet another field.

The wind picked up. Out of breath, they staggered to a stop and collapsed onto the wet ground. Rain slashed at their faces, and their shoes were filled with water. They huddled together in silence, watching the field behind them to see if they were followed. Marguerite couldn't stop shivering.

Finally they decided they were alone. "Isn't it wonderful to be a part of a well-executed plan?" Marguerite said sarcastically through chattering teeth. "What shall we do next?"

CHAPTER TWENTY-NINE
ESCAPE

Marguerite pulled off her beret, wrung it out, and slapped it back on her head. "Do you think London has broadcast our second alert yet?"

Guy shrugged. "Who knows? I have no idea where we are, but I think Ville de Pommes is in that direction." He tipped his head to the right just as a bolt of lightning flashed, followed by a deafening clap of thunder. They crouched under dense hedges that offered only partial shelter from the downpour.

"We have to get out of this storm," she shouted. "Instead of Ville de Pommes, maybe we should find Perdu and the Cave?"

Guy nodded. "Good idea. We'll stay warmer if we're moving." They stood up and began walking west. The downpour grew heavier, soaking their clothes until they stuck to their skin, but they kept moving. Gradually the countryside grew more familiar. They slogged through another muddy field and suddenly Marguerite gripped Guy's sleeve.

"Look! The path to the Cave!"

"I see it. Let's pray it's not full." She was so cold and wet she almost didn't care. At least it would be shelter.

At the entrance Guy stopped and cautiously pulled the door open far enough to see inside. They felt their way along the tunnel to the inner door, and when Marguerite switched on her flashlight, she stared in wonder. Everything was exactly as she had left it.

"There are lanterns and matches upstairs," she said. "I'll get them." She found a kerosene lantern and a stack of dry towels. She threw one to Guy and set the lantern on a table. "I'm going back upstairs to change out of these wet things."

She hung up her wet dress and jacket, found a dry nightshirt, and went back down the stairs barefoot. Guy stared at her for a long moment. "Marguerite, you're beautiful."

She touched her head. "Ah, *non*. My hair is soaking wet."

He stepped in close and touched her shoulder. "Your wet hair is beautiful, too. But what's this?" He lifted the medal that hung around her neck.

"Dr. Morel gave it to me. It's a St. Anthony medal. He gave it to me because it was special to him."

"Morel is fond of you, I think." Gently he stroked his forefinger along the scar on her face.

She flinched away. "Don't touch that. It makes me feel disfigured."

"*Non*. Cervantes said that wounds received in battle bestow honor, they do not take it away. Don't shrink from it. You should be proud." Very slowly he bent his head to kiss the mark.

Marguerite kissed him back. "I love you."

"I know," he said quietly. "Are you cold?"

"And exhausted."

"We should try to get some sleep. Tomorrow may be worse than today."

She touched his shoulder. "When do think the storm will end?"

He laughed softly. "Do you care?"

"*Non*. Not as long as I am with you, I don't care."

Without a word, Guy pulled two mattresses together, piled blankets on top, and blew out the lamp. "Come to bed, Marguerite. Being together will keep us warm."

They clung to each other in the darkness, listening to the storm outside. "When this is over," he whispered, "I never want to be apart from you."

Her throat tightened into an ache. "I pray it will end soon, Guy. I want France to be free, and I want us to be together."

* * *

A clap of thunder awakened her. Guy was still asleep, so she slipped out of his arms into the chilly air and lit the lantern. His damp shirt hung over a chair and on impulse she put it on. It was cold at first, but her body warmed it. It would be dry before he woke up. She rolled the sleeves up to her elbows, crept downstairs, and cracked open the outer door.

The sky was grey as slate. Surely the invasion would not take place today. She turned back to Guy and the safety of the Cave.

He was awake, just pulling on his pants. "Where's my shirt?"

"Here." She pointed at her chest. "I'm drying it for you."

An odd expression crossed his face and he moved toward her, slipped his hands inside the shirt, and smoothed his fingers over her skin. Very deliberately he slipped the buttons free, spread the garment wide, and let it fall to the floor. He looked into her eyes. "You know, this is my only shirt." He ran his hand over her bare shoulders and down her arms.

She looked up at him. "Sooner or later," she whispered, "we must leave here and rejoin our mission."

"I agree," he murmured. "I choose later."

* * *

Marguerite opened her eyes and stared up at the ceiling. Many people had found safety here, but she had never appreciated the Cave more than she did at this moment. She smiled. With Guy she had found more than safety.

Guy rolled onto his side and kissed her slowly. "What are you thinking about?"

"I'm thinking it's ironic that to live free means we must risk death. Does everything worthwhile in life cost so much?"

"I don't know the answer to that, Marguerite. I only know that what we have together is worth fighting for."

She gave him a long look. "What should we do next?"

"We got the first alert from London, so we know the invasion has started. We didn't hear last night's broadcast and we won't hear tonight's, either. But I know what our mission is."

"Tell me," she said.

"We are to cut the telephone lines south of Cabourg. But we were supposed to get cable cutters and a map at the meeting yesterday, so now we have to get to Cabourg and connect with their Résistance."

She considered that for a moment. "We should start for Cabourg after the storm."

The storm broke mid-morning. Marguerite slipped her handgun into her pocket and they loaded their Stens. "How are we going to reach Cabourg?"

"I gave that some thought last night," Guy said. "Nobody stops or questions the displaced people walking on the roads. If we break down the Stens and wrap them up, maybe to look like a baby, we might get through."

"A mother would also have a bag for the baby," Marguerite pointed out. "We can put food and ammunition in it."

When they finished packing, Marguerite stepped outside and gazed at the fields, so fresh and green in the early June sunlight. Thousands of Allied planes droned overhead, and from every direction came the sound of bomb explosions. *Mon Dieu. Are they English? American? Who are they dropping their bombs on?*

Close to Cabourg, the foot traffic suddenly thinned and Marguerite began to grow uneasy. Then they rounded a curve and saw a heavily guarded roadblock.

"What should we do?" she whispered.

"Go back," Guy ordered.

But it was too late. One of the guards waved them forward. Marguerite clutched her bundle. "We can't get caught with the Stens."

They turned away from the roadblock, but a shout from behind stopped them. "*Halt. Halt!*" A dark grey military transport truck with an iron cross painted on the door thundered past, then braked in front of them. Six soldiers piled out, pointing their rifles.

Marguerite's throat went dry.

A red-faced officer stepped down from the truck. "What are you doing here?" he demanded.

"We are on our way to Cabourg," Guy answered calmly.

"To my *maman's* home," Marguerite added.

"There was heavy Résistance activity here last night," the officer snarled. He studied Marguerite. "What are you hiding there?" He gestured to the bundle in her arms.

"My…my baby. She's asleep."

"May I take a look?"

Marguerite shrank away from him. "Please don't disturb her. The airplanes and the bombs make her cry, but she is asleep now."

"Don't worry, I won't disturb her." He stepped in close.

Her mind raced. There were too many of them to use their pistols. She turned away, but the officer grabbed her arm. She struggled to break free until a soldier stepped behind her and nudged her with his gun barrel. The officer peeled back the blanket and jerked at the sight of the disassembled Stens.

"Hands in the air, both of you!" One of the soldiers searched them, found their handguns, and tossed them on the ground next to the truck.

"You Résistance scum," the officer barked. "Kneel! Keep your hands on your head!" He unholstered his Luger and circled them slowly without speaking. Each time he passed behind Marguerite, she thought she would scream. He could shoot them here and now and no one would ever know.

"We need only one of you to talk. That makes the other one superfluous, but which one? Who wants to speak?" He stopped behind Guy and waited.

The silence roared in her ears. "Leave her alone," Guy shouted. "She knows nothing. I'll tell you everything, just let her go."

"*Nein.*" The officer laughed. "In Germany, we are gentlemen. Always the ladies are first." He pressed the muzzle of his gun to the base of her brain. She squeezed her eyes shut and waited. *There will be no pain,* she thought. *Only a light that will take me to Papa.*

The gun dug into her neck. "What do you have to say?"

All at once she was completely calm. It was over. No more hiding. No more killing. No more pain. She would die now, as the banshee had foretold. A feeling of serenity came over here. Her girlhood, her life, was over.

She reached for her St. Anthony medal. "I have something for you."

"What is it?" he asked suspiciously.

Without looking back at him, she removed the medal from around her neck and held it out. "It's a St. Anthony medal. St. Anthony is the Patron Saint of Lost Causes," she explained. "I thought it was for me, but perhaps it's actually for you. "

"That is just like you French papists," he hissed. "You terrorize the countryside. You lie, cheat, kidnap, and murder and then you offer me some useless piece of metal. I need to remind you that I have the gun and you are on your knees. You need this medal more than I do."

"Take it," Marguerite insisted, her voice calm.

"*Nein,*" he shouted. "You need to— "

A submachine gun erupted and the officer's words were cut off. Two German soldiers on her left crumpled, and Marguerite and Guy instinctively flattened themselves on the ground. She had been prepared to die, but now . . . Now she wanted to live. She wanted to cut telephone wires and help to free France!

The four remaining Germans began returning fire. Four shadows began running away through the hedges to the left.

"Go get them," thundered the officer. "You stay with me."

Three of the soldiers started after the gunmen. After they disappeared into the hedgerows the firing slowly became fainter. Then two dark figures walked through a hedge opening on the right, their hands raised. Looking into the bright sun, Marguerite couldn't see them clearly. One was short, a woman, she realized as they drew closer. The other was a man wearing a black beret.

"We surrender!"

When she saw their faces Marguerite gasped. Bérénice and José! They exchanged a silent look but did not kneel. Almost imperceptibly Bérénice tipped her head toward the soldier closest to her. José edged near the officer, then abruptly took two quick steps and launched a well-placed kick at him. Bérénice attacked the other.

Both Germans fell. Guy and Marguerite snatched up their weapons, and José fired a short burst into the back of each soldier, then motioned to them. "Follow us."

They ran across three fields and through the bordering hedges to a small stone house at the far side of yet another field.

"How did you find us?" Marguerite panted at the building entrance.

"We thought you would try to reach Cabourg," Bérénice explained as they entered. "We knew you had to come this way, so we waited at the roadblock. We had one team draw most of the Germans off to the left, and José and I came from the right."

"Well," a male voice boomed from the rear of the room. "You're with us again."

"Richard!" Marguerite threw her arms around his solid body. "Red, I can't believe it's really you."

He frowned. "Are you all right?"

"I think so. I thought we were both dead back there."

"And you, Guy? Are you all right?"

"I am. Now I'm ready for anything."

"This is our command post," Richard said, suddenly all business. "When it gets dark we'll go out in pairs to cut telephone lines and destroy railroad tracks and bridges."

"Did we get the second alert?" asked Marguerite.

"*Oui*, last night."

"Could Guy and I be one of the teams?"

Richard nodded. "I didn't know if you would find us, so I didn't count on you. Guy, look at this." He unfolded a map and pointed to a marked area to the south. "The two of you could move south and west and cut these three lines, here. Start with this one. It's the main trunk line from the beaches to the Ville de Pommes communications center. Other teams are cutting the lines around the town to isolate the military headquarters." He shot Guy a quick look. "Do you know the difference between a power line and a telephone line?"

"*Oui*."

"*Bon*. Because the first telephone pole you encounter will have power lines on it as well. Cut the first line, then go west across here . . ." He tapped his forefinger on the map ". . . and cut this line, here."

Guy nodded.

"And if you can," Richard went on, "cut this third line, here. José and Bérénice will be with you. Keep moving west until you come to these railroad tracks, but stay out of sight. If the Germans see you up on a telephone pole, they'll shoot."

Guy nodded. "Where are the cable cutters?"

"With the guns and ammunition. We've been collecting material here for weeks." He pried up two floorboards to reveal cable cutters, explosives, guns, and ammunition. Richard pointed at the cache. "The handguns are behind the ammunition boxes."

Marguerite reached in, located half a dozen Sten clips, and handed them to Guy. The cable cutters were too cumbersome and heavy to lift.

"José, come over here." They all crowded around and Richard again pointed at the map. "Your mission is to demolish this railroad bridge, here. A straight section of track crosses the ravine and continues north to the coast. Between the edge of the ravine and this road here, oak trees and thick brush hide your approach. It's the best place we could find to set explosive charges on the tracks. Your team will come from the east through this hedgerow field. When you get to the western edge, hold up and check for sentries."

José bent closer to the map and frowned. "Sentries? Where will they be, on the bridge?"

Richard nodded. "Be careful. Military trains use this bridge to bring troops and supplies to the coast. Guy, while you're cutting the telephone lines José and Bérénice will be your cover." He darted a glance at Marguerite. "Remember that the Germans operate trains at night. Don't get caught out on the bridge with a train coming. There is only one set of tracks on the bridge and nothing else, no road, no walkway, so there is no way to avoid a train except to climb over the side until it passes. It's dangerous because the bridge will shake, and we don't want you tossed off and into the ravine."

Marguerite gripped her hands tight together. "When do the trains run?"

"They operate sporadically. We tried to get hold of their schedule, but they keep them well guarded and they change constantly. Lately we've had a little too much success in ambushing military targets," he said dryly.

"How do we help José and Bérénice?" Guy asked.

"Shoot any soldiers on the bridge. When it's clear, José will set the explosive charges from the British." He surveyed them with unsmiling eyes. "Is everyone agreed?"

"Agreed," Guy and José answered in unison.

Marguerite located two .45 caliber handguns and two magazines. Then the four of them sat outside studying Richard's map, waiting for nightfall. Partisans dribbled in from the fields. Richard met each of them at the door, asked if anyone was hurt, and formed more teams, mixtures of *Réfugié* and OCM members.

Allied bombs continued to explode around them, some close enough to make Marguerite jump. As darkness fell, the tins of black grease came out and everyone coated their faces and hands. Then Richard stood before them.

"We have waited four years for this day. After you complete your assignments, meet in the town of Saint Annellet-sur-Mer, at the intersection of Route de Port-en-Bessin and Route de Fornginy."

His gaze rested on each of them for a moment. "May God be with you. *Vive la France*."

"*Vive la France*," the teams chorused.

Richard turned and thrust his Sten into the air. "This is our time."

CHAPTER THIRTY
PAYING THE PRICE

June 5, 1944

The teams smeared their faces with black grease and moved out in all directions. Marguerite and her team hiked east toward the telephone lines, listening in growing unease to the shells exploding in the distance. They avoided paved roads, railroad tracks, and towns, where the Allies were dropping tons of bombs. Occasionally the flaming tails of rockets streaked toward some distant target.

It was tough going in the dark fields, squeezing through hedges in the thick blackness while avoiding German patrols. Spotlights lit the undersides of thousands of lumbering bombers and agile fighters. All around them echoed the crack of artillery, the drone of aircraft engines, anti-aircraft bursts, the swoosh of rockets, and earth-shaking bomb explosions. Machine gun fire erupted from the fighters overhead, which was answered by anti-aircraft fire from the ground.

They slogged across pastures where the mud was so dense Marguerite's boots made a sucking sound at every step. Each time a bomb detonated near them, they flung themselves face down on the ground. She was muddy and sticky and full of both fear and resolve. *I hope we can cut these lines before we get killed.*

The first telephone line bordered a deserted road, and Marguerite gasped when she saw it. She craned her neck to peer up the 25-meter-high wooden pole. "Are all four of those wires telephone lines?"

"*Non*," Guy said, his voice tense. "Three are power lines. If I touch the wrong one, I'll be electrocuted."

Marguerite caught her breath. "Then how do you know which one to cut?"

"The three lines connected to glass insulators are power lines. The telephone line is the one without insulators." He dropped the cable cutters and his Sten, drew his .45, and held it down at his side. "I'm going to have to shoot the insulators and bring down the power lines."

"Someone will hear us!" she warned.

"Not with all these explosions going on around us."

He raised his revolver, took careful aim, and fired. The insulator shattered, and the first line snaked to the ground. The second line fell, and when it touched the already downed line, a white flash blinded her. Both lines writhed on the ground and then lay still.

Guy snatched the cable cutters and quickly snipped each one, then shinnied up the pole and squeezed the cutters on the telephone cable. Marguerite heard a snap and the line drifted down.

"José, I'm going to cut a segment out of the cable," Guy explained when he descended. "We'll drag it into the woods and hide it so the Nazis can't easily repair it." At the next pole he again clambered up and severed the line. José grabbed one end and Guy the other, and they dragged it into the woods.

All around them Marguerite saw the glow of fires, and the spotlights illuminating the undersides of the slow-moving Allied bombers were mesmerizing. Occasionally one plane burst into flames and she watched, horrified, as it fell out of the sky and plummeted toward the ground, trailing fire. This was followed by a giant burst of light at it hit the earth. *So much death!*

"Let's get to the next line," Guy ordered. They stumbled across field after sodden field and after another half hour, they found the next pole. This one would be easier to cut because it was located underneath the power lines, but the lines paralleled the nearby road, which was heavily traveled.

Once again Guy climbed the pole, but just as he opened the jaws of the cable cutter, Marguerite heard a truck engine. "Someone's coming!" she yelled.

Everyone but Guy scrambled to grab their Stens and the backpack full of explosives and dive into the thick brush. Above them, Guy hugged the pole. *Mon Dieu, if they see him they will shoot.* She lay in the undergrowth and readied her Sten with shaking hands.

A German staff car drove by, followed by three military transports. The trucks whined past them, but the last of the transports slowed to a stop on the shoulder of the road. Marguerite held her breath.

An officer got out and issued orders to his men. "Two of you get up this road to the railroad tracks," he barked. "Follow the tracks to the bridge and stay there to guard against saboteurs. Shoot to kill!"

Two privates dropped down out of the back of one truck, jogged up the road, and vanished. The rest of the troops climbed out and walked about aimlessly, stretching their legs. Over their heads, Guy clung to the telephone pole.

Sweat dampened Marguerite's shoulder blades. *God help him if he's captured.* After an agonizing delay, the soldiers piled back in the truck. The driver started the engine, pulled back onto the road, and sped off to catch up with the rest of the caravan.

Guy then cut a section from the line overhead and let it drop to the ground, where José and Bérénice dragged it to the ravine. "Now," he said when he rejoined them, "we go due west to find the third line."

They circled back into the wet fields and after half an hour came upon the last line. Guy cut it, and Marguerite did a little dance. *We did it! We cut all three telephone lines!*

Guy dropped his cable cutters and turned to José. "From up on the pole I could see the railroad bridge. It's not too far that way." He pointed into the darkness.

They hiked to the gorge at the edge of a field and followed the ravine until the bridge loomed ahead of them in the moonlight. The wooden trestle spanned a deep canyon, and the railroad tracks cut between two hedgerows with thick brush and scrub oaks on both sides. They crept up to the hedgerow bordering the tracks and spread themselves flat on the berm.

Marguerite peeked through the vegetation at the bridge. It had been repaired recently; a section of the wood looked new and it smelled of creosote.

"Demolishing any one of the supporting timbers will start a chain reaction," José whispered. "That will collapse the entire bridge."

Guy pointed. "And look! Richard was right. The tracks are the only thing on top of the bridge. No roads or maintenance walkways on either side."

"Right," José muttered. "Setting the charges will be dangerous."

Marguerite squinted to see through the dark. "I don't see the guards."

"Over there," Bérénice said in a low voice.

The tiny red glow of a cigarette moved erratically up and down. An air burst above illuminated two dark, helmeted figures smoking at the side of the bridge closest to them. The opposite side was too far away to see any guards.

"What do we do about the guards?" she murmured.

Guy touched her shoulder and the four huddled together. "José, take Bérénice and make your way down to the north end of these hedgerows. I'll squeeze through here and shake some brush to distract them."

José nodded and shouldered his backpack.

"Marguerite, cover me, but watch the tracks to see that José and Bérénice get across the rails and through those hedgerows on the other side. Once they're safely across, tap me on the shoulder."

"What do we do then?"

"You and I will draw the guards away while José sets the charges and Bérénice rigs the detonator. José, work your way up on the far side of those hedges. We'll give you ten minutes to get safely across the tracks and then we'll draw the guards away."

José gave a thumbs up and he and Bérénice quietly slipped away. When they reached the north end of the hedgerow, José waved, struggled through the hedge, and disappeared. Guy crawled forward on his belly and shook the bushes. The two soldiers tossed down their cigarettes and peered into the darkness.

"We've got their attention," he breathed.

José and Bérénice stole unobserved across the tracks and into the brush, and Marguerite moved to Guy's side and tapped his shoulder. "What now?" she whispered.

"We split up and I'll attract the guards' attention again. When they come within range, we cut them down. If there are guards on the other side of the bridge, they will charge across and make easy targets."

Marguerite's heart thumped under her jacket. Guy signaled for her to crawl some distance away and hide in the brush, and then he spoke in a loud voice. "We can blow it from here."

Both sentries swung toward them, and now Guy whispered audibly, "Philippe, watch out for the guards."

The sentries crouched, separated, and advanced toward them from two directions. When the closest man moved past her less than 20 meters away, she stood up, fired a short burst, and dropped back to the ground. The soldier crumpled in his tracks.

Guy fired his Sten, but the second sentry had retreated to cover. Then a burst of gunfire came from the other side of the tracks, and the sentry fell into the ravine. Bérénice stood up and waved.

They all gathered on the north end of the bridge. Marguerite watched the other side for more soldiers, but none came. José stood ready with a lump of doughy plastique explosive in his hand; Bérénice uncoiled a wheel of thin wire as he moved away from her.

"José, I'll cover you as you place the charges," Guy called.

Both men walked out onto the bridge between the rails, Guy in front with his Sten and José following with the plastique. They stepped from railroad tie to railroad tie until they reached the third wooden support from the end of the trestle, and then José went down on all fours and disappeared over the side.

Suddenly Marguerite heard the faint sound of a train in the distance. Horrified, she stood up and stepped onto the bridge. "A train is coming!"

Across the ravine, smoke puffed from a locomotive engine as it chugged around a curve and headed toward the bridge. Guy eased himself over the side so the train could pass, but at that moment an odd sound overhead caught Marguerite's attention. She looked up to see two small flaming rockets streaking toward the ravine. Just as the locomotive steamed onto the bridge, two tremendous explosions rocked the trestle.

"Get off the bridge!" she shouted. "They're bombing the train!"

Another pair of rockets streaked toward the engine. One exploded on the ravine wall, the other on the crossing support timber 20 meters below the engine.

The train kept coming. Guy and José scrambled onto the tracks and started to run to safety. Marguerite raced to the end of the bridge, gripping her Sten, but she could do nothing. The locomotive was gaining on them. *Oh, God, they won't make it.*

A panting Bérénice joined her just as two more rockets hit another support. The trestle shuddered. One set of timbers snapped in two and smacked into the adjacent support, setting off a chain reaction. The entire bridge began to buckle. The tracks dipped toward the collapsing structure, and the railroad cars slowly tipped sideways toward the ravine.

The steam engine was almost on top of Guy and José, but as she watched, the locomotive slowed almost to a stop and then rolled backward as the bridge began to buckle and twist. With a groan that became a roar, the remaining supports snapped like matchsticks, and the entire bridge tumbled into the ravine.

Like a cat clawing to get over a wall, the locomotive wheels spun as, one by one, the boxcars fell into the ravine, dragging the engine backward. At the last instant, Guy and José dove forward and grabbed the last railroad tie.

Marguerite and Bérénice plunged forward to grasp their wrists. While the two men dangled at the edge of the gorge, the entire trestle and the locomotive engine vanished into a cloud of steam on the ravine floor.

Guy and José scrambled up onto the severed railroad tracks and the four of them stared into the canyon, watching the steam dissipate and the glowing red coals from the engine's firebox scatter across the ravine floor.

Suddenly brakes screeched behind them and a guttural German voice shouted. "*Halt!*"

CHAPTER THIRTY-ONE
CAPTURED

"Quick," Guy whispered. "You two go that way, we'll go this way." Bérénice and José disappeared into the brush across the tracks, and Guy snatched up his Sten. They crouched low and crawled back to concealment behind the hedgerows. A moment later she heard the short blast of a submachine gun.

She clutched Guy's arm. "We have to go back."

"*Non*. We need to get out of here."

"We can't leave them!" She started back toward the bridge but Guy grabbed her shoulder. "*Non!* We must think of the mission."

"The mission's done," she snapped. "They might need us."

"We don't know that." He dragged her away and began to push her ahead of him away from the ravine, working their way alongside a hedgerow. Roaming spotlights pierced the dark sky and bursts from German antiaircraft guns illuminated hundreds of Allied aircraft headed inland. *Mon Dieu, it's the invasion.*

"You there," a thick voice shouted. "*Halt!*"

Guy spun around. "Stay here," he whispered. "I'll draw them off." In the next moment he was gone.

Small arms fire erupted ahead of her, and Marguerite edged in the opposite direction. She stopped when she realized she was headed back toward the destroyed bridge, which by now was probably teeming with soldiers. Terrified, she backtracked, found a depression in the hedges, and crawled in. *Has Guy gotten away? Is he looking for her?* She listened hard but heard nothing.

She dared not leave her hiding place, so she decided she would wait until dawn. She hugged the ground and thought about Guy and the others. *They must get away. They have to.*

All night the ground trembled with explosions. She lay in her hiding place until the sky lightened, and by then the explosions to the north were getting louder. *What was happening?* Finally she couldn't stand not knowing and crawled out.

"*Halt!*" a voice shouted.

Slowly she turned to face a squad of four soldiers with rifles pointed at her. A German lieutenant stepped forward and a cold hand closed around her throat.

"It looks like we have one of the saboteurs. There are some people at headquarters who would like to talk to you. Let's go."

They found the pistol in her skirt pocket, forced her wrists together in front of her, and snapped on handcuffs. Two men roughly pushed her to the edge of the field and shoved her into the back seat of a dark grey Citroën with a German military cross painted on its side. The lieutenant got in next to her.

"Do you know how many people you killed tonight?" he yelled.

"I didn't kill anyone. The Allies destroyed the bridge."

"You are out after curfew and you have black grease on your face. That's enough to get you interrogated and then shot."

Marguerite bit the inside of her cheek. She knew what interrogation meant. *I must keep them questioning me for 24 hours. Just 24 hours.*

The car sped toward Ville de Pommes. A line of six German tanks rumbled by going the opposite direction, and she twisted around to see them disappear toward the coast. She knew the Allies would be bombing anything that moved; she prayed they would hit the car she was riding in and spare her the ordeal she knew was coming.

A caravan of transport trucks overtook them and disappeared down the road. More military transports roared by going the opposite direction.

They don't know what they're doing! She smiled to herself. *Cutting the telephone lines has created chaos.*

The sun was up when they stopped in front of military headquarters in Ville de Pommes. People were going to work, opening bakeries, polishing the windows of cafés. She climbed awkwardly out of the car and a soldier propelled her up the steps. All at once the lieutenant stopped her and yanked her around to face the curious crowd gathering in front of headquarters.

"Private, go inside and get a wet cloth. Let the people of this town see who we have captured."

The driver bounded up the stairs and returned with a dripping towel. As the lieutenant roughly scrubbed the grease from her face, she stared out over the heads of the gathering crowd. She could hear something; the sounds were far away but unmistakable.

The invasion! She smiled. *I can face whatever is coming knowing that I have helped.*

The lieutenant jerked around her to face the crowd. She stood erect, her head up.

"Look! It's Marguerite Auriol," someone cried. "Marguerite Auriol!"

The lieutenant sniffed. "*Gut.* We have an identification. Inside, Marguerite Auriol. We have questions for you." He pushed her through the military headquarters entrance.

She stepped into the office where all was chaos but without the accompanying ringing telephones. Only one phone seemed to be working. Secretaries and German officers took turns speaking into the receiver and scribbled notes; as soon as they hung up, the phone rang again. In the middle of the room, Simone LaVaque was in line to use the single working telephone and she looked up.

"Marguerite? What are you doing here?"

"You will not talk to the prisoner!" the lieutenant ordered.

"Prisoner?" Simone blinked, but she kept her puzzled gaze on Marguerite.

She refused to look at Simone. *Traitor! I hope Simone LaVaque knows what she's done. She had better escape with the Nazis when the Allies get here.*

"You, Private! Take the prisoner down to the interrogation room."

The guard gripped her arm and pushed her past Simone's desk and down the stairs. When the basement door opened, Marguerite gagged at the overwhelming stench of vomit and urine.

At the bottom of the stairs were six small cells with barred doors backed up against the basement wall. All faced a large plywood cube with a shiny chrome handle on the door. Only one of the cells was occupied; the female prisoner looked up when Marguerite was led in. The woman had two black eyes and her lips were cut. There were odd-shaped bruises around her neck.

There was no sign of Bérénice, Guy, or José. *I will believe they escaped. I cannot think about the rest.*

The guard yanked off her handcuffs while the jailer opened an empty cell and shoved her inside. "You will not speak to the other prisoner." He locked the door behind her. “A *Milice* specialist will be here to question you soon.”

She sank down on the narrow bench and tried not to sob. *Oh, God, what will it be like?*

She inspected her tiny cell for some way to escape, but there were no windows and only the one door, and it was locked. An artillery shell exploded outside. She prayed that Ville de Pommes would be liberated soon, with or without her.

I will endure until . . . until I am either dead or liberated. She clenched her fists and waited.

CHAPTER THIRTY-TWO
THE MARCH INTO HELL

The door at the top of the stairs opened and footsteps descended toward her. A tall, thin, unsmiling man dressed in black and wearing a wide-brimmed felt fedora appeared carrying a black leather bag in one hand and a manila folder under his arm. A uniformed guard followed at his heels. They walked past the jailer to the wooden cube where the guard opened the door and switched on a single bare light. It cast a hard light on a straight-backed chair.

Marguerite flinched. The interrogation chair had leather straps on the arms and legs and another at throat level. A small table stood beside the chair; a wheeled, backless stool rested beside it.

The tall man removed his hat to reveal a completely bald, colorless head. She saw that he was missing his eyebrows and she wondered if he had a disease. He set the black bag on the table and began arranging a collection of chrome instruments on the table. Next, he took out a small gas burner and placed it beside the instruments.

"I am ready," he said softly to the guard. "Bring me Clarisse Bassat."

The woman cowered at the back of her cell. "*Non! Non!*" she cried. "I've told you everything I know." The jailer unlocked the cell and she began to sob. Marguerite's entire body went cold.

Two soldiers dragged the woman out while she twisted and kicked at them. They shoved her into the wooden cube and threw her into the interrogation chair. One guard held her arm down while the colorless man buckled the leather strap to her wrist.

"Please," she begged. *"Please."*

Once her wrists and ankles were secured they buckled the leather strap across her throat. They closed the door and left her alone with the colorless man. At first there was silence, and then Marguerite could hear her pleading. Her voice was faint and muffled, and then suddenly it stopped. A muted scream echoed from the cube, followed by more pleading, and then more screams. Awful screams. Shudders ran up her spine and she clapped her hands over her ears.

The screams went on and on. *Mon Dieu, what is he doing to her?* She rubbed her thighs with perspiring hands. *What will he do to me?*

At last there was silence, and the colorless man opened the door. The two soldiers stepped in, unstrapped the unconscious woman and dragged her out, then dumped her on the floor of her cell. Her hair was matted with sweat, her wrists red and bloody from the restraints. Black burn marks covered her arms, and open wounds on her bare back oozed with blood. Marguerite thought she would throw up.

They locked the woman's cell door, and the colorless man pointed his chin at Marguerite. "All right, bring *her* in."

She scrambled to the back of her cell as they unlocked the door. Each of the soldiers grabbed one of her arms and propelled her into the wooden cell and the interrogation chair. She thrashed and kicked, but they held her down while the colorless man buckled the leather straps around her wrists and ankles. His last act of preparation was to fasten the strap tight around her throat. His arms were as hairless and pale as his head, and his hands were like ice. He had very thin lips and his pale grey eyes were expressionless.

She bit him and he slapped her face, hard. "*Sich niederlassen*!" he shouted. Then he pulled the strap tighter across her throat.

"I...can't...breathe," she panted.

"You can breathe well enough to talk," he snarled.

She stretched her neck up and wagged her head back and forth to get enough slack to pull in air. The guards closed the door and left her alone with the colorless man. On the table lay a horrifying collection of shiny clamps, forceps, needles, and scalpels. And the gas burner. Marguerite shuddered.

The man squatted on the stool and opened the folder. "So, Marguerite Auriol, we finally captured you." He leafed through the file and glanced up at her, then clasped a clammy hand on her forearm. "The Gestapo report says you are suspected of being the terrorist Patrice Cerne. Is that true?"

She looked away from him. *I will not tell him anything.* She clenched her fists.

The colorless man studied her hands and smiled. "So, we have decided to resist."

Immediately, she opened her fists and relaxed her hands.

"That won't work, *Fraulein*. You have already given yourself away."

"I . . . don't know this Patrice . . . whatever her name is."

His meaty fist slammed into her mouth. She had never been struck in her life. At first she was humiliated and then she was infuriated that this man would dare to touch her. She felt her lip swell and she tasted blood. She glared at him, then spit blood in his face.

His reaction was genuine surprise, then he chuckled and wiped his face with a handkerchief. "You will learn that when you are good, you get a little reward. And when you are bad, well . . . " He raised himself slightly off the stool and drove his fist into her solar plexus.

She couldn't breathe. She struggled to pull air into her lungs, but her diaphragm would not cooperate. She felt nauseated. She tried and tried to pull in air, but the strap around her neck made the effort a struggle. Little by little she was able to suck in a breath. The colorless man was laughing.

"Now that is what happens when you're bad. And since you seem to be a person who likes pain, I have these." He reached down to his bag, retrieved a set of brass knuckles, and laid them on the table next to his instruments. "The next time you are bad, I put these on. Now let's try again . . . " Without warning, he smashed his fist into her right eye.

He threw back his head and laughed again. "You didn't expect that, did you?"

He is enjoying this too much.

She began to sob. He stood and slipped the brass knuckles onto his right hand. "Crying is not allowed. Are you going to be bad?"

She stared at the gleaming metal on his calloused knuckles and shook her head. With great effort she stopped crying, but she could not control her trembling mouth. Her eye was swelling shut.

"That's better." He removed the knuckles and set them back on the table. "Now, where were we? Ah, that's right, you were about to confess to being Patrice Cerne."

Marguerite squeezed her eyes shut, shook her head, and waited for the next blow.

"Now, don't be shy. I also want the names of the rest of the *Réfugié* and OCM members you've been associating with."

Another blow smashed into her face. Her bottom lip split and blood dribbled down her chin. She began to pant. *They already know I'm with the Résistance. Could I admit to being Patrice? What could happen?*

"Let me see if we can convince you this way." He reached in his trouser pocket and produced a match, struck it, and lit the wick on the burner. It burned blue as the gas hissed through the nozzle, and he adjusted the flame. Carefully he selected a flat instrument and held it over the flame while he spoke in a slow, quiet voice.

"They say the most painful experience is being burned. For some reason the nervous system reacts intensely to burns. I don't know why, but I find this a most effective tool." He gripped her elbow and pressed the red hot instrument on the inside of her forearm.

She screamed. He lifted the instrument away, and she could not control her choking sobs. He sent another blow to her midriff and she forgot about the burn on her arm and struggled to breathe. Nausea swept over her, and she turned her head to one side to vomit.

It went on and on. At one point she heard someone screaming and realized it was her own voice. *I can't last much longer. I cannot. How long has it been?*

She woke up in her cell, wondering if she was finally going to die.

She lost all perception of time. Later they came for her again. As they unlocked her cell door, she tried to think. *Two hours? Twenty?*

The questioning started all over. Blows drove the breath from her lungs, and the gas burner heated his metal instruments. She smelled her own flesh burning. *Mon Dieu, I cannot stand this. How much time has passed? Have I told him anything?*

She could not hold out much longer. She prayed she would not break before the 24 hours were up, but her mind was fuzzy with pain. Could she last?

She would try.

The colorless man was growing frustrated. She could tell because his punches were sharper and they came more often. Now he was using both hands, hitting her jaw first from one side and then the other.

She swallowed hard after the last blow and struggled to stay conscious. Then she thought she heard someone pounding on the wooden door and a male voice. "Sir! Sir, I must speak with you."

"Not now," the colorless man spat. "I'm busy."

"But Sir, we have orders to evacuate the prisoners!"

He flung the flat instrument across the room and yanked open the door. "What did you say?"

Marguerite opened her eyes to see Simone standing outside with a soldier; she was holding out some papers. She glanced at Marguerite and quickly looked away.

"We have orders from Vichy to evacuate Ville de Pommes," Simone said. "Patrice Cerne and Clarisse Bassat are to be evacuated to Vichy for trial. These orders are from Pétain himself."

The colorless man snatched the papers and scanned them, shaking his head.

"*Milice* cars are coming to transfer them," Simone added. Her ordinarily silky voice sounded tight.

Marguerite closed her eyes and let her head rest on the back of the chair. *Liberation is so close and now they're taking me to Vichy for more torture. So be it.* She looked up at Simone and tears welled up in her eyes. *Damn you. You were once my friend.*

"Who is coming to take the prisoners?" demanded the colorless man.

"They didn't say."

"I'm going with them."

Simone pursed her lips. "You are to evacuate with the rest of us."

"These are my prisoners!" the colorless man snapped. "I will go with them to Vichy."

The soldier stepped in and unstrapped Marguerite while the colorless man watched in disgust. As soon as the strap around her neck was loosened, she sucked in a deep breath and tried to stand. Her legs buckled. Simone reached to catch her, but Marguerite righted herself and pulled away.

"Don't touch me."

She struggled to her feet and stared at Simone out of her good eye. The jailer pushed her back into her cell and locked the door. She tottered over to the bench and collapsed.

"I see no transfer orders," shouted the colorless man as he leafed through the papers.

"They're on my desk." Simone accompanied him upstairs while the sentry kept watch.

Marguerite curled up in a fetal position and fought blinding pain and nausea. Her face throbbed; her chest ached from the beatings. After a long time, she heard footsteps.

The sentry unlocked Clarisse's cell, and a *Milice* agent in civilian clothes handcuffed her while the colorless man watched. The woman was barely conscious and unable to walk out of her cell without assistance. Then someone unlocked Marguerite's cell door and snapped handcuffs on her wrists.

"What will happen to us?" she asked.

"The prisoners will not speak!" yelled the colorless man.

The *Milice* agent answered. "More interrogation in Vichy, and then a trial. If they spare you, you will be sent to Drancy for processing and then to the women's work camp at Ravensbrück."

She and Clarisse were taken upstairs where Marguerite saw papers burning in metal wastebaskets and boxes of files being carried out the front door. She averted her gaze from Simone as she passed her desk. "You will regret this," she murmured.

Another blow to her chest and Marguerite was on her knees, vomiting. "Prisoners will not speak," the colorless man spat.

She fought her way upright and stumbled toward the door. *Dear God, don't let him hit me all the way to Vichy.*

Outside, the headquarters staff was loading files and equipment into a line of trucks. A crowd of villagers watched in unsmiling silence. Marguerite spied Jenna Benault, Dr. Morel's receptionist, standing next to her *lycée* teacher, *Mademoiselle* Huet. The two women clung to each other, their faces chalky, as Marguerite was escorted past.

With a supreme effort she raised her chin and squared her shoulders. *God be merciful to them, if not to me.*

Two black Citroëns waited, their engines running. As they drew closer, a *Milice* agent emerged from the rear seat of the first car. He wore a tan trench coat and a hat with the brim pulled down over his eyes. *Odd.*

A soldier propelled her toward the car, and as she moved forward the *Milice* agent looked up at her with horrified eyes.

Guy! Oh, my God, Guy!

"Get in," he snarled.

She stared at him, but he wouldn't look at her.

She began to sob. "That is not allowed," the colorless man snapped. He drew his fist back, but Guy stepped in between them.

"There will be plenty of time for that later," he said barring the colorless man with his arm.

She lifted her manacled hands and wiped her tears with her sleeve. Furtively she glanced back at the second car, and the man holding the door for Clarisse stole a look at her.

Mon Dieu, Uncle Pierre!

She broke down and wept again.

"We will take it from here," said Guy to the colorless man.

"*Nein.* I am accompanying these two. They are my prisoners."

"Then get in front. I will stay in back and guard this prisoner."

The colorless man watched as Clarisse was loaded into the second Citroën, then stalked around the car to climb into the front seat and settle himself next to the driver. Marguerite continued to sob. He twisted around in his seat. "I have a solution for that crying."

Marguerite gazed at him through her tears. The man glanced at Guy. "Are you sure you have her secured?"

Guy said softly, "Oh, she is very secure."

"Then let's go."

The two-car caravan pulled away from the curb and accelerated, turning north on the road toward Perdu and Charentais. "You are going the wrong way," the colorless man said.

Guy pulled a pistol from his trench coat pocket, leaned forward, and pressed it to the man's neck. "Actually, we are going the right way. *You* are going the wrong way." The driver reached over and retrieved a revolver from the colorless man's coat.

"By the way," Guy said in a calm voice. "I don't know if you've been properly introduced to my fiancée, Marguerite Auriol. Now, may I ask who it was that was beating my future wife?"

She didn't think it possible, but the colorless man turned white as milk. "I— I was operating under orders."

Guy smashed his pistol across the man's ear, then leaned over the front seat and hit him again. Marguerite grabbed his arm with her manacled hands. "That's enough. He's unconscious."

Breathing hard, Guy gazed at her, his eyes filling with tears. "Stop the car."

The driver pulled over on the deserted country road. The trailing Citroën parked behind them. Guy dragged the colorless man's body out, searched his pockets for the handcuff keys, and freed Marguerite's wrists.

Uncle Pierre helped Clarisse out of the second automobile and Guy unlocked her cuffs, then handed his revolver to Marguerite.

"Do you want to do it?" He glanced at the colorless man on the ground.

Marguerite passed the revolver to Clarisse. "You do the honors."

Clarisse studied the weapon and then smiled. She limped over to the inert form, dropped to her knees, and pressed the gun barrel to his temple. She fired a single shot, then spit on the corpse.

Marguerite rubbed her wrists and fought dizziness. “Could someone explain to me how you got us out?”

“Yvonne Callion called the OCM on the wireless dropped by the British,” Uncle Pierre said. “They parachuted the sets to us so we could communicate when the telephone lines were cut.”

“But how did Guy get here?”

Guy touched her arm. “After you were captured at the bridge, I went back to the stone house. Richard had a wireless, and he put me in touch with Pierre. Your uncle picked me up at my father’s house, and we planned the rescue with the help of the OCM.”

Marguerite shook her head. “How did you arrange the prisoner transfer papers? You would have had to… *Mon Dieu, Simone!”*

Her uncle nodded. “Yvonne and Simone worked out the *Milice* ruse, and Simone typed up bogus orders and transfer papers.”

Marguerite swallowed. “I was so hateful to her.”

“It worked better that way,” Guy said. “That way you didn’t have to act.”

Her uncle waved everyone back into the cars. “We need to get out of here. Guy, take Marguerite to the Cave so she can recover. I need to return to Caen with the OCM.” He pointed to the other driver. “You come with us and bring Clarisse. We’ll return her to the OCM. They’re going to care for her.”

Guy helped Marguerite back into the car, put it in gear, and pulled onto the road. When they reached the Cave, he walked Marguerite in and found the lantern.

She collapsed onto a cot and closed her eyes. *It’s over. My ordeal is over and I didn’t break.* “I’m cold,” she murmured.

“Lie still,” Guy ordered. He inspected her burns, cleaned them, and covered her with blankets. Still she couldn’t stop shaking. After a long while, she drifted off, but when two big explosions went off quite close, she sat bolt upright. “What was that?”

Instantly Guy was on his feet. “Artillery. *Non*, wait. Those are tanks! There is a battle is going on in the Perdu farmyard!”

The explosions were punctuated with reports from machine guns and other small arms. When Marguerite heard German voices she froze. The Nazis were making a stand. Guy found a pair of Stens, loaded them, and handed one to Marguerite. “Just in case,” he said quietly.

The gunfire above went on for an hour, and then it was quiet.

“What do you think?” Marguerite whispered.

“I don’t know,” Guy responded in a low voice.

All at once they heard the scream of a dive bomber, and an explosion rocked the Cave. Another bomber thundered overhead, followed by an even larger explosion. Dust and dirt rained down on them and they crawled under a table.

"Rückzug!" a man shouted. *"Rückzug!"* German voices. The sounds faded, and after a time they heard the grinding of tanks.

And voices in English!

She shook Guy. "They're English! *Mon Dieu*, can it be the Allies?" She grasped her Sten with both hands. "Let's go up and help."

"*Non,*" Guy said. "There's a battle going on up there. Two people can't just pop out of the brush with Stens; they'd be killed either by the Allies or the Germans. Besides, you can hardly walk."

"But they're here! The Allies are here!"

The gunfire diminished, but the voices continued to speak in English. Guy touched her shoulder. "I think now we can go up to the hilltop and see what's going on. Marguerite, can you manage the climb?"

She gave a shaky laugh. "I am going to run up that hill so fast you won't be able keep up with me!"

Guy grinned. "Not in the shape you're in you won't. Let's make a white flag and wave it before we come charging out of the brush."

They emerged from the Cave and Guy helped her up the hill. As they stepped out of the brush, Guy waved the flag, and three British soldiers swung their rifles toward them.

"Don't shoot! Don't shoot!" Guy shook the flag at them. "We are Résistance."

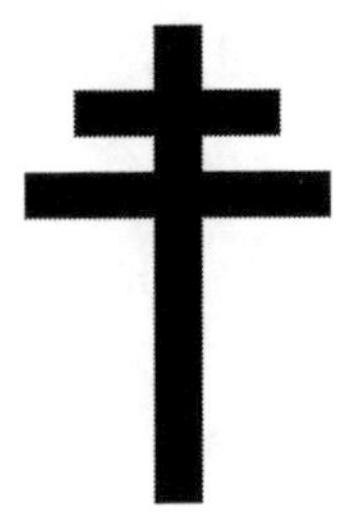

CHAPTER THIRTY-THREE
INTEGRATION

In the Perdu farmyard, Marguerite limped from one British soldier to another, unable to stop her tears. Some of them hugged her with a little too much zeal, but she clutched her ribs and kept smiling.

"Marguerite, stop," Guy admonished. "You are not strong enough for this."

"But I am, Guy. I want to thank all of them."

"You should sit down. He gestured to the remains of the bunkhouse. "Then they can come to you."

More exhausted than she realized, she sank onto the only bunkhouse step that still remained. A sergeant walked over with a concerned look on his face. "*Mademoiselle*, are you all right?"

"*Oui*, I am fine." She held one arm across her ribcage. "I'm still a little tried from . . . from being interrogated by the *Milice*, but oh! I am so happy to see you here!"

"The *Milice*! A Frenchman did this to you?"

"*Oui*. Could I lie down?"

"Sergeant," Guy said. "She needs medical help. Can we get a stretcher?"

The sergeant signaled for a medic and litter bearers, and Marguerite let them load her onto a stretcher. "Oh, *merci*," she sighed. "*Merci* for coming."

The bearers grinned, and to her surprise one responded in French. "We are glad to be back in France, *Mademoiselle*."

Guy picked up her Sten and walked beside the stretcher. "Where are you taking her?"

"First we'll take her to our combat aid station. Once she is released she will go by ambulance to the command post, and then on to Bayeux and the Free French command post."

At the aid station a medic checked her for broken bones and cleaned and dressed her burns and puncture wounds. "Who did this to you, *Mademoiselle*?"

"The *Milice*."

"Jesus!" He finished bandaging her arm. "Jesus Christ Almighty!" She thought his voice grew hoarse.

They loaded her into a military ambulance, drove her toward the coast, and stopped at a large military field operation. The ambulance halted in front of a large tent with a red cross painted on the top, and she emerged into the sunlight and blinked.

Tents bloomed all over the field and hundreds of uniformed men and vehicles milled about. Huge stacks of supplies were neatly arranged in rows beside the tents and a steady stream of military trucks, vans, and troop carriers kept arriving from the north. Other vehicles departed to the south.

How did they get so much here so fast?

Guy helped her to a cot where a British nurse smiled at her. *"En français?"* she inquired.

Marguerite looked up at her. A British nurse! A woman! "*Oui, merci*. This is Guy Massu, my fiancé."

"*Bonjour*, Guy." She inspected Marguerite's face, ran her fingers gently over her jaw, and felt her ribcage. "You've been beaten pretty thoroughly." She unwrapped the bandages on her arms and her breath hissed in. "How did this happen?"

"I was captured and . . . interrogated."

The nurse gaped at her. "Oh, *Mademoiselle,* I'm so sorry to ask. You are the first torture victim I've ever seen."

Marguerite tried to smile. "I will be all right. They did not break me."

"You have too many bruises. You must rest here, and I'll have an aide bring you something to eat."

Marguerite tried to sit up, but her chest hurt and she couldn't take a deep breath without pain. "We must get to Bayeux."

"Not quite yet, *Mademoiselle*. You are not well enough to travel."

Guy draped a blanket over her. "Marguerite, I'm going over to the command post and see if anyone else from *Réfugié* has been found by the

Allies."

She caught his hand. "Find out about Bérénice, José, and Richard. If Red is there, ask him about *Maman* and Germaine." When he left she tried to relax, but her mind raced. It was too much.

Hours later, Guy stepped into the field hospital and stood beside her cot. "There is no news. Do you think you can you travel now?"

Marguerite struggled to sit up. "*Oui*, I think so."

"A truck is leaving for Bayeux in ten minutes. I think we should go to the Free French command post and ask about *Réfugié*. See if anyone has turned up."

She swung her feet over the edge of the cot and stood up, steadied by his arm. "Then let's go. I cannot bear not knowing." She followed him to a line of large supply trucks and waited until the sergeant waved them forward. Guy helped her climb into the back, and they rode the 20 kilometers seated on a hard wooden bench. She grimaced with the pain and he held her all the way.

From the back of the transport she could see a continual stream of tanks, towed artillery, troop transports, and command jeeps heading inland. Columns of troops tramped along both sides of the road going in the same direction.

A huge French flag hung on either side of the Grand Hotel Bayeux's imposing stone entrance. She and Guy walked in carrying their Sten machine guns, and all conversation ceased. A uniformed French officer intercepted them. It was the first French soldier in uniform she had seen in four years. She wanted to kiss him!

"Puis-je vous aidez?"

"We are Résistance," Guy said. "We were told to report here."

"*Bonjour*. I am *Capitaine* Mondel."

"I am Guy Massu and this is Marguerite Auriol. During the Occupation she was known as Patrice Cerne."

He gave Marguerite a sharp look. "Patrice Cerne from the radio?"

She nodded. "*Oui*, the same."

"You are the third Patrice Cerne who has reported here since yesterday," he said, his voice skeptical.

She smiled. "I assure you I am the only real Patrice Cerne. I can prove it."

"*Trés bien*. I will take you to the interview room." He relieved them of their Stens and led them to an empty room with chairs lining the walls and a single table in the middle. Three uniformed French officers filed in, along with four enlisted men. One officer opened a file.

"Identify yourselves, *si'l vous plait*."

Guy spoke first. "I am Private Guy Massu of the French Army. I escaped from a German prisoner of war camp in 1940 and joined the Résistance."

The officer turned to Marguerite. "And you? You claim to be Patrice Cerne. What is your real name?"

"Marguerite Auriol."

"Why are your arms bandaged?"

"I was captured. The Germans turned me over to the *Milice* in Ville de Pommes, and I was tortured."

The officers glanced at each other. "To which Résistance cell did you belong?"

"*Réfugié* at first," she said. "Then we merged with the OCM in Caen."

"Who is the leader of *Réfugié*?"

"There are two," Marguerite explained. "Richard Markey and also my uncle, Pierre Auriol."

The officers whispered among themselves and finally one rose, leaned across the table, and shook both their hands. "Welcome, Marguerite Auriol and Private Massu. If you do not mind, we have more questions."

Guy bent toward her and spoke near her ear. "Are you up to more?"

She nodded. "I will try. We have to get this over with and find Red."

Guy answered questions about the history of *Réfugié*, who the members were, what they did, and what happened to the ones they knew about. After an hour, Marguerite touched his sleeve. "I'm getting dizzy. Could we stop for today?"

The senior officer ordered an enlisted man to get *Capitaine* Mondel, then turned his attention to Marguerite. "You should get some rest, *Mademoiselle*. We will talk more tomorrow."

Capitaine Mondel escorted them to a nearby hotel and spoke to the concierge, who gave them the room key.

"Tomorrow we will decide what to do with you," *Capitaine* Mondel said at the entrance to the elevator. There is a café nearby. Order whatever you wish and charge it to the room. *Bonsoir*." He gave a short bow and was gone.

At the café they ordered *coq au vin* and *tarte aux pommes,* but Marguerite was too tired and sore to enjoy it. It was enough to be with Guy in a clean room with no explosions or the sound of gunfire outside. They slept all night without waking.

The debriefings continued over the next three days as Marguerite gained strength. The French officers asked about the activities of their relatives, their friends, and their coworkers at both Caen and Ville de Pommes. Of particular interest was the LaVaque family. Where had Jean LaVaque gone with the bank's money after the Germans arrived? Did he return? Did he join the Nazi party? Did he support the Résistance? Did Giselle LaVaque, Simone's mother, entertain the Nazis? When did Simone begin working for the German military? What did she do?

Marguerite soon realized that separating patriots from collaborators would take years of interviews and research. Each day Guy checked with the Free French headquarters for any word of Bérénice, José, or Richard or Marguerite's uncle. She couldn't stop worrying about *Maman,* and as the days passed she began to lose her appetite.

At last the questioning was over, and that afternoon *Capitaine* Mondel escorted them to his office. "It is our custom to offer Résistance members commissions in the Free French Army. If you accept, we will assign you duty that will keep you together as much as possible."

"I want to go home to Ville de Pommes," Marguerite blurted. "My mother and my cousin are missing; I want to go home so they know where to find me."

"That area is currently occupied by the British Twelfth Army Group, *Mademoiselle*. I understand you are a nurse?"

"*Oui*, that is correct."

"May I suggest a commission as First Lieutenant in the French Medical Corps? We will assign you as Medical Liaison Officer to the American Civil Affairs Division. Once the British combat troops around Ville de Pommes move on, this American division will move in to maintain order and establish civilian justice. We need French officers to work with the Americans to pacify the area and sort out patriots from collaborators."

"I am not sure I am up to that," said Marguerite. "I need to give it some thought."

"*Bon*." He turned his attention to Guy. "You already belong to the French army. We will adjust your rank to First Lieutenant. We will also attach you to the American division in the Ville de Pommes area; you will represent the Free French Army to the American military."

Guy looked at Marguerite, then back to *Capitaine* Mondel. "May we talk in private?"

"*Oui,* of course." He excused himself.

"What do you think?" Marguerite asked when they were alone.

"You want to go home, and that's what they're offering."

"But if I go to Ville de Pommes as a nurse, I will still want to search for *Maman* and Bérénice. I cannot do both."

He leaned close and drew his thumb across her cheek. "You forget that I will be with you. I can search for your mother and Bérénice while you are concentrating on your duties."

She closed her eyes and smiled. "All right, let's do it."

Guy called *Capitaine* Mondel back. "We accept."

"*Bon*. You can start here." He opened his desk drawer and pulled out a folder. "Here is a list of suspected traitors and criminals in the Ville de Pommes area. We plan to investigate and possibly prosecute them."

Marguerite scanned the list of names and the charges. The name of Yvonne Callion and her mother, Thérèse, leaped out at her. "Why do you want to prosecute the Callion women?"

"They are the owners and operators of Callion Construction. They made a lot of money from forced labor."

"Yvonne Callion was a member of the OCM. She smuggled plans for the German beach defenses to me and I passed them on to British intelligence. She helped me escape from the *Milice*. She should be decorated, not prosecuted."

She ran her finger down the list. "Here I see Dr. Morel listed, to face charges for the murder of Lieutenant Lastrange."

"*Oui*."

"But Dr. Morel didn't kill Lastrange. I did. Dr. Morel hid me when the Nazis were after me. When Lastrange discovered me, I shot him and Dr. Morel helped me escape.

Capitaine Mondel leaned back in his chair and folded his arms. "*Mademoiselle* Auriol, do you see why we need you in Ville de Pommes? You are someone we can trust."

Within the hour she reported to the supply center for a uniform. "The Free French do not have our own women's uniforms," the supply officer explained. "Instead we have adopted the American Women's Army Corps uniform and we add a French tri-color patch on the shoulder."

Even the smallest size did not fit her, but it took only a few hours for the uniform to be altered, and then she and Guy were on their way to headquarters in Bayeux. Soon she would be in Ville de Pommes where she belonged. And soon, she prayed, she would find *Maman*.

CHAPTER THIRTY-FOUR
JUSTICE

"Marguerite!"

She looked up at Guy from the little room at military headquarters in Bayeux where she was enjoying a cup of coffee. *Real* coffee!

"The British have taken Caen."

"Truly?" She shot to her feet and hugged him. "How soon before the Allies liberate Paris?"

"Soon. The Americans are moving into Ville de Pommes today. You've been assigned to go with them, so you need to finish your coffee and pack up."

"You are not coming?"

"*Capitaine* Mondel has a mission for me—nothing dangerous, but it's something I must do. I'll meet you at the Cave tomorrow."

She loaded her duffel into the first truck in the caravan and allowed an over-polite American MP to help her into the transport along with the rest of the office staff. She was going home at last! No one would recognize her in this uniform; she looked like any American in a WAC uniform, but it didn't matter. *I will be home.*

The truck ground to a halt in the Ville de Pommes town square in front of the building where she had been tortured by the *Milice*. People thronged the main street, and when the truck began to unload the American soldiers, the crowd began to cheer.

"C'est les Americaines! Les Americaines!"

The town looked . . . tired, Marguerite thought. Bullet holes pocked some buildings; others showed bomb damage. And the townspeople! *Mon Dieu*, they looked gaunt and thin, but their expressions were exultant. Tears stung under her eyelids. How good it was to see them.

Securing her helmet on her head, she climbed down and stood in line helping to unload supplies to be carted into the building. Because her ribs were still sore, she lifted only the smaller boxes. Inside the offices she passed Simone's old desk. *Where was she now?*

When she went outside for another load, an old grey-bearded man she didn't recognize stared at her. He pointed at her French tri-colored shoulder patch and whispered something to his companions

All at once a woman beside him shouted, "*Elle est francaise! Une soldat de la France!* She's a French soldier!"

People surged toward her. Two men grasped her around the waist, hoisted her up onto their shoulders, and paraded her around the square. *"Vive la France,"* they shouted. *"Vive la soldat de la France!"*

She was the first uniformed French soldier in Ville de Pommes in four years. She choked back tears and tried to balance herself and hold onto her helmet. "We're free, we're free!" a man yelled. "*Vive la France.*" Someone began singing the *Marseillaise.* A few townspeople joined in, tentatively at first, and then everyone was singing. "*Allons enfants de la patrie . . .*"

Women pelted her with flowers, and men reached up to shake her hand. Streams of townspeople joined the throng, and people hung out of second- and third-floor windows. Marguerite's throat ached.

Then she spotted Jenna Benault and *Mademoiselle* Huet on the edge of the crowd, hugging each other and weeping. Marguerite asked to be put down, walked up to the two women, unbuckled and removed her helmet. *Mademoiselle* Huet clutched her chest. "*Mon Dieu,*" she screamed. "It's Marguerite Auriol!"

An instant silence descended on the crowd, and then murmurs began to echo around the square. "Marguerite Auriol! It's Marguerite Auriol!" Shouted cheers broke out again, and once more the men raised her onto their shoulders and circled the square. The crowd began to chant. "Mar-guer-ite, Mar-guer-ite." She looked down at the pandemonium in the street and thrust her fist in the air. "*Vive la France!*" she shouted through her tears.

A tall American MP waded through the crowd, helped her down, and set her on her feet. She blotted her wet cheeks with the sleeve of her uniform. The MP bent down to her. "Lieutenant Auriol, a mob has broken into a house on the outskirts of town and three women are trapped inside. Could you come and calm things down?"

He helped her into a jeep with two other MP's, and another jeep full of soldiers followed them to the stone wall in front of the LaVaque home. A jostling crowd surrounded a flatbed truck where three straight-backed chairs had been positioned.

A group of men dragged the women out of the house. Marguerite recognized Yvonne Callion, Simone LaVaque, and Simone's mother, Giselle. "Nazi whores," a pregnant woman shouted. Women from the crowd climbed onto the truck bed and pulled up the terrified trio, tearing at their clothes and cursing at them. Four men forced the women onto the wooden chairs.

Mon Dieu, what was happening? "Stop!" Marguerite shouted. Her cry was drowned out.

"Let's give them Coiffeur Forty-four," a gaunt woman cried. Marguerite reached the truck just as a bent old woman with a pair of scissors grabbed a handful of Simone's blonde hair and began to hack it off. Two men pinned a struggling Yvonne and Giselle in the chairs.

Non, not Simone! If it were not for her, I would be dead now. Marguerite clambered up onto the truck bed and faced the chanting townspeople. "Sergeant," she shouted over the noise, "get their attention."

He turned to the MP at his side. "Private, fire two blanks over their heads." The soldier loaded two charges into his pistol, aimed it above his head, and fired into the air.

The shots stunned the crowd into silence. Marguerite raised her arms. "I am Marguerite Auriol. You all know me. My Résistance name was Patrice Cerne." She pointed to Simone. "You cannot harm this woman. She saved my life."

"She is one of them, a man challenged. "A collaborator. And so is that one." He pointed to Yvonne.

"Non, I tell you. Yvonne Callion worked with the Résistance. She risked her life to smuggle German plans to the Allies. She should get a medal for what she did for France."

An MP sergeant climbed up onto the truck bed, pushed the men away from Yvonne, and hauled her to her feet. He handed her down to a private, and three more MP's muscled their way through the crowd to escort her to their jeep, where they stood guard over her. As she passed Marguerite, their glances caught and held.

Then Marguerite turned back to the truck and watched, horrified, as the old woman roughly shaved Simone's head. She knew Giselle would be next; she had to do something.

"Who is in charge here?" she shouted.

A man's voice boomed from the LaVaque house. "I am."

She could not see who had answered, but the throng turned toward the figure who stood on the porch step, his hands fisted on his hips. "I am in charge here," he yelled.

Richard! She couldn't believe it. She fought her way to him. "Richard!" Tears flooded her eyes. "I thought you were dead."

"Marguerite! *Non*, I am very much alive. And as you see . . . " He gestured toward the flatbed truck ". . . we have business to attend to."

"But Richard . . ."

He signaled for the women to continue. One yanked Giselle out of her chair, and Marguerite clenched her jaw. She gripped Richard's arm. "Stop them!"

He stepped forward and spoke in her ear. "*Non*. Does Simone's single act in saving you from the *Milice* erase four years of collaboration? Not in the minds of the townspeople."

"But surely there is forgiv— " A raucous cheer drowned her words, and when she looked back to the truck, Simone cowered in her chair, her head completely bald. The old woman was now shearing off Giselle's hair. *My God, how terrible for her!*

"Red, listen to me. You don't understand."

He snaked his arm around her shoulders and called to the crowd. "Our work here is finished. Get the women off the truck and send them back to their homes to live with what they have done."

Two MP's pulled Simone and Giselle off the truck bed, and they stumbled up the steps into the house while the townspeople shouted insults at their back. Marguerite couldn't help feeling sorry for them both. *From now on, every time they showed their faces in town, at the bakery, the café, even the bank, they would feel the hatred of the townspeople.*

Richard descended the steps and called out, "José, return that truck to its owner."

José? "Red, is that José? *Our* José?"

He nodded.

"Where is Bérénice? I haven't seen either of them since— "

"I can't explain now, Marguerite. I'll talk to you later."

She left Richard to check on Yvonne in the jeep. Her friend was pale and shaking, but she wore a tremulous smile. "Marguerite, you saved my life. I thought they were going to hang us!"

"Yvonne, how did you get mixed up with the LaVaques?"

"Everyone in town thought I was a collaborator. Richard suggested that my mother and I move in with Simone because it was the only safe place in town.

But this morning all those people broke through the gate and dragged us out of the house. Richard tried to get control of the mob, but it wasn't until you came that they settled down."

"Where is your mother?"

"Hiding in the cellar. I need to go in and see if she is all right."

"I am glad you are both safe," Marguerite said, touching her arm.

"What about you?"

"I am well, except for the burns and sore ribs. But those are small things compared to what others have suffered."

"And Guy? Where is he?"

"Both of us are assigned to the Americans here. They sent him out of town on a mission."

Yvonne hugged her and began to cry. "What . . . what will happen to Simone and her mother?"

"They will have to live among people who regard them as traitors," Marguerite said slowly. "They will have to hide in their house until their hair grows back. They will never get back the respect they had before the Occupation. I don't think the people of Ville de Pommes will ever forget."

Yvonne mopped at her eyes. "It seems awfully harsh."

Marguerite nodded. "They collaborated with the Nazis. Have you any idea how many people *Réfugié* had to smuggle out of Ville de Pommes to save them from their Nazi friends?"

Yvonne nodded. "I understand."

"Yvonne, they know you worked for the Résistance, so you are safe here now."

"*Merci*, Marguerite. Thank you for speaking up for me."

An hour later Marguerite found Richard in front of the LaVaque house, addressing a dozen men. He reached his big right arm around her shoulder and pulled her close. "You had a question?" he intoned.

"Red, I need to know about my mother. And about Bérénice. Where are they? Are they all right?"

Richard excused himself from the group. "Gentlemen, I have business with Lieutenant Auriol." He led her away from the crowd, then turned to her.

"Bérénice is safe at the Cave. She and José are working with me."

"What about *Maman?* And Aunt Germaine? Have you any news about them?"

"*Oui*, I do." His face looked suddenly grave, and Marguerite's body went cold.

CHAPTER THIRTY-FIVE
JUSTICE FOR ALL

"Marguerite, the news is not encouraging." Richard paced back and forth, his usually booming voice sounding oddly subdued. "We've made contact with Germaine and your mother. They're still in Paris, and they are both all right, but things there are beginning to break down."

"Break down? What does that mean? What is happening?"

"The American Army is approaching Paris from the east and the British are pressing down from the north. It is true that many Germans are evacuating, but the Nazis are still fighting for control of the city. Germaine and your mother have taken refuge at the hospital."

"Can you get them out?"

"*Non.* The area around the hospital is under siege and it is dangerous. The Résistance and the Germans are fighting in the streets; the Résistance controls some parts of the city, but the Germans control other parts. The Résistance is gaining, but it's slow."

Marguerite clutched his arm. "But it will end, won't it? It *has* to end."

"It will end, yes. It's just a matter of time."

Sick at heart, she turned away. Richard said *Maman* and Aunt Germaine were safe, but . . . for how long?

Days dragged by, then weeks. She tried to keep her mind off the battle raging in Paris, but each night she clung to Guy and wept. "The war is over, isn't it? Why are the Germans still fighting?"

No matter how he tried to comfort her, she grew more and more despondent. Every evening they huddled in the Cave before the radio, listening for news and praying it would be over.

"We will not be married until your mother and Germaine can stand up with us," Guy announced one evening. "And also my father."

"And Dr. Morel," she added. "I will bicycle to his clinic and ask him tomorrow."

Two days later, Richard appeared in the Cave with news. "The telephone lines have been destroyed. Probably sabotage, but who can tell? We have lost contact with the hospital where Germaine and your mother have taken refuge. There is less fighting in the streets, but— "

"Could we go to Paris and rescue them?" Marguerite interrupted.

He hesitated. "Not yet. We should wait until the Allies get there."

"How long will that be? Red, I must do something! I cannot just sit and wait."

"Yes, you can," he replied. "After all the things you have been through, you can do this."

Disheartened, that night she sat in the circle of Guy's arms and heard the BBC announce that Paris would be liberated in the next few days. The next morning they went to find Richard.

"It is over!" Marguerite cried.

"It isn't over," Richard replied. "There is still fighting in parts of Paris, and the Germans still occupy half of France." She started to cry. "But it's a good start," he said hastily. "And tomorrow, I will drive to Paris and find Germaine and your mother."

"I will come, too," Marguerite announced.

* * *

The Peugeot crept toward the hospital through the fighting in the streets of Paris, moving toward the hospital one car length at a time. When they got close enough to see the building, a bomb exploded at the front entrance, shattering windows on the ground floor, and Richard braked. "Get down!" he shouted.

Marguerite crouched next to Guy and began to pray for her mother and Aunt Germaine. Richard swerved the vehicle to avoid the barricades, built using bricks torn up from street, and she flinched at sporadic bursts of gunfire. Richard began to swear in some language Marguerite had never heard. Through all the *Réfugié* operations she had never heard him swear. His face was like a mask.

Hours passed while he edged the car forward inch by inch. Civilians were running in every direction, and then all at once there was a lull in the gunfire. Marguerite looked to the west and saw what looked like American soldiers. When they drew closer she saw they wore the Cross of Lorraine patch on their sleeves. French soldiers!

"Richard, look! They're French!"

"Ah," he said. "*Bon.*" She thought he smiled, but she couldn't be certain. Then she spied a line of tanks. Smoke hung above the buildings, but as the tanks rolled up the street, Marguerite saw they were American.

People began to pour into the street from everywhere, singing and shouting and hugging everyone, especially the American soldiers. She wanted to sing with them, but she was sobbing.

More tanks rumbled along, and gum-chewing soldiers in khaki uniforms tossed chocolates and candy to the children lining the sidewalks. A church bell started to ring. Other bells joined in and soon the air filled with a thousand peals announcing liberation. Women threw flowers at the soldiers, who lifted laughing girls onto their vehicles. French flags appeared from apartment balconies, and it seemed everyone was kissing everyone else—old men, girls, even young boys. Marguerite kissed Guy and then leaned over and kissed Richard's bristly cheek.

Suddenly he pointed ahead. "Look there," he breathed.

Two women stood on the sidewalk in front of the hospital. Two women in faded dresses, gripping small suitcases in their hands.

"*Maman!*" Half laughing, half weeping, Marguerite clambered out of the car and ran to her mother and enfolded her in her arms. "*Maman*, are you all right? What about you, Aunt Germaine?"

"*Oui*, I am as well as can be expected," her mother said. And Germaine . . ."

But her aunt was enfolded in Richard's strong arms.

"Don't cry, *chou-chou*," her mother admonished. "Just take me home."

* * *

The first thing *Maman* did was to inspect the kitchen in their new farmhouse. Then they climbed in the truck and drove to the Cave at Perdu, where they gathered to eat. Marguerite helped her mother dust off the table and set out plates, and then Bérénice and José came in through the tunnel with a gaunt but smiling Uncle Pierre. They talked and cried and drank calvados and ate warm bread and cheese until Richard and Guy came in bringing Aunt Germaine and Dr. Morel.

Midway through the celebration Richard rose and asked for quiet. “I have an announcement,” he said.

The room fell silent and Marguerite wondered why he looked so serious.

He cleared his throat. “There is joy in the fact that all Frenchmen live in France. And now the Irish want the British out of Ireland, and I believe they need my help. Maybe I can help to convince the British that Ireland is for the Irish.”

“And perhaps some French,” Germaine added quietly. She took Richard’s hand and squeezed it.

“I don’t understand,” said Marguerite, staring at the two of them.

Aunt Germaine smiled at her. “I am going to Ireland with Richard.”

“But . . .” Marguerite began.

“Richard fought for Ireland’s independence in the twenties, for Spain in the thirties, and for France in the forties,” her aunt said. “I think it’s time he returns home.” She stretched up to kiss his cheek, and Marguerite was certain she saw the big Irishman blush.

“My work here is finished,” he said. “The rest is for you and your children to do.” He slipped his arm around Germaine’s waist. “Who knows, maybe we will grow apples in Ireland and produce Irish calvados. And I am thinking of starting a career in politics. What do you think?”

Marguerite grinned at him. “God help the British,” she quipped.

CHAPTER THIRTY-SIX
PEACE

Marguerite confronted her cousin where she stood drying a platter in the new Perdu kitchen. "Bérénice, I'm serious. Simone saved me from horrible torture. Please, come to lunch with us today. Do it for me."

"*Non. Non, non, non!* I will not be seen with her."

Marguerite grasped her hand. "Simone saved my life, Bérénice, and the war is over. This is about Ville de Pommes now. About healing. We have to forget and move forward."

Her cousin took a deep breath. "All right, I'll do this for you. But I will never forgive Simone for four years of collaborating with the Nazis. Never."

"I'm not asking you to. I'm asking you to think about the future, not the past."

The smell of fresh lumber and paint hung in the air inside *Café Angele*. Marguerite walked slowly to a table at the back of the café, an odd sense of loss tugging at her. Those old times, before the Nazis came, could never be recaptured.

She and Bérénice waited in silence, and then Simone LaVaque entered, looked around apprehensively, and started toward them. Conversation in the crowded café ceased, but Simone looked straight ahead.

"That one has a lot of nerve," someone muttered. Bérénice stared at her.

Simone slid into an empty chair and kept her eyes on the table. "*Merci* for inviting me," she said hesitantly.

"I didn't— " Bérénice began. Marguerite kicked her under the table, and her cousin bit her lip.

"*Bonjour*, Simone," Marguerite said, her voice quiet.

A waiter brought a carafe of white wine and four glasses. After an awkward wait Yvonne Callion appeared in the doorway. Marguerite waved her over.

"*Bonjour*," Yvonne said as she took the unoccupied chair.

"*Bonjour*, Yvonne," Marguerite and Bérénice said in unison.

"I am glad we are here together," Marguerite began. "We have all been scarred by the Nazi occupation; I thought the four of us should meet as we used to." She swallowed hard. "The last time I was here was the day the café was bombed."

Yvonne reached for her hand. "What is done during wartime is terrible. Everything changes."

"True," Bérénice acknowledged with a sharp glance at Simone. "We all had to do terrible things."

"We did terrible things for France," Marguerite interjected. "For our freedom from the Germans."

"*Oui*," whispered Simone. "You are right. We should try to move on."

Marguerite smiled at her. "Simone, I owe you my life for rescuing me from the *Milice*."

"I— I had to do it, Marguerite. I couldn't stand to watch— " She broke off.

"We are all different now," Marguerite said. "We will never forget the bad times, but now we must look ahead to what we want for the future."

"I want to spend time with my mother," Yvonne said instantly.

"I want to be with José," Bérénice confessed. "And grow apples."

"I want to grow my hair out," Simone said quietly.

"I want to marry Guy," Marguerite said. "As soon as possible."

Marguerite filled the glasses, and the four young women solemnly raised them to each other.

EPILOGUE

In 1949, on the fifth anniversary of D-Day, a Paris newspaper assigned a reporter to travel to Ville de Pommes and write an article on the Résistance and the famous Patrice Cerne. Marguerite had reluctantly agreed to the interview, and she and Guy met the reporter on the front porch of Charentais.

The reporter asked endless questions about Marguerite's experiences during the Occupation. Throughout the afternoon she reflected on her life and the lives of all of them under the Occupation, the death and destruction she had witnessed, the terrible things she had done. So much of it was difficult to think about or discuss.

"We fought for a free France," Guy offered at last.

Then a blond, blue-eyed boy of four years ran up and crawled into his father's lap. Marguerite reached to tousle his hair.

"This is our son, Antoine," she said. She gave the reporter a long look.

"This is why we fought."

ABOUT THE AUTHOR

J. Walter Ring is a member of the Historical Novel Society of North America, Napa Valley Writers Club, and Sherlockians of Napa, California. He is published in "America in World War II" and "Nuclear Plant Journal," and he works as a stringer for the Napa Valley Register. He holds a B.S. degree in electrical engineering from Purdue University and has completed graduate work in nuclear engineering at Indiana University. He also holds a master's degree in business administration and has taught at Cerritos College. Recently he returned to France to conduct research for this book.

Mr. Ring lives in Napa, California.

44436206R00141

Made in the USA
Charleston, SC
28 July 2015